PATT
BUCHEISTER

TILT AT WINDMILLS

D0039838

Silhouette®

SPECIAL EDITION®

Published by Silhouette Books New York
America's Publisher of Contemporary Romance

To Kathy (Johnson) Becker, who has given me
the gift of friendship for over thirty years.

Don Quixote's adventure of the windmills:
"It is clear," replied Don Quixote (to his squire Sancho),
"that you are not experienced in adventures. Those are
giants, and if you are afraid, turn aside and pray whilst I
enter into fierce and unequal battle with them."

Don Quixote
Cervantes

SILHOUETTE BOOKS
300 East 42nd St., New York, N.Y. 10017

TILT AT WINDMILLS

Copyright © 1992 by Patt Bucheister

All rights reserved. Except for use in any review, the reproduction
or utilization of this work in whole or in part in any form by any
electronic, mechanical or other means, now known or hereafter
invented, including xerography, photocopying and recording, or in
any information storage or retrieval system, is forbidden without
the permission of the publisher, Silhouette Books, 300 E. 42nd St.,
New York, N.Y. 10017

ISBN: 0-373-09773-5

First Silhouette Books printing October 1992

All the characters in this book have no existence outside the
imagination of the author and have no relation whatsoever to
anyone bearing the same name or names. They are not even
distantly inspired by any individual known or unknown to the
author, and all incidents are pure invention.

®: Trademark used under license and registered in the United
States Patent and Trademark Office and in other countries.

Printed in the U.S.A.

PATT BUCHEISTER

was born and raised in Iowa and has since lived in California, Hawaii and England. After moving nineteen times in the twenty-four years of her husband's career in the U.S. navy, she has settled permanently with her husband in Virginia Beach—near the Atlantic Ocean and her two married sons. Due to extensive traveling over the years, she has a wide range of places and locations to use in her novels.

Along with her writing, she has a variety of interests, primarily painting in her studio and learning a form of martial arts called t'ai chi.

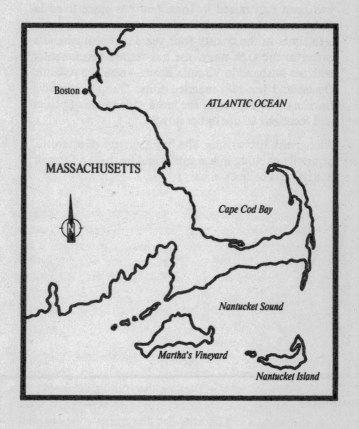

Chapter One

Of the one hundred people attending the private party in Ballroom Three at a large hotel in downtown Boston, ninety-nine guests were having a great time. It was a Friday night, the beginning of the weekend when the daily grind could be put behind them until Monday. Crowds of revelers were lined up at the long buffet table and at the bar, or dancing, flirting, drinking champagne and generally having a good time.

Except for one man.

He was standing near the closed double doors watching every person entering or leaving, his eyes alert, his expression serious as his gaze roamed the room thoroughly. He wasn't eating or drinking or talking. He was searching.

Rudd Lomax hadn't attended the party to be sociable. Nor was he in the mood for polite chitchat or interested in following up the provocative glances he received from a number of women. He didn't even notice them, which only acted as a challenge to the women who couldn't accept that a man could possibly resist their charms. It wouldn't have mattered if the women stripped off every stitch of their clothing in an attempt to get his attention. He would have looked, but that's all he would have done. He might not be interested, but he wasn't dead.

An attractive woman, who was wearing a red leather dress that left nothing for an imagination to do, stopped in front of him.

"Hi."

His gaze flicked over her. "Hi," he murmured, then resumed surveying the crowd.

Undeterred, the woman smiled and said, "You're going to ruin my evening if you're waiting for your wife."

Since she wasn't going to be easy to shift, he said, "I'm waiting for Ellen Sheridan. Do you know her?"

"Sure," she replied easily, recovering quickly from whatever disappointment she might have been feeling. "I saw her over by the buffet table a little while ago."

"Thanks."

She reached out and touched the small, gold-key tie tack on his tie with a manicured finger. "I'll be glad to keep you company in the meantime."

"That's a pretty offer, but I'll have to pass."

She shrugged, the simple action rearranging the leather briefly. "Maybe later."

Rudd didn't bother commenting one way or the other.

His reason for being at the hotel on that particular night wasn't to have a good time, but to find a woman. Not just any woman. One specific woman. A silver-haired, green-eyed woman whom he hadn't seen in six months. So far, he wasn't having much luck. The surroundings and the occasion didn't help much. The lighting in the ballroom was muted, the crush of people packed in like well-dressed sardines.

One advantage in not finding Ellen the minute he arrived, the only one he could come up with while he'd searched the ballroom, was that it gave him extra time to think of how he would put his proposition when he finally did see her. For the last couple of days, he'd gone over several scenarios of how he would approach her after he'd decided she might be the solution to his problem. Considering he hadn't seen her in over six months, she might not even remember him. That could complicate matters.

Somehow he didn't think she'd have forgotten him any more than he'd forgotten her. He couldn't see how she could forget being struck by lightning—which was how he'd felt.

When Rudd had first arrived at the hotel, he'd threaded his way through the crowd in the ballroom for about an hour without even a glimpse of her. He finally gave up and chose a spot near the door. Waiting wasn't one of the things he was very good at, but he didn't have any other choice. She would have to leave by the door at some time or other, and he would be there when she did. He didn't want to think that she might not even be at the hotel at all. The receptionist at Carstairs Designs had said this was where Ellen would be tonight, and he could only hope the chatty woman had known what she was talking about.

He didn't have to worry about recognizing Ellen even though he hadn't seen her in six months. Ever since that one meeting, her face had appeared in his mind every night when he closed his eyes, affecting his sleep and his hormones. Even when his world had been abruptly turned upside down by a phone call from his ex-wife's attorney, Ellen had stayed in the back of his mind like a haunting melody. He had found himself hearing her husky laughter in his dreams. At odd times, he would find himself thinking about how quickly she'd brought him to the brink of desire when he'd kissed her. His reaction to her then had been as strong as a tidal wave rolling over him until he was drowning in unfamiliar, yet pleasurable, sensations. He'd never felt anything like it before or since.

The powerful way he'd responded to her had been one of the reasons why he'd turned away from her six months ago. He'd had his life all mapped out, and there wasn't any room for detours.

It was also one of the things he'd had to consider when he decided to ask for her help. There were no guarantees he wasn't about to jump into the deep end again, but he was going to have to take that chance.

She was the only woman he knew who could speak Spanish fluently.

The fact that he was physically attracted to Ellen would have to be set aside—and that wasn't going to be easy. No matter how many silent lectures he'd given himself over the last few months, he hadn't been able to stop thinking about her. The way her image had clung to his mind had given him second thoughts about contacting her. More than second thoughts. He was up to about two hundred. He hadn't planned to ever see her again. In fact, he'd tried very hard during the last six months to put her out of his mind...without any success. Now a strange twist of fate had seen to it that he was going to bring her back into his life.

Looking into the crowd, his gut clenched suddenly. He'd finally found her.

It was as though all the lights in the ballroom focused on one particular woman in the crowd. He almost groaned aloud when he felt his heartbeat quicken involuntarily. One of the paper streamers radiating out from the ornate crystal chandelier had come loose from its taped mooring on the wall and flapped against Ellen's cheek. She reached up to brush it away as though it were an irritating fly buzzing around her face. His stomach tightened as he watched the movement of her hips under the shimmering blue fabric of the dress she wore as she stepped around a tall man to duck away from the hanging streamer. The claws of attraction dug further into him when he caught the smile she sent in the direction of the man's companion.

He'd never met anyone who smiled as much or as often as Ellen Sheridan did. It was as though she'd been given a smile the day she was born and had never had a reason to turn it back in.

Another man hugged her briefly, then kissed her cheek. Rudd came away from the wall. His immediate reaction was to yank the man away from her. Rudd took a step toward Ellen, then stopped abruptly. He had no right to stop her from kissing every man in the room if she wanted to, and he forced himself to stay where he was.

His gaze never left her as she made her way across the crowded floor in his direction. The lights from the crystal chandelier overhead glanced off her unusual shade of gray-blond hair. One of the visions that had haunted him was how her hair appeared as though it had been coated with a light mist of fog when he'd sat across from her at a candlelit table in the restaurant when they'd had dinner together.

As he watched another man kiss her, he remembered how soft her skin had felt under his fingertips, the way she'd moved against him on the dance floor, the desire that shuddered down his spine when he heard her husky laugh.

He sucked in his breath as he fought the stab of desire tightening his body. Damn, he thought ruefully. He hadn't even talked to her or touched her, and he was already feeling a strong tug of attraction. Where was that famous self-control his ex-wife had hated?

Ellen disappeared out of his sight for a moment, and he used the time to try to cool down. It had taken only one glimpse of her, and he was responding like a teenager with hormones in overdrive. It was the way she'd affected him six months ago, and the main reason he'd resisted the temptation to see her again.

In the five years since his divorce, he hadn't exactly lived like a monk. But the women he'd dated and occasionally took to bed were the type to enjoy the moment without expecting a lifetime commitment. The last thing he'd needed was an involvement with a woman, especially this woman who didn't appear to be the kind of woman to have an affair. And that was all he would have been able to offer Ellen then—or so he'd thought at the time.

Then he hadn't fully appreciated her obvious pleasure in being with him. He'd been too busy fighting his own reactions. Now, he found himself wanting her to look at him that way again.

He left his position against the wall and started to make his way through the people between him and Ellen.

Peering around a man who had to be at least seven feet tall, Ellen caught a glimpse of the woman he was obviously propositioning. His object of conquest had a massive head of startling red hair piled on top of her head. Her hairstyle was a tribute to the hair spray industry. She was only a couple of inches shorter than the giant, but her hair almost brought her up to the man's height. Ellen smiled to herself as she heard the woman deftly turn down the poorly executed offer of a festive romp in one of the rooms upstairs in the hotel.

Ellen wasn't particularly surprised she couldn't put names to their faces even though the occasion was a party in her honor. If it was anyone else except Tiffany Allison hosting the party, Ellen would expect to see mostly her own friends, but that wasn't how Tiffany operated. The world was Tiffany's oyster, and she tried to get as many people into her shell as would fit.

Feeling as though she were a midget attending a convention of basketball players, Ellen gingerly worked her way through the clusters of elbows and solid bodies, trying to keep the glass of champagne in her hand from spilling. Shaking her head in bemusement, Ellen wondered where Tiffany had found some of the people attending the party. She was beginning to think her friend had chosen the guest list according to height. There didn't appear to be anyone under six feet except Tiffany and herself.

A woman ducked around her tall companion and called out to her. "Happy birthday, Ellen."

Smiling faintly, Ellen replied automatically to the greeting she must have heard at least fifty times since she'd arrived, "Thanks."

Her smile faded gradually to be replaced by a rueful twist of her lips. She hadn't had a problem about turning thirty until someone had casually reminded her that she was over a quarter of a century old by five years. For some strange reason, that statement made Ellen feel she should be assessing her life, adding up what she'd accomplished so far to determine whether the total was adequate. In some people's minds, especially her father's, what she'd accomplished so far might not amount to much in the material sense, but she was relatively satisfied with her life. Her bank account might not register a gigantic balance, but she wasn't borderline destitute, either. She had a terrific job as a fabric designer, a comfortable apartment in a nice area of Boston, and a number of friends. Her health was good, and she owned a car that ran more times than not. It wasn't a bad total for a woman her age or any age.

There were a few things missing from her life that she'd expected to have by age thirty, but she'd learned early not to expect too much. Then she wouldn't be too disappointed. Like almost every other adolescent girl, she'd once dreamed about having a happy home complete with children and an adoring husband, but the fates had decreed that she should do without them for the time being.

A sharp elbow accidently stabbed her in the ribs, which effectively yanked her back to the present.

The man the elbow belonged to turned around. "Sorry, Ellen," he said with an apologetic grin. "How's the birthday girl?"

"Bruised. How are you, Tony?"

"Dry. I've been trying to get to the bar for a refill, but evidently I'm going against the current. Now I know how a salmon feels."

Ellen could sympathize. About fifteen minutes ago, she'd aimed for the exit, but for the last ten minutes she hadn't been able to even catch a glimpse of the red sign over the door. It was times like this that her five feet, four inches were a definite disadvantage. She glared at the glass of champagne in her hand. The glass was only half empty or half full, whichever way she wanted to look at it. She certainly didn't want to consume any more liquid, considering the strain she was under at the moment.

As she stepped past a man who had flung his hand out while he chatted with the woman in front of him, she slipped the glass of champagne into his hand, smiling when his fingers automatically closed around the stem, then struggled on, minus the champagne.

If screaming for help would do the trick, she might have tried it out of desperation except the noise level had reached about 120 decibels almost an hour ago. Along with the crescendo of conversation from a hundred people, there was a three-piece band whose amplifiers were churning out music at an ear-splitting level.

If she didn't find a nice, quiet rest room soon—or even a noisy one—she was going to give new meaning to the word *stress*.

Faced with a wall of tall, warm bodies, she closed her eyes and wished for a modern-day Moses to part the sea of bodies. When Ellen opened her eyes again, all she could see directly in front of her was a tiny, gold-key tie tack attached to a maroon tie knotted at the collar of a crisp, white shirt. Her gaze remained on the tie tack as she took a tentative step to the left. She became fascinated when the tie tack stayed in front of her as the man stepped in the same direction. When she sashayed in the opposite direction, she wasn't too surprised when the tie tack went right along with her.

It was that kind of a night.

When she again stepped to the right, she collided with someone built as solidly as an oak tree and almost as tall. The gold-key tie tack shifted quickly between her and the man about to run her over. A strong arm slid around her waist and guided her effortlessly out of the immediate crush, miraculously finding a spot where she could actually move her arms.

Impressed by his evasive moves, she raised her head to thank her Knight of the Golden Key. Her smile faded slowly as her gaze met the man's blue eyes. Familiar sapphire blue eyes. She'd seen that same assessing look before, too. Her heartbeat rocked, then thudded heavily, painfully, in her chest. The steady intensity of his gaze bore into her, leaving her fighting for breath.

Of all the people she hadn't expected to see tonight, Rudd Lomax was at the top of the list.

That he'd been on Tiffany's guest list was just as hard to believe. A little over six feet tall, he met the height requirement Tiffany apparently had set for the evening, but Rudd certainly didn't qualify as a friend. At least not hers. Which left the possibility he was a friend of Tiffany's. Any party Tiffany gave included a variety of people, a blend of business associates and reciprocating social invitations. She wondered which category Rudd Lomax fell in.

The light gray suit he was wearing was similar to the one he'd been wearing the last time she'd seen him although this one had tiny, almost indistinct, stripes. His thick, black hair was as neatly trimmed, his deep blue eyes as compelling and direct as she remembered. As before, he didn't automatically smile, his expression one of solemn assessment. It hadn't taken her long to discover his smile was like a precious gem, only brought out to be admired on rare occasions.

When he'd told her he was a research chemist, she'd surmised that it might be his nature to weigh every fact, to reserve judgment until all the variables were known, in his personal as well as his professional life. Since she'd met him only that one time, her assessment could be completely off base. Then again, she could be right on the money since he wasn't any more generous with his smile now as he'd been then.

She also remembered how solid he'd felt against her when he'd held her during the one and only time they'd ever danced together.

The one and only dance during their one and only meeting.

She gave him a polite smile. Her pride refused to let him see it had mattered that he'd never wanted to see her again.

"Well, fancy meeting you here," she said lightly. "How are you, Rudd?"

In order to hear what she was saying, he'd leaned down closer to her, his head only inches from hers. She became aware of his masculine scent and the heat emanating from his tall body so close to hers.

"I'm fine," he responded when he lifted his head to look down at her. His gaze roamed over her deep blue cocktail dress and her blond hair pulled back at the nape of her neck. "There's no need for me to ask how you are. You look even more beautiful than the last time I saw you."

Another time she would have enjoyed hearing a compliment from him. This wasn't one of those times.

Changing the subject, she said, "I'm surprised to see you here. I didn't realize you knew Tiffany."

Raising a brow, he asked, "Isn't that a lamp?"

"A person. Tiffany Allison. She's the one who's giving the party." Deciding to get right to the point instead of skirting around it, she asked, "If you don't know Tiffany, why are you here, Rudd? Did you take a wrong turn in the lobby?"

His gaze held hers. "I'm here because you're here."

She had no idea what that meant. At the moment, there were more urgent matters she was concerned about that took precedence over curiosity.

"Well, I'm trying to get out of here." She smiled faintly. "You wouldn't happen to know where I could find the exit, do you?"

It was clearly not what he'd expected her to say. "It's about ten feet to your left. Are you leaving the party?"

"Temporarily. If I can ever get to the door." She took a step away, then glanced at him over her shoulder. "Thanks for the help a minute ago."

He stopped her progress with a hand on her wrist, closing the distance between them. "I'm coming with you. Now that I've finally found you, I don't want to take the chance of losing you in this crowd again."

His touch sent shock waves of heat down to the bone. It required an enormous effort to keep from jerking her arm to break the hold he had on her, even though his grip wasn't all that tight.

"I would rather go by myself."

He bent his head toward her, obviously unable to hear her. "What did you say?"

Raising her voice, she said firmly, "I don't need any company where I'm going."

His mouth tightened in an angry line as she was jostled by a woman trying to get by. "This is ridiculous," he growled. "I'll be damned if I'm going to shout at you all night."

He slid his arm around her waist to clamp her to his side as he guided her through the crowd. When they reached the door, Rudd opened it and pushed her gently out of the ballroom. There were only a few people milling around in the broad hallway outside, the sound of conversation a mere whisper compared to the din they'd left behind them.

Ellen saw a small sign jutting out from the side of a door about twenty feet away and breathed a quiet sigh of relief. "Thanks for the bulldozer service, Rudd. I would probably still be trying to get out of there."

The strain in her voice wasn't entirely due to the fact she had an urgent need to use the ladies' room. Seeing Rudd again had been a jolt she was still trying to recover from without a great deal of success. It must be because her self-esteem was a little sensitive from all those comments about turning thirty, she rationalized. Seeing an old flame shouldn't affect her so strongly. Especially when he'd been more of a brief spark than a full-fledged flame.

Rudd was looking at her with a puzzled expression, baffled by the humor making her green eyes dance. He dropped his arm, no longer touching her except with his steady gaze. "There's a coffee shop in the hotel. We could talk there without having to yell at each other."

She bit back the urge to ask him what in the world they could possibly have to talk about.

"I don't think so. I have a more urgent priority at the moment," she said, glancing at the sign indicating the ladies' room, then back at him with a raised brow.

A corner of his mouth curved upward when he realized what she meant. "I'll wait here for you."

"There are plenty of women inside the ballroom who would be more than willing to keep you company, Rudd. Why don't you mingle? You might get lucky."

Then she walked away from him.

After Ellen took care of her pressing problem, she had a silent, heart-to-heart chat with herself about her reaction to seeing Rudd Lomax. Seeing him again was a surprise she could have done without. It had taken her an astonishing amount of time to get over the humiliating fact she'd been remarkably easy to forget six months ago. Maybe it was ridiculous to harbor resentment from a chance encounter just because it hadn't led to anything more, but she did. She didn't want to go through that crushing disappointment again. It wasn't in her nature to turn the other cheek once she'd been slapped. It was a lesson she'd learned early in life, and one she wouldn't forget again.

Ellen had seen him only once; the day they'd met when she'd shared her umbrella with him outside a popular restaurant as they were waiting in line for available tables. Since she was ahead of him, she'd invited him to join her at her table when she was allowed in. It had seemed the most natural thing in the world to be with him. Something vital had happened to her the moment their eyes first met. She hadn't been able to put a name to the emotion that had struck her like the powerful flash of a lightning bolt. Labels hadn't mattered; the depths of her feelings had.

Unfortunately, he hadn't felt the same way.

As she washed her hands, she thought about his rejection. She should be used to being brushed off, considering her father was a master in making her feel less than necessary. It had somehow been worse when Rudd had never made a move to contact her again—until tonight.

She studied her reflection in the mirror over the sink, smiling slowly at her image. You're a big girl now, she reminded herself silently. So things don't always work out the way she wanted. That was life. She should have learned something from her experiences with her father. She'd never been able to change her father's attitude toward her, nor could she make Rudd feel something he didn't feel. Acceptance of the cards she'd been dealt was one thing. To leave herself wide open to be dealt another losing hand was quite another.

She'd tried to put that night down to a moment of insanity. There'd been an unreal quality to the time she'd spent with him, a moment out of time. Even now it was hard to accept that she would willingly have gone to bed with a man she'd known for only a couple of hours. And even harder to accept that he'd known she felt that way. And he had rejected her. Her hard-won confidence had been badly shaken and had taken longer than it should have to recover.

All this soul-searching was a waste of time, she decided, making a face at herself in the mirror. She wouldn't be all that surprised if Rudd wasn't waiting for her even though he said he would. Six months ago, he'd said he would call her and he hadn't. She wasn't going to put much credence in anything he said.

When she left the ladies' room, she felt the impact of his eyes watching her, a strange, intense expression in their depths. She was both relieved and disappointed to find him still waiting for her, making her wonder if she would always have these contradictory feelings about Rudd.

In that split second when their eyes met, she knew she was still too vulnerable where he was concerned. There was no way she was going to leave herself open to him again. He would have to find someone else to play with tonight. It wasn't going to be her.

Her fingers gripped her small clutch purse as though she were physically holding on to her resolve. Six months ago, she'd welcomed the rush of sensations he'd created within her. Now she was wary and cautious, unwilling to walk into his path without gearing up her defenses.

Stopping directly in front of him, she said, "I didn't think you'd still be here."

"I said I'd wait."

"That doesn't necessarily mean you would." Irritated with herself for referring to the past even indirectly, she added, "I'll take a rain check on the coffee, Rudd. Tiffany has gone to a lot of trouble to arrange this party for me. The least I can do under the circumstances is to be there."

"What's the occasion?"

She was puzzled by the odd, strained note in his voice. "It's my birthday. What did you think it was?"

"It wouldn't be unheard of to be celebrating an engagement."

In her case, it would be a miracle, she thought cynically. "If you didn't know I would be attending my birthday party, how did you know where I'd be?"

"I remembered you telling me where you worked, so I called your office this afternoon. The woman who answered told me you'd left early to get ready for a party at this hotel. She neglected to tell me it was your birthday that was being celebrated."

"That was probably Patsy. She would have made a great town crier."

A corner of his mouth lifted slightly. "She saved me a lot of time."

Considering he'd had six months to look her up, she thought it odd that he was suddenly in such a rush to see her. Tilting her head to one side, she asked, "Hard up for something to do tonight, are we?"

"If I were, this isn't what I would have chosen as a way to spend an evening. I told you earlier. I came here tonight to see you."

"Well, you've seen me. I'll look forward to seeing you again six months from now, since that appears to be the time limit you've set for renewing acquaintances." She held out her right hand in a polite social gesture. "It's been interesting, Rudd," she managed, pleased with the cool dismissal in her voice. "Maybe I'll run into you again sometime."

Rudd took her hand, but not to give her a polite handshake. Curling his long fingers around hers, he slowly drew her toward him.

"I haven't wished you a happy birthday."

She stiffened when his hand went to her waist to keep her positioned in front of him. Panic clawed through her as she saw him lower his head toward her.

"A simple happy birthday is sufficient," she said tightly, as she twisted her head to one side before he could kiss her.

His hands came up to frame her face, forcing her to look at him. "You didn't object when other men kissed you earlier," he murmured close to her mouth. "Why should I be left out?"

She was amazed she could still articulate. "They were friends."

His thumbs stroked her soft skin. "And I'm not?"

She smiled faintly. "No, Rudd. I wouldn't call you a friend. An acquaintance maybe, but definitely not a friend. Friends stay in touch with each other."

Something flickered in his eyes as he lowered his gaze to his hands cupping her face. "I'm touching you now."

She closed her eyes as an explosion of pleasure jolted through her when he covered her mouth with his. The first touch of his lips was light, almost teasing, yet devastatingly powerful. Then his intention changed as he gained access to the warmth within her mouth.

Ellen heard a soft moan as he invaded her mouth, and realized the sound had come from her. This assault to her senses was nothing like the tepid pecks on the cheek she'd received from other men tonight. The impact of the kiss made her feel as though she were standing in water, and his mouth was creating a powerful electric current throughout her whole system.

Even though she was caught up in the sensual glory of his kiss, she was dimly aware of a strange, almost desperate quality in the way he took her mouth. She dismissed the thought as ridiculous. There was no reason she could think of why he would be desperate to kiss her.

Self-preservation had her spreading her palms over his chest to resist him. It was a little late to protest now, when he had to be aware she hadn't been exactly fighting him off during the last few minutes, but it was the best she could do.

Her reaction was pure instinct. She didn't want to be given a gift that would be taken away at the end of the evening.

When he raised his head, his blue eyes were dark with arousal. A muscle in his jaw clenched as he stared into her eyes, then he murmured, "Happy birthday, Ellen."

It was an effort not to laugh at the simple phrase she'd heard all evening, afraid it would come out slightly hysterical. "Thanks," she managed, wishing she didn't sound so breathless. "If you'll let me go, I'd like to return to my party."

"I understand. What you need to understand is that I'm going with you."

Proving to herself she could learn from past mistakes, she asked with a trace of irritation, "Why?"

"I came here tonight to talk to you. That's kind of hard to do if I'm not with you." When he saw the wary skepticism enter her eyes, he asked, "Why do you find that so hard to believe?"

Controlling her temper, she said quietly, "I might have given you the impression I was just another dumb blonde six months ago, Rudd, but I'm not stupid. When a man fails to call a woman after saying he will, it generally means he isn't interested in seeing her again. It's one of those unwritten rules in the dating code, a rather obvious one. Please don't insult me by trying to make me think you've suddenly discovered a need for my company after all this time. I won't buy it. If you're at loose ends tonight, I suggest you chat up some of the women attending my birthday party. There are a number of attractive, single women here who would be more than happy to keep you entertained without expecting a lifetime commitment or a phone call tomorrow.''

Before he was able to explain she was the only one he wanted to be with, a petite woman poked her head out the door behind him, catching Ellen's attention. The woman's gaze searched the opposite end of the hall first, then looked in their direction. When she caught sight of Ellen, she smiled broadly and gestured impatiently with her hand.

''Ellen, Tiffany's looking for you. She's sent out a search party.''

Pulling her arm free, Ellen walked away from Rudd and slipped through the open door. She didn't look back to see if he followed her. This time she was going to be the one to walk away. Her pride insisted on it.

Chapter Two

It took a few minutes for her to become accustomed to the torrential waves of sound again after the relative quiet in the hall. At least the band was no longer playing, which brought the noise to a halfway tolerable level. The musicians were standing around on the small stage with their instruments blissfully silent. The reason they weren't earning their fee was because a woman was standing in front of the microphone, one of the spotlights highlighting the ruby-and-diamond necklace she wore around her neck. The woman was clad in a stunning red dress, her blond hair several shades darker than Ellen's and arranged in a casually elegant twist.

Smiling at the sea of faces in front of her, Tiffany announced, "Grab your significant other and gather around, everyone."

Ellen couldn't help smiling. Giving orders was only one of Tiffany's talents, but one she used often.

Tiffany's gaze roamed around the room. "Ellen Sheridan. Come out, come out wherever you are. It's time to pay the piper."

Groaning inwardly, Ellen walked toward the stage, wondering what horror Tiffany had in store for her. It was bound to be embarrassing, considering Tiffany's offbeat sense of humor. Oh, well, she thought philosophically. This seemed to be her night for surprises. She shrugged inwardly. She might as well get this over with. She wasn't about to let anyone say she wasn't a good sport.

Heads began turning in her direction. She was amused when the crowd parted in front of her to allow her access to the stage. She could have used this magical transformation a little while ago when she'd been trying to find the exit.

Everyone was smiling broadly in anticipation of the entertainment. Tiffany was known for providing unusual diversions, with emphasis on the word *unusual*. Ellen had the sinking feeling this was going to be an evening she wasn't about to forget for a long time.

When Ellen reached the stage, she accepted Tiffany's extended hand to assist her up onto the platform. The bright spotlight nearly blinded her as she stood beside her friend, but it also made it nearly impossible for her to see the faces in the crowd gathered around the stage. That was definitely a plus.

However, she could see Tiffany's expression all too clearly. The diamond hair clip Tiffany was wearing in her blond hair glittered almost as much as the expression of mischief in her brown eyes. It was a look Ellen had learned to dread since grade school.

Keeping her voice low, Ellen warned, "Before you get too carried away, I want to remind you it's not too late for me to tell your mother what happened to her prize Ena

Harkness rosebush the night you tried to ride Harold Henderson's motorcycle.''

Tiffany's laughter was magnified by the microphone, filling the room with the rich sound. With amusement in her tone, she spoke to the crowd. ''As most of you know, we are gathered here to celebrate the auspicious occasion of my dear friend Ellen Sheridan's birthday. Ellen and I have been through puberty, college exams, and numerous broken hearts together. For those of you who don't happen to know her, she's the artist who designed the series of sheets and pillowcases called Tropical Forest put out recently by the Carstairs Design Portfolio. Many of you are probably sleeping with her,'' she said in a low, sultry voice, pausing pointedly before adding, ''designs on your beds without realizing it.''

Ellen groaned audibly and covered her eyes with her hand, removing it when Tiffany continued speaking. She knew it was better to face whatever Tiffany had planned for her with her eyes wide open.

''To show how much we appreciate you coming here tonight, we are going to entertain you with a song we performed at a charity function my mother sponsored when we were sophomores in college.''

Ellen leaned forward and said loudly into the microphone, ''No, we aren't.''

Applause and catcalls came from the assembled crowd who were more than ready to be entertained, no matter how badly. *Especially* if it was done badly.

''See?'' gloated Tiffany. ''They want to hear us sing.''

''That's because they've never heard us sing.''

''If you've forgotten the words, just wing it. I've heard the memory is one of the first things to go as you get older.''

"I'm only two months older than you, Tiffy," she said sweetly, using the nickname Tiffany had hated since grade school. Her friend simply grinned back at her. Ellen sighed heavily. "All right. Let's get this over with. My birthday cake had better be fantastic."

Tiffany chuckled as she turned Ellen to face away from her and stepped behind her. Signaling the band, she placed her hands at Ellen's waist and began to sway back and forth as the band began the introduction to the song "Sisters".

Rudd's gaze never left Ellen as she and Tiffany performed the duet with apparent ease. The two women's movements were synchronized and graceful as they sang and danced their way through a routine obviously familiar to both of them. Even from his vantage point some distance away, Rudd could see the amusement curving Ellen's mouth as she went through the performance.

Just the sight of her smile had his guts twisting into a hard knot.

As Rudd watched Ellen, he couldn't help smiling faintly at the antics of the two women on the stage. It was an automatic response, one he'd had before when he'd met her. She had made him smile from the first moment he'd seen her holding the umbrella over his head. She'd seemed like a ray of warm sunshine on a cold, rainy day. There was nothing coy or false about her. Her natural enthusiasm for life had been as intoxicating as the finest Tennessee whiskey, filling an emptiness he never knew was inside him.

When he'd met Ellen before, she'd looked at him with warmth and anticipation, her expression a soothing balm to his raw emotions. He'd always been a logical, clear-thinking man who analyzed every move before he made it, but she had knocked caution into a cocked hat the moment she'd first smiled at him.

At the time, he hadn't fully appreciated her obvious pleasure in being with him. He'd been too busy fighting his own reactions. Maybe there was such a thing as a second chance.

His smile faded as he remembered what she'd said to him a few moments ago. Ellen hadn't pulled any punches when she let him have it for the cavalier way he'd treated her six months ago. The amazing thing was, he didn't think she was lambasting him because of a bruised ego. He sensed she would honestly liked to have seen him again and had been hurt when he obviously hadn't felt the same way. He wondered what she would say if he admitted to her that he'd had more than a few bad nights remembering how she'd tasted. Or if he told her how he'd picked up the phone a couple of times and punched out her number only to hang up before it rang at her end.

He grimaced. She probably wouldn't believe him, not that he could blame her. It would come out sounding like some corny line or feeble excuse.

When he'd come searching for her tonight, he hadn't given any thought to the possibility he could hurt her by asking for her help. He'd only been thinking of Katie.

The sound of clapping brought his attention back to the stage. Like a magnet, his gaze centered on Ellen. He had to remember why he was there, why he needed Ellen. Not for himself. For Katarina Maria Lomax. His daughter.

In order to be able to communicate with Katie, he would use the one woman who could arouse him by simply being in the same room. Hell, he admitted, all he had to do was remember the feel of her in his arms and his body reacted.

Loud enthusiastic applause bounced off the walls. The women on the stage clasped hands and bowed deeply, grinning at each other as they waited for the raucous cheering from their audience to die down. It took awhile.

Rudd pushed himself away from the wall with the intention of going to the stage to persuade Ellen to leave with him now. He'd taken two steps when he saw Tiffany approach the microphone again. Glancing in the direction of a cluster of waiters dressed in white jackets standing near a folding screen that partitioned off a corner of the room, she instructed, "Get your fire extinguishers ready, guys. It's time to bring out the birthday cake."

Tamping down his impatience, Rudd stayed where he was as the hotel staff wheeled out the most enormous cake he'd ever seen. It took two men in front of a low platform on wheels and two more waiters pushing from behind to maneuver the cake in front of the stage. Lighted candles blinked and wavered around the third tier.

As Ellen stared with wide eyes at the huge cake, Tiffany began to sing "Happy Birthday" into the microphone and was joined by the assembled crowd.

Except for Rudd, who never took his eyes off Ellen.

In order to blow out the candles, Ellen had to walk around the cake as she blew them out one by one. The moment the last one was extinguished, Tiffany announced, "This cake has a special filling that I'm sure you'll all enjoy. I know Ellen will." Raising her voice, she yelled, "Open, Sesame!"

As the drummer played a loud drumroll, the crown of the cake folded back and a man wearing a tuxedo, complete with a top hat, appeared from the depths of the cake, a bouquet of red roses in his hand. A high platform with steps leading up to it was wheeled over to stand beside the cake, and the elegantly dressed man used it to climb down. On the stage, he removed his hat and gave Ellen an elaborate formal bow before presenting her with the bouquet of roses.

Rudd felt something uncomfortable clench in his stomach when he heard Ellen's laughter over the wolf whistles and cheers of the crowd as she curtsied mockingly. Not an easy trick in a tight dress, but she managed to do it with style and grace. Every muscle in his body tensed when he heard the band begin to play a throbbing, rhythmic tune more appropriate for a striptease than a waltz. If the guy in the tuxedo started to strip off his clothes, Rudd wasn't sure just what he would do, but he would definitely do something.

It wasn't necessary for him to do anything. The man kept his clothes on, and simply led Ellen out onto the dance floor as everyone backed off to give them room. Rudd's fingers curled into fists at his side as he watched Ellen place her arm on the other man's shoulder and move in unison to the music and the graceful movements of her elegantly dressed partner.

Pain in Rudd's jaw made him realize he was clenching his teeth as he watched Ellen in another man's arms. Great, he thought irritably. Just what he needed was to start feeling possessive and jealous of any man who touched her.

Tearing his gaze away from her, he glanced at his watch. Short of picking her up bodily and carrying her out of there, he was going to have to bide his time.

An hour later, his small supply of patience had been used up. Ellen had danced with just about every man there. At least it seemed like it. Now it was his turn.

She was smiling at the tall man she was dancing with when Rudd tapped him on the shoulder. When she saw who was cutting in, her smile faded. It was as if a light illuminating her eyes had been extinguished.

When Rudd slipped his arm around her slender waist to bring her close, he could feel her resistance as she held herself stiffly in his arms. "Having a good time?" he drawled.

She met his gaze, her expression wary. "Yes, I am," she replied politely. "Are you?"

"Not particularly. I'm ready to call it a night."

"Then why are you dancing with me?"

A corner of his mouth curved upward. "Because it's the only way I could get to you. You haven't left the dance floor in over an hour."

"I like to dance."

"Obviously," he murmured, his gaze going to her mouth briefly before raising to meet her eyes. "Do you want to say anything to your friend Tiffany before we leave?"

"*We* leave? Since when am I going to leave with you?"

He ignored her question. "I hope you didn't come with someone else. It would make it much easier for you to come with me without the complication of having to tell your escort to disappear."

Ellen stopped dancing. Dropping her hands, she stood stiffly in front of him. "Have you been sniffing something strange in that laboratory where you work? What makes you think I would go anywhere with you?"

"Because you're curious why I would look you up after six months' time."

For a few seconds, she simply stared at him. Then she sighed deeply. "How sad. You've lost your mind."

"You could be right," he said dryly. "You didn't answer my question. Did you come with someone else?"

"You never asked me that question. You said you hoped I didn't come with someone else."

"Do you usually remember what everyone tells you word for word?"

He'd be surprised, she thought. If called upon, she could recite practically every syllable he'd said to her during their previous meeting.

"It's a gift," she muttered, unwilling to give an inch.

Prying nails out of granite had to be easier, he decided. "How are you at answering the questions you're asked?"

"Would you like to see some of my report cards from school?"

"I'd like you to answer a simple, straightforward question," he said irritably, unable to keep the frustration aggravated by desire out of his voice. "Did you come to the hotel with someone or did you come alone?"

"I came alone."

"If you've made any arrangements to go home with anyone else during the last couple of hours, I'd appreciate it if you'd tell him to forget it. I need to talk to you about something important, but not here."

Giving him a wary look, she asked, "What do you want to talk about?"

His gaze was serious, his voice slightly husky as he announced, "I want you to come away with me for the weekend."

Chapter Three

Had it been anyone else, Ellen might have thought he was joking, but Rudd's tone was completely serious, his gaze solemn and unyielding. For a man who was proposing what she assumed was an illicit weekend, he didn't sound very enthusiastic. Or romantic. Perhaps if she'd known him better, she would have been able to determine whether or not this was a standard approach of his.

Or if he was certifiably nuts.

The only way she would find out why he would suddenly want to spend the weekend with her was to ask. "Is this some type of initiation rite into the Brotherhood of Crazy Chemists? Look up a past acquaintance and try to whisk her off for two days of scientific experiments? If it is, you'll have to choose someone else. I'm not going to cooperate."

"It has to be you," he said seriously. "I have a personal favor to ask of you, and it would mean going to Nantucket for the weekend if you agree to do it."

One of her friends called out a birthday greeting to her, and she automatically smiled back and raised a hand in response. Turning her attention back to Rudd, she asked calmly, "What's the favor?"

He took her arm and drew her toward the ballroom exit. "It's impossible to talk here without being interrupted every other minute."

They were almost to the door when Tiffany broke away from the group of people she'd been talking to and approached them. Ellen felt Rudd's grip tighten on her arm as though he were afraid she would leave him the first chance she got. She found a smile to give to her close friend. If it was a little ragged around the edges, it was the best she could do.

Tiffany glanced at the man at Ellen's side. "I don't believe we've met, and I find that interesting since I thought I knew everyone I invited to the party."

Ellen introduced them. "Tiffany Allison, this if Rudd Lomax. He crashed your party."

"How inventive of you," Tiffany said with a grin. "Are you running away with the guest of honor?"

"Yes," he replied with a crooked smile. "At least I'm trying to, but she's not being very cooperative."

Tiffany chuckled. "Maybe I can help. Giving Ellen choices doesn't always work, which is why I just go ahead and make plans she can't get out of no matter how much she fusses later."

"I'll have to remember that," he drawled, his gaze resting on Ellen.

Tiffany's eyes glittered almost as brightly as the brilliant stones in her necklace. "If I'm any judge of men—

and considering I've been engaged twice to jerks that's a debatable point, but I like to think I am experienced enough with the male of the species at least to render an accurate opinion—I doubt if you need my advice on how to handle a woman."

Before Rudd had a chance to reply to Tiffany's statement, Ellen interjected, "As much as I'm enjoying having you two talk about me as though I'm not here, I would rather not be discussed as though I'm some stubborn, complicated tool that needs careful handling."

Tiffany's laughter was one of pure enjoyment. To Rudd, she said, "Isn't she cute when she gets huffy?"

Ellen couldn't help the smile that automatically broke through the stern, disapproving expression she'd been trying to maintain. "I'm not the one who's full of hot air." Changing the subject before Tiffany saw fit to hand out any more bits of wisdom to Rudd, she asked, "Are we still on for Tuesday?"

In a loud, exaggerated whisper, Tiffany leaned toward Rudd, saying, "She always changes the subject when she's losing an argument." Resuming her natural tone, she turned her attention to Ellen. "I'll pick you up at your office at noon with my charge cards in one hand and a bag of sandwiches from Truman's Deli in the other. We can eat in between spending sprees. If we can't find a pair of turquoise shoes during our lunch hour, we'll have to try again after work."

"This time, bring a sample of the material used in your dress so we can match the color. We've returned three different pairs of shoes on three separate occasions."

"It's not my fault that Danielle has chosen that odd shade of turquoise for her maid of honor. At least Dani made it easy for you. The royal blue dresses the bridesmaids wear is a relatively easy color to match."

Chuckling, Ellen said, "And makes me look like a cross between Alice in Wonderland and a streetwalker."

"But you look so cute in it," Tiffany quipped with a grin, using the one word she knew Ellen would hate. Tiffany gave Rudd an assessing glance. "How do you feel about weddings, Mr. Lomax? Would you be willing to dress up like a peacock for the woman you love? Or maybe you already have. I didn't think to inquire if you were married or not. Since you haven't let go of Ellen the whole time we've been talking, you're either free to hang on to whatever woman you want or you're cheating on your wife."

"There's no wife to cheat on," he answered with amusement at Tiffany's less than subtle inquisition.

"Good. I wouldn't want Ellen to be hurt by some low-life who's only playing with her affections. You should be warned. I can get real mean with people who hurt my best friend."

He met her gaze and held it for a long moment. "I'll keep that in mind. Now, if you'll excuse us, there's something I want to discuss with Ellen."

Tiffany wasn't given the opportunity to reply one way or the other. Ellen was propelled through the open doorway without any chance of holding further conversation with her or anyone else. Glancing back over her shoulder, Ellen saw her friend's look of surprise. Then Tiffany made a circle using her forefinger and her thumb for Ellen's benefit. Ellen wasn't sure whether Tiffany was showing her approval of Rudd or the fact that Ellen had made a conquest during the evening. Since Ellen had never mentioned the one and only time she'd been with Rudd before, her friend wouldn't have recognized his name or realized the significance of his attending her birthday party uninvited.

She could have refused to leave the ballroom with Rudd by staging a revolt of sorts, but he'd been right on target earlier when he'd said she was curious why he'd suddenly reappeared after such a long absence.

Her pride wanted some answers. Her heart wanted an explanation.

A few minutes later, Ellen was standing next to Rudd at the cloakroom where he'd handed over his claim check, then asked her for hers. The clock on the wall inside the room was visible from where Ellen was standing, and she saw that it was twenty minutes after midnight. It was no longer her birthday.

But apparently the surprises weren't over yet.

Since Rudd obviously was preparing to leave the hotel, this was a good time to tell him she was willing to hear what he had to say, but it wasn't necessary to leave to do so. There was a certain safety in numbers.

"Rudd, I'm not..."

He cut off any protest she was about to make. "Wait until you hear what I have to say before you turn me down."

He slipped his trench coat on after handing her a lightweight shawl the attendant had given him. Frowning as he watched her drape the shawl around her shoulders, he muttered, "The temperature in Boston in October is not exactly balmy. Is that all you wore?"

She glanced down at the delicate shawl, then met his gaze. "What did you expect me to wear with a cocktail dress?" she asked mildly. "A parka?"

He took her arm and pulled her toward the entrance of the hotel. "Women," he muttered under his breath.

Unabashed, Ellen said soothingly, "I know. We really are a pain in the butt sometimes, aren't we? You have to admit, though, that we are nicer to look at than those little white mice you chemists practice on in your laboratory."

"You've been watching too many Vincent Price movies about mad scientists. I don't do any research that involves using animals."

"I'm glad to hear it," she commented as she accompanied him to the door. He didn't know it yet, but she didn't plan on leaving the hotel. She would walk with him to the door, then say goodbye. "What exactly are you working on with all those bubbling test tubes at your disposal? Are you growing anything interesting in the petri dishes?"

Work was the last thing he wanted to talk about right now. "Nothing you'd be interested in."

Ellen could almost hear the door slam closed in her face; his reply had been that definite in shutting her out.

She stopped walking and faced him with her hands on her hips. She gave him a look cold enough to freeze Boston Harbor. "I know H_2O from kumquats, Mr. Wizard. Don't patronize me. I'm quite capable of following an intelligent conversation without having to grab a dictionary to look up every other word."

Her spirited attack surprised him. He remembered her statement earlier about him thinking she was just another dumb blonde. Apparently, the question of her intelligence was a touchy one. He found himself wondering who or what was responsible for her defensive attitude.

Without realizing he was doing it, his hand stroked her arm in a soothing motion. "I'm not patronizing you, Ellen. The technical details of the study of soil pollution are not generally considered polite conversation."

Refusing to be totally placated, she said, "It is if the person you're talking to is interested. Never mind. Forget it. I was foolishly following Rule 'Seven-A' of *The Palmer's Etiquette Guide* my father made me memorize. The chapter heading was 'Dealing with Reticent or Difficult Dinner Companions.' We aren't having dinner, but I thought it fit.''

Rudd glanced down at her, amusement flickering in his eyes. ''Your father made you memorize a book of etiquette?''

''Chapter and verse. I even had to take a written test.'' She grinned up at him. ''I got every question correct except for the one about seating arrangements for royalty. I didn't think it would ever come up. My father did. I now know the proper seating arrangements if you ever invite the queen of England over for dinner.''

''I doubt if the occasion will ever come up.'' He shook his head in bemusement. ''Is your father a teacher?''

''Hardly,'' she said drily. ''He's more Clarence Darrow than Mr. Chips. He's a lawyer.''

Her last name clicked in his mind. ''Your father is Paul Sheridan.''

Since he'd made a statement and not a question, she didn't feel the need to reply.

He did. ''In all the articles I've read about Sheridan, I don't recall any mention of him having a daughter.''

''I'm not surprised. He's not even aware of it himself most of the time.''

She turned her head away from him when she heard her name being called, so she was unaware of the strange look Rudd was sending her way. She heard Rudd mutter something under his breath, but she ignored him as she watched one of the men she worked with approach her, his new wife clamped close to his side.

''I'm impressed, Jack,'' she drawled, glancing at the coat he was wearing. ''I thought you were always one of the last to leave a party.''

"I'm coming, not going. I only went out to my car to get a pack of cigarettes. That's when I noticed the front left tire on your car is flatter than my bank balance."

Ellen groaned. "Please tell me you're joking."

"Sorry. I'd never kid about a flat tire. I wouldn't know the difference between a lug nut and a pecan nut, but Sam and Barry and some of the other guys from accounting are huddled around your car waiting for me to bring them your keys to the trunk."

"I'll call the auto club." Catching Jack's glance at the man beside her, she introduced them. "Rudd Lomax, this is Jack and Sonya Quebec. Jack works at Carstairs in the art department, and Sonya is his bride of two months."

After Rudd shook Jack's hand and acknowledged the woman beside him with a nod of his head, he assured the other man, "I'll take care of Ellen's tire problem."

"You might have to stand in line. There's quite a group forming out there." To Ellen, he said, "I know I've already wished you a happy birthday, but consider it said again. You never did say how old you are."

"I'm too old to dance until dawn and too young for Social Security."

Laughing, Jack walked away with Sonya still adhered tightly to his side. Ellen felt Rudd's fingers clasp her elbow as he began to walk toward the entrance of the hotel, drawing her along with him.

"Rudd," she protested. "You don't have to help change the tire. I pay a hefty premium to belong to an auto club. I might as well get my money's worth and give them a call."

He shook his head. "I can have it changed before they even leave the garage."

"But..."

He sighed heavily, stopping near the door where a uniformed member of the hotel staff was waiting to open it for them. "Don't fight me on this, Ellen. It'll only take a few minutes to change the tire. You'll need your car in order to drive home. I'll follow you to your place, then we can talk without any interruptions."

She tried again. "I don't—"

"Now you do," he said succinctly without letting her finish. Again. "Show me which car is yours, then you can wait in my car where you'll be out of the cold."

She had to take two strides to each of his as he swept her through the entrance. "I never realized you were so bossy."

He looked down at her, clamping one arm around her waist to give her the protection of his body. The temperature had fallen considerably since he'd entered the hotel earlier. "I prefer to think of myself as being efficient rather than bossy. Which direction to your car?"

She gestured to his left. "Over there. It's the ten-year-old red Mustang parked about four cars from this end. The one where those five guys are standing."

"Mine's the gray Jaguar in the row behind yours." When they reached her car, he fished his keys out of his pocket and held them out to her. "Start the engine and turn the heater on."

She didn't take his set of keys. "I'm going to help."

"Ellen," he said with forced patience. "It's about forty degrees out here, and you don't even have a decent coat."

Her chin went up as she faced him. "Then we'd better get to it, hadn't we."

"You are one stubborn lady." Without giving her a chance to respond to his statement, he added, "I need your keys."

While she was opening her purse, he shrugged out of his trench coat and wrapped it around her. When he drew the collar up around her neck he didn't let go of the ends, his gaze holding hers for a long, electric moment. Then he dropped his hands.

Ellen was going to object to the use of his coat on principle, but the additional covering was a blessed relief from the chilly air. Handing him her keys, she muttered, "And you think *I'm* stubborn?"

He took her keys. "That's one thing we seem to have in common."

Clutching the front of his coat to keep it closed, Ellen walked beside him to her car. When Sam and the others caught sight of her, she had to endure good-natured teasing about her older model car. Rudd was automatically accepted into the fold when Ellen told them he had the necessary keys to get the trunk open. Like a pack of lions scenting new blood, the guys she worked with hovered around Rudd, asking questions instead of making any moves toward the trunk. With a deftness Ellen had to admire, Rudd managed to get the crew organized while fielding their questions without actually telling them anything significant about himself.

Barry, who was more comfortable with a calculator in his hand than a tire jack, kept her company several feet away from the activity.

"It looks like I'll have to tell Marcy Lou not to worry about setting you up with her cousin from Philadelphia. You're doing fine on your own."

"He's just an acquaintance, but you can still tell Marcy Lou to forget the cousin from Philly. Try to get it across to your wife that I don't really need the hassle right now."

Barry's gaze went to Rudd, who was handing a tire iron to Sam. And looking at Ellen. "You might have one whether you want it or not. A hassle that is. He's hardly taken his eyes off you."

She'd noticed, too, but put a different connotation on the attention from Rudd. "That's because I have his coat."

Chuckling, Barry shook his head. "I think it's more than that, but if it makes you feel safer, go right ahead and believe it."

"Thanks, I will. Why don't you go help them now that they're almost finished?"

"What a good idea."

Ellen leaned against the fender of a neighboring car. She slipped her arms into the sleeves of Rudd's coat and wrapped them around her waist to try to keep in as much body heat as possible. The late hour was catching up with her. Tiffany had told her once that she had a Cinderella complex. For Ellen, the party was over when it struck midnight. Tonight was no different.

Rudd's sudden arrival had taken its toll, too. Occasionally, she'd indulged in visions of how she would act if she ever saw Rudd again; cool, offhand, maybe even pretend she couldn't remember who he was, but she would always be in control of whatever reaction she would have.

It was much easier to imagine her reactions than to actually carry them out. This time was going to be different. She wasn't going to be as open as she'd been before or as much of a fool to expect too much. She wasn't going to be left wondering, hoping, hurting again.

It wasn't the first time she'd had to deal with rejection. And it probably wouldn't be the last. At least with her father, she knew why he'd shut her out of his life. Rudd's rejection, on the other hand, was a complete mystery. One minute he'd kissed her as though she were the most sensual, exciting woman he'd ever known. Then he'd left her at her door and had never attempted to make any sort of contact with her. Until tonight.

The sound of metal clanking against the pavement brought her gaze back to Rudd and the other men. Rudd was getting his hand wrung by the volunteer pit crew. Sam called out to her, "I want you to know I don't get down on my knees for many women, Ellen."

With tongue in cheek, Ellen answered, "I'm deeply honored."

"So, can I have that new drawing pen we chipped in and got you for your birthday?"

Laughing, Ellen turned him down. "Sorry. You'll have to settle for a simple thank-you."

He raised his hand and grinned back at her. "Consider it another birthday gift. See you Monday at work."

Ellen watched them head back to the hotel, then turned to Rudd. He lightly slapped his hands together to brush off the debris from handling the tire. As he returned her keys, he said, "You have some interesting friends. I've been grilled, drilled, and pitched to buy an insurance plan."

"Sam's moonlighting for his father-in-law's insurance company. He drives us all crazy with annuities and stuff he thinks we should buy."

"You can drive your car now. I'll follow you to your apartment."

"It's late, Rudd." She removed his coat and handed it to him. "I'm going home. Alone."

"Dammit, Ellen. I need to talk to you."

She walked around the front of the car and unlocked the door. "And I need to get some sleep. Thanks for the help with the flat tire, Rudd." She lifted a hand in a silent farewell and slid in behind the steering wheel.

Rudd stood in the parking lot as she drove away. She was going to see him again. He would guarantee it.

Chapter Four

Early the following morning, Ellen let herself out of the apartment building where she lived and headed for the park across the street. On Saturdays, it wasn't usually crowded until later in the day so she wouldn't have to dodge around baby strollers, bicycles, and parents with children in tow. Once she was there, she executed a few stretching exercises, then began to jog along the path she usually took.

The morning mist had dampened her gray sweat suit and her hair, and perspiration dotted her forehead by the time she'd been running for twenty minutes. She lifted a hand in greeting to the elderly man who was sitting on one of the park benches. He nodded his head and tipped the brim of his hat as he always did. He was one of the regulars who came to the park every morning, like the white-haired woman in the pink jogging outfit who was now stepping lively ahead of Ellen.

This morning Ellen ran longer and farther than usual, but no matter how much distance she covered, she couldn't outrun her thoughts. They were with her every inch of the way.

Usually she used the time to plan her day or work through a problem she was having with a design. This morning she could only think about seeing Rudd again. She kept going back to everything he'd said, the expression in his eyes when he said he wanted to talk to her as though he had something important to tell her.

She slowed to a walk and wiped off some of the moisture by sweeping her forearm across her face. Placing her hands on her knees, she bent over to make it easier for her to catch her breath. Instead of clearing her mind, her run in the park had only made her realize she'd been running even harder last night when she wouldn't let Rudd tell her what he wanted. Even now, thinking over the previous evening, she doubted if she would have done anything different.

Straightening up, she made a startled sound when she saw the man who was standing in front of her.

The collar of Rudd's brown leather jacket was pulled up around his neck, and his hands were shoved into the side pockets. Below the jacket that came to his waist, he wore jeans, *tight* jeans, that clung to his lean frame.

Vanity had her wishing she didn't look like a drowned rat. Pride had her lifting her chin to meet his gaze.

"You do tend to pop up in the most unlikely places, Rudd."

"I could say the same for you," he drawled. "Before you ask, I found out where you were from your neighbor. She poked her head out her front door when she heard me knocking on your door and told me I'd find you here."

"I'll have to have a little chat with Mrs. Kravitz."

"I would have waited until you got back. She just made it easier. I still want to talk to you."

"I gathered that."

When she didn't move, he suggested, "We would be more comfortable in your apartment than standing here."

Wrapping her arms around her middle, she tried to control the shiver that wasn't entirely caused by the cold. "Why don't you tell me now and get it over with?"

"As I said before, you are one stubborn lady," he muttered. "Not here. In a few more minutes, you'll be an ice cube."

Closing the distance between them, he took her hand and drew her along with him. Ellen didn't try to talk as she walked beside him. She needed all the breath she could muster in order to keep up with his long strides. Seeing him had altered her heartbeat and made her hope again.

When they reached his car, which was parked at the curb across the street from her apartment, Rudd unlocked the passenger door and assisted her into the front seat. Out of the wind and cold, she instantly felt warmer. Her gaze remained on Rudd as he walked around the front of the car and slid behind the wheel. As soon as he shut his door, he stuck the key into the ignition and started the engine.

The tension came back, even stronger than before. "Don't start the car, Rudd. I'm not going anywhere with you. You said you wanted to talk. So talk."

He raised a brow as he looked at her, surprised at her strong reaction. "I'm starting the engine so I can turn the heater on."

She relaxed somewhat until she saw the condition of his hand as he placed it on his thigh. The knuckles were scraped and red.

The sound of Ellen's exasperated voice brought his head up. "What did you do to your hand?"

"It's nothing. I knocked a couple of layers of skin off on the pavement when I was changing your tire last night."

"I'm sorry," she said, feeling it was inadequate but unable to come up with anything better.

"It's not your fault. I was trying to turn one of the lug nuts and my hand slipped. If I'd had the sense of a gnat I would have let your friend, Sam, do it instead of trying to come off as some macho jerk. I wanted to be the one to change your tire, not Sam or any of the other guys. Sounds like something from the school playground, doesn't it? Trying to show off for a girl's attention."

Rudd saw the amusement in her eyes and found himself responding to it as he had six months ago. He felt his tension slacken, and all she'd done was smile at him. For the first time in what seemed like forever, he felt his muscles relax.

He decided to get right to the point before she took a notion to hop out of the car. "Remember I said I wanted you to go away with me this weekend?"

She nodded. "It was the most unusual offer I had last night."

"I have a good reason for wanting you to go to Nantucket with me for the weekend. She's four years old. My daughter, Katie."

Ellen continued to look at him, showing no signs of surprise, shock, or even curiosity. "Go on."

"Two months ago, my ex-wife was killed in a car accident in Spain. She'd gone there to live after the divorce." He tried to keep the anger out of his voice and knew he'd failed when he added, "About a week after Cynthia died, I received a phone call from my lawyer informing me that she had left a will stating if anything happened to her, I was to have full custody of our daughter."

He paused before going on, but when Ellen still didn't make any comment, he continued. "I wanted to get on a plane and fly to Spain the moment I'd heard about Cynthia's death, but my lawyer said I wouldn't be able to have custody of Katie until all the paperwork was done, and that was going to take time. He advised me to wait until the legalities were taken care of before going over to get her."

He ran his fingers through his hair in an impatient gesture. "It was unbelievably complicated with two governments to satisfy, a lot of legalities to be observed, a passport for a minor to be issued. Finally, I was given the okay to go to Spain to bring her back. That's when I discovered I was going to have some problems trying to make her understand me. She only speaks Spanish, which I suppose is understandable under the circumstances, but difficult to get around since I don't speak the language. I was finally able to bring her back with me, but I haven't been able to communicate with her."

It didn't take a light bulb flashing in front of her face to make Ellen realize why Rudd had come to the party to find her. It wasn't because he'd suddenly developed an uncontrollable passion for her. Instead, he came looking for her because he'd remembered she had told him how she'd been raised by a Spanish housekeeper. How stupid could she be? she thought wearily. She should have learned her lesson six months ago, but apparently she hadn't. There was a small part of her that had hoped he'd come looking for her for a completely different reason.

She asked quietly, "Is this where I come in?"

He nodded. "I thought if you came with me to Nantucket, you could act as an interpreter between me and Katie. I have a summer place on the island. I thought it would be quieter and less confusing to take Katie and her nanny there, rather than bring her to my place in Boston.

She has enough adjustments to make without having to get used to a strange, large, busy city. It's quiet there and relatively private."

Ellen thought it was a strange decision for him to make. Instead of saying so, however, she asked, "How often have you seen her?"

"Every weekend since she arrived from Spain. Four weekends."

He'd misunderstood her question. She'd wanted to know how many times Rudd had seen his daughter since she was born. Maybe the answer would have been the same even if she'd phrased her question differently.

"And you want me to go to Nantucket for a weekend and act as an interpreter. Have I got that part right?"

He nodded. "I haven't been making much progress the way things are now."

"Aren't you expecting too much out of one weekend?"

"It would be a start. The way things are now, Katie's Spanish nanny translates every word I say. Señora Santana's made no secret of the fact she disapproves of me, so I can't be sure she's giving Katie an accurate translation. I don't know if Cynthia had said something about me to the nanny or whether the woman has simply made up her own mind that I am the bad guy who's taken them away from their home in Spain. Either way, Katie's nanny is only making the situation more complicated by not cooperating when I'm trying to get to know my daughter."

Ellen looked out through the windshield at the lights of the parking lot. If he'd wanted to get to know his daughter, he could have made an effort before this. He'd had four years, for crying out loud, she thought disgustedly.

After a moment, she asked, "Why me? You don't even know me very well, Rudd. What makes you think I would be an adequate interpreter between you and your daughter?''

He didn't hesitate. ''There isn't any one else I know who can speak Spanish. I do know you. I trust you. Will you do it? I realize it's a lot to ask, but it would only be for a weekend.''

She felt like arguing a point or two, like how he could possibly know whether or not he could trust her. Since his past experience with her consisted of sharing a meal, the most he could have formed an opinion on was the fact she had decent table manners. That fact certainly hadn't impressed him in the past, considering she'd never heard a peep from him until he dragged her out of the recesses of his memory because he happened to remember she spoke Spanish to the waiter in the restaurant where they'd dined together.

She realized that it didn't matter that he trusted her. She didn't trust him not to hurt her again.

As much as she hated the thought of his young daughter feeling lost and alone and unable to communicate with her own father, Ellen stalled at giving him an answer. ''Your ex-wife obviously spoke English. She had to learn from someone. What about your daughter's grandparents? Your ex-wife's parents?''

''Cynthia's father was an American. Her mother, Spanish. They were both killed in a camping accident when Cynthia was seventeen. She lived with her grandmother until she left Spain to attend school in Boston.''

''Is that how you met her?''

He nodded, which was the only response he was going to make on that subject. ''Her grandmother was in the car accident with Cynthia. They both died instantly. There are various aunts and uncles, but they're in Spain and Katie is here. Cynthia obviously hadn't taught Katie English since my daughter doesn't seem to understand a word I say."

After thinking for a few minutes, Ellen said, "I could put you in touch with the housekeeper who raised me. Mercedes is retired now but would know of someone who could help you with your daughter."

"No," he said roughly, then tempered his explosive reply by adding, "I don't want a stranger. I want you."

If only that was true, she thought ruefully, understanding the ironic twist of his statement even if he didn't. "I'd be a stranger to Katie as much as anyone else. Mercedes or anyone she recommends would be, too."

He stubbornly stuck to his choice. "It has to be you."

"I'd like to think about it."

The only sign Rudd gave that indicated he didn't like her answer was the way his fingers tightened around the steering wheel. "How long do you need to think about it?"

She could sympathize with his impatience. What she still didn't understand was why he'd parked his daughter so far away.

She didn't back down from her stand. "If you'll give me your phone number, I'll call you," she said, aware of the phrase being similar to the one he'd given her six months ago.

Rudd slowly relinquished his grip on the steering wheel and leaned back against the leather upholstery. "I guess I don't have any choice."

Something in his voice had her asking, "You didn't expect me to go with you today, did you?"

With a twist of his lips, he drawled, "It was a thought."

He reached overhead to take a business card from behind the visor. He also took a pen from the gear console between them and wrote his home phone number on the back of the card. Then he handed it to her.

"You can reach me at the number on the back late Sunday night. That's when I return from Nantucket. I'm on my way there now. If you haven't called me by then, I'll phone you early in the week."

She took the card and held it in her hand without looking at it. "I can't promise I'll be ready to give you my decision by then."

He looked at her briefly, then shifted his gaze to the card she held in her hand. "I'll call, anyway."

For several seconds, she studied him, trying to gauge what he was thinking, but his expression gave nothing away. When she realized she was looking for some sign of disappointment, she reached for the door latch. He couldn't express what he didn't feel. Impatience maybe, even frustration, but the idea that he regretted she wasn't immediately accepting his offer was ridiculous. It wasn't personal, you nitwit, she scolded herself. He simply wanted her for his daughter's sake, and she would be better off wishing for the moon than hope for something more personal between them. If she did agree to spend the weekend with him and his daughter, she was going to have to accept a lot less from him. It would be foolish to expect or hope for more.

When he made no move to stop her, Ellen opened the door and stepped out. She heard him say her name, but she continued to shut the door, effectively cutting off whatever it was he wanted to say. He'd already given her enough to think about; she didn't need any more.

Chapter Five

The restaurant on the top floor of one of the high-rise buildings in downtown Boston was one of those places where the waiters spoke in subdued tones and the tables, covered with crisp, white tablecloths, looked like they would keel over if more than two plates were put on them.

Ellen sat across from her father, pretending to enjoy the skimpy serving of whatever it was he had ordered in immaculate French. Those were the only words Paul Sheridan had spoken other than to wish her a happy birthday, two words more than he usually said to her.

When his secretary had called Ellen at work that morning to issue the invitation for lunch with her father, she had been astounded enough to agree to meet him. Surprise had given way to a mixture of other emotions, mainly irritation, as the luncheon progressed. A man with well-manicured nails and hair and perfect table manners, Paul Sheridan was dressed impeccably as usual. The image he presented had been carefully calculated from the color of his silk tie to the razor-sharp crease in his tailor-made suit. He kept his attention on his meal without once looking at Ellen or attempting to make conversation.

Ellen refused to fill the silence with inane chatter although she was tempted to fiddle with the silverware, which she knew drove him crazy. The cold stares she would get for her trouble would at least be a reaction to her presence, which was more than she'd gotten since she arrived. She barely resisted the urge to tug at the hem of her pewter gray skirt or check the lapel of the matching suit jacket to make sure it was lying flat. Her father always had that affect on her, making her feel as though something was always out of place with her appearance. Sometimes it was. Appearances had always meant a great deal to her father, and Ellen hadn't ever had the same priorities as he did—which was only one of the many bones of contention between them.

More for her own sake than to please her father, she'd dashed home and changed out of her work clothes while a taxi waited out front. Meeting her father wearing a pair of slacks and a cotton sweater would only antagonize him and remind him again of the type of work she did. Another bone for him to chew on.

Knowing from years of experience that her father would get to whatever it was he wanted to say eventually, she let her gaze roam around the room. Most of the tables were occupied with men like her father, in business suits without wrinkles or lint daring to cling to the expensive cloth. What conversation existed was muted.

Which was why she searched for the source of a robust laugh that suddenly rang out.

An older man seated at one of the tables near the wall of windows was laughing uproariously at something his companion had said. When she slid her gaze to the man across from him, she almost dropped the glass of wine she'd raised to her lips.

Rudd's amused eyes met hers, and he lifted his glass in a mock salute.

"Do you know that gentleman, Ellen?"

The sound of her father's deep voice had her jerking her head around. With great care, she set the glass of wine down on the table. "Yes, I do."

"And in what capacity would you know Professor Michaels? I don't recall mathematics ever being of any interest to you."

The insult was more in the tone than in the actual words. "It still isn't. I'm referring to the other man at the table."

For the first time, Paul Sheridan looked at his daughter directly. He carefully placed his napkin on the table and pushed his chair back. "I would like an introduction to Professor Michaels. Perhaps your friend would do the honors."

Knowing it would be easier to deflect a charging elephant than to try to talk her father out of going over to Rudd's table, she rose to follow him. She was aware of Rudd's gaze on her as she walked toward his table. What she didn't see was her father pausing to speak quietly to one of the waiters who nodded briskly, then hurried across the room in the opposite direction.

As she approached the table, Rudd stood up and the older gentleman did the same. "Hello, Ellen."

"Hello, Rudd." She hated this, but she didn't have any choice. "I'm sorry to disturb your lunch, but my father would like to meet your friend."

Rudd's sharp glance caught the strain in her eyes. Even though he didn't know the cause of it, he set out to ease it. He held out his right hand toward the tall man standing stiffly next to her. "How do you do, Mr. Sheridan? I'm Rudd Lomax."

A long time ago, Rudd's father had told him he could tell a lot about a man by the way he shook hands. In this instance, Rudd's impression was of a piece of granite: cold, hard, and without emotion.

Instinctively, Rudd slipped his hand around Ellen's, not one bit surprised to find her fingers curled into a fist. After a moment's hesitation, she relaxed her fingers and clung to his hand.

While he made the introductions, Rudd unobtrusively stroked his thumb over the indentations her fingernails had made in the palm of her hand.

He looked down at her. "I'd like you to meet one of my college professors, who thinks he knows everything there is about numbers even if he has to make it up, Professor Louis Michaels." Raising his gaze, he said, "Professor, this is a friend of mine, Ellen Sheridan."

Tufts of white hair bristled out from above each ear and matched the bushy eyebrows over the brightest blue eyes Ellen had ever seen. Extending her free hand to the older man, she said, "I'm pleased to meet you, Professor Michaels."

The professor took her hand but instead of shaking it, he lifted it and touched her knuckles to his mouth. "My pleasure, Miss Sheridan. Numbers aren't nearly as fascinating as a beautiful woman."

Chuckling, Rudd introduced the tall man standing stiffly at Ellen's side. "And her father, Paul Sheridan."

Turning to Ellen's father, the professor offered his hand and a polite smile. The professor's smile faltered when a flashbulb exploded the moment he took Paul Sheridan's hand. "What in the world?"

"I hope you don't mind, Professor Michaels," Ellen's father stated in an ingratiating tone that implied the professor should be flattered, not insulted. "I had my photographer on hand to record giving my daughter her birthday gift. I didn't want to pass up this opportunity to also have him take a picture of this occasion as well. I'm having a brochure made up to give out as a press release for my upcoming bid for the Senate and would consider it an honor if you would allow me to use a photo of our meeting."

Rudd could feel Ellen stiffen even more and wondered how that was possible. Her posture was as brittle as thin ice. Her expression was as frozen as her stance, her customary smile noticeably absent.

The professor wouldn't thank him for what he was about to do, but he couldn't stand to see Ellen like this.

"Why don't you and your father join us, Ellen?"

She turned and looked at him as though he had just lost his mind. "We've intruded enough," she said with difficulty.

As though she hadn't spoken, her father gestured to one of the waiters to bring more chairs to the table. Turning his back on Ellen, he said, "I've admired your work for years, Professor Michaels. I would enjoy talking to you about some of the work you've done for the budget committee."

If Paul Sheridan didn't catch the puzzled look the older man sent in Rudd's direction, Ellen did. "The professor was having a private lunch with his friend, Paul. We would be interfering."

Her father slowly turned his head toward her. "It is for the gentlemen to say, not you. Perhaps you should take this opportunity to return to your job. I'm sure our conversation would only bore you to tears."

The message couldn't have been clearer if it had been a ten-foot high neon sign. She took her cue. Summoning a stiff smile, she gave a brief nod in the professor's direction. "If you will excuse me, Professor Michaels. It was a pleasure to meet you."

"And you, my dear. Rudd, why don't you see Miss Sheridan down the elevator. I'll order coffee and fill Mr. Sheridan in on the budget woes of our government." Making a gesture with his hand, he waved them off. "Take your time. I would, if I was your age."

As Rudd led her away from the table, he leaned over and said softly, "I'm going to owe the professor a big one for this."

"You should stay with your friend. It's not his fault my father wants to use him for publicity."

Guiding her past the maître d', Rudd tightened his grip on her hand. "It's not your fault, either."

When they reached the bank of elevators, Ellen tried to free her hand without any success. "You don't need to see me out of the building, Rudd. Return to your friend and finish your lunch."

"I think you need a friend right now more than he does. The professor can handle your father."

She gave him a sideways glance as the elevator doors opened. Then she stepped inside. A number of people crowded in behind them and Rudd released her hand, sliding his arm behind her as they were pushed toward the back of the elevator. With each stop the elevator made, more people joined them until it was full. When the doors opened on the ground floor, Ellen and Rudd had to wait for everyone else to get out before they could move.

In the lobby, Ellen turned to Rudd. With as much dignity as she could muster, she asked, "Could I have my hand back, please?"

"No."

That wasn't the answer she expected. "Why not?"

"Because then you'll just walk away like you did Saturday morning. I'm learning that I need to hold on to you if I want to keep you with me."

His tone had been light, his words teasing. Hers was tight, her words excuses. "I need to get back to work, and you need to rescue your friend."

He shook his head. "What you need is something to eat. Maybe a little food will put some color back in your cheeks and the light back into your eyes."

"I just had lunch. Remember?"

"Yes, and you didn't eat it."

The last thing she wanted from Rudd was sympathy. "If you're feeling sorry for me, it's not necessary. I don't feel a bit bad about not getting my picture taken with my father."

"He's not exactly a candidate for Mr. Warmth, is he?"

The humor in his voice eased past her defensive pride. "Apparently, he's a candidate for the Senate," she said dryly.

Rudd tilted his head to one side so he could see her face. "You didn't know, did you?"

"I do now."

He heard the flat tone of her voice and responded to it. "Let's get out of here." When he felt her resistance under his hand, he said, "We could both use a breath of fresh air. You heard the professor. I don't need to hurry back."

Short of having a tug-of-war with him, Ellen had no choice but to follow him when he started toward the front entrance of the building. She was only too glad to be leaving, anyway. Meeting with her father always left her drained. She always came away feeling inadequate, which made her angry with herself because she knew she wasn't.

Childhood pain never seemed to go away when the child grew up—it only dimmed with time.

With an ease she envied, Rudd guided her through the heavy, noon crowd of people scurrying either to the nearest watering hole or back to the grind. About halfway down the block, he ducked into a doorway. He pushed the door open and ushered her inside ahead of him. By some miracle, there was an empty booth available near the back, and Rudd headed for it, gently guiding her toward it with a hand at her waist.

Standing to one side, he waited until she was seated, then slid onto the plastic cushion beside her. She'd clearly expected him to sit across from her and had to hastily move over to give him room.

Rudd was pleased to see that color had come back to her face, even if it was caused by irritation. He would use whatever it took to erase that frozen expression she'd had since he first looked up and saw her sitting across from her father. Surprise had given way to anger as he'd seen the way Paul Sheridan had ignored her as though she were one of the chairs pulled up to the table.

"Did you really design the sheets with the foliage and tropical birds all over them?"

Ellen turned her head and met his gaze, surprise widening her eyes. "If they have the Carstairs Design Studio label on them, then yes, I did. Why?"

"Maybe that's why I found myself thinking of you last night when I was in bed. I have your sheets on my bed." He brought his hand up to her neck and began to stroke the taut cords under his fingers. "But then again, maybe it wasn't the sheets at all. I've thought about you for the last six months."

Ellen was saved from having to make a comment by a young man who approached the table wearing a towel

knotted around his waist and carrying two large plastic
cards that served as menus. Casually tossing the menus
onto the table, the waiter gave them a friendly smile and
babbled off the specials of the day with colorful descriptions of how each dish was prepared.

Rudd glanced at Ellen, silently waiting for her to order.
After she'd chosen the chicken salad sandwich, he ordered the same. And coffee, one black and one with
cream. He had made the order automatically, unaware
he'd remembered she took cream in her coffee.

She noticed.

With the menus and the waiter removed, Rudd returned to the subject of her work.

"How did you get into designing fabrics?"

The look she gave him bordered on skeptical, as did her
tone. "Are you really all that interested in fabric designing?"

"Why would I ask if I wasn't?"

Since it was a safe topic and better than talking about
her father or Rudd's daughter, she went along with the
subject. "When someone buys a painting, there are only
a few people who will enjoy looking at it when they hang
it in their home. I liked the idea of having my work seen by
more than just a few, with the added benefit of creating
something people would use instead of simply adorning a
wall. To make extra money while I was in art school, my
roommate and I used to hire out with a couple of interior
design firms that wanted hand-painted tiles and sinks.
When I graduated, I had a portfolio of designs I'd done
when I applied at Carstairs. I got the job, and I've been
there ever since."

He wondered if she realized some of her tension had
dissipated. Not wanting it to return, he kept away from the
subject of her father. "In a way, that's what I try to ac-

complish as a chemist, to have some effect on the environment. The work I do could help make changes in soil conservation all over the country.''

The sandwiches were delivered with a flourish, the coffee cups set down without a drop being spilled even though the waiter was rushing about.

Because she really wanted to know, she asked, ''Were you one of those dreadful little boys who went around blowing up their parents' home with their chemistry sets?''

''Afraid so. I was the terror of Cedar Street in a little town in New Hampshire. Mothers used to ban their children from playing with me after I accidently singed off Billy Smith's eyebrows when I mixed the wrong compounds when we were trying to make gunpowder.''

Fascinated, Ellen asked, ''What happened? Did you get punished?''

''I couldn't sit down for a week.'' He took her hand and brought it up to her plate. ''Eat,'' he ordered. Then he continued telling her of other episodes of destruction and occasional successes with his early explorations into chemistry.

Satisfied to see her finish off the last of the sandwich, he ended by telling her how his father had found a way to control his son's adventures. ''My dad sent me to a summer camp that catered to science fanatics. The mad scientist became a serious student without experimenting with things that could endanger the neighborhood.''

She heard the humor and the affection in his voice when he spoke of his father. She had learned a long time ago that her relationship with her father was the exception, not the rule. There was no envy, only curiosity when she listened as he related other incidents from his childhood.

When the waiter plopped the check down on the table as he whizzed by, it made Ellen realize their lunch was coming to an end. To emphasize the point, she glanced at the slim watch on her wrist. "I've enjoyed the meal, Rudd, but I have to get back to work." Hesitating to bring up the incident with her father, she said, "And you have a harried professor waiting for you who will be ready to tear out what little hair he has left."

"Don't."

Startled, she blinked. "What?"

"Look so guilty and miserable. You aren't responsible for your father's actions."

"But I'm responsible for my own. I didn't have to bring him over and interrupt your lunch."

He smiled faintly as he slipped his hand into the inner pocket of his suit coat and withdrew his wallet. "From what little I've seen of your father, I think he would have found another way of having his picture taken with the professor. You should be more upset because your birthday celebration was interrupted."

"I can live without having the photographer record the touching scene of Paul Sheridan handing his only daughter a scarf his secretary had chosen."

"How do you know it was a scarf if you never got your present?"

"It's always a scarf."

Rudd stood up and extended his hand to assist her. He didn't let go of her until they were outside the restaurant.

Ellen flagged down a taxi she saw coming in their direction. As the cab stopped at the curb, she turned to Rudd and held out her hand. "Thanks again for lunch, Rudd."

"You keep running away from me. Why is that?"

"It's your imagination."

He shook his head but didn't argue. "I'll phone you later."

She met his steady gaze. "I still don't think it's a good idea for me to go to Nantucket with you."

"We'll talk about it later." He smiled and flicked a glance at the waiting cab. "Your meter's running."

Rudd stood on the sidewalk, oblivious to the people brushing by him as he watched the taxi pull away and meld into the traffic. Then he retraced his steps back to the French restaurant he'd left earlier.

He was going to have to make it up to the professor somehow for putting him through what had promised to be a supremely boring time with the overbearing lawyer. Hell, he'd even sit through the opera with the professor tonight if that's what it would take. It was worth any sacrifice on his part since he'd been able to make the haunting sadness in Ellen's eyes disappear.

He never wanted his own daughter to look at him with the cool wariness Ellen displayed when she was with her father. With Ellen's assistance, he would get to know Katie and have the close relationship he'd had with his own parents and possibly have a relationship with Ellen as well. The attraction between them was strong, whether Ellen was ready to admit it or not.

He wanted Ellen to come to Nantucket for his sake as well as his daughter's. She was just going to have to adjust if she thought he was moving too fast in a direction she didn't think she wanted to go.

Rudd sat on the edge of his bed and listened to the recording on Ellen's answering machine for the third time since he'd arrived home after dropping the professor off at his hotel. He hung up without leaving a message.

Glancing at the small clock beside his bed, he scowled. Where in the hell was she at eleven o'clock at night, damn it? He'd left two previous messages saying he'd called and asking her to phone him back when she got in. Either she hadn't gotten back, wasn't going to call him, or was there the whole time and ignoring his call.

He kicked off his shoes and piled a couple of pillows up against the headboard of his bed before leaning back. Even though he had to get up early to drive the professor to the airport, he knew he wasn't going to be able to sleep for a while.

Two minutes after he'd last looked at the clock, the phone rang. He picked it up even before it quit ringing.

"Ellen?"

"Hello, Rudd. You left a message for me to call you."

He could hear the weariness in her voice. "Are you all right? I was getting worried when you didn't answer."

There was a pause on the line. Then she said, "I was next door in Mrs. Kravitz's apartment. This is the anniversary of her husband's death six years ago, and she doesn't like to be alone."

He repeated his question since she hadn't answered it. "Are you all right?"

"Of course," she replied. "Why wouldn't I be?"

He could think of several reasons, but he didn't give her any of them. "The professor asked me to tell you he'd rather have had his picture taken with you than your father."

A soft chuckle came over the line. "I bet he really keeps the coeds hopping on campus. Has he forgiven you?"

"There was nothing to forgive. He had a great time. He said your father was just the right equation for a politician. I would have phoned you earlier than I did, but I took the professor to the opera tonight. One of his few passions other than mathematics."

"But not yours?"

Tucking the receiver in the crook of his neck, he crossed his arms over his chest. "My passions are a bit more basic."

She chuckled again. "I'm not going to touch that at this hour after listening to Mrs. Kravitz relive every day of her marriage with Sonny The Steamroller Kravitz. Especially her honeymoon, in colorful detail. Apparently, Sonny was as active in the bedroom as he was in the boxing ring."

Recalling his brief meeting with Ellen's neighbor, Rudd tried to picture the tiny ancient woman as a match for Sonny and failed completely.

Along with the humor, he could hear the weariness in her voice. "We'll discuss basic passion another time when you aren't so tired. How about tomorrow night?"

There were a few seconds of silence. "I still haven't made up my mind, Rudd."

"I want to see you, Ellen. And it has nothing to do with helping me with my daughter."

"Good night, Rudd," she murmured, then hung up.

Rudd lowered the receiver slowly, not giving in to the urge to slam it down, which would have been more satisfying. She didn't believe him. After meeting her father and seeing the way the older man had manipulated his daughter, it wasn't too surprising that Ellen expected the same from him.

He was just going to have to show her she was wrong.

Chapter Six

Ellen gave up trying to sleep when the clock on her bedside table told her it was a few minutes before six. Usually on Saturday mornings, she enjoyed the luxury of sleeping in as long as she could. However, this morning was going to be an exception.

After gulping down two cups of coffee, she returned to her bedroom and tugged on a pair of faded jeans and a baggy, gray Cambridge University sweatshirt over a tailored white shirt that she tucked into the waistband of her jeans. She slipped on a pair of old jogging shoes, not because she was going to go for a run, but because she didn't care if they got wet.

Taking a pail from under the sink, she filled it with water and a squirt of detergent before tossing in a fat sponge. She grunted with the effort of lifting the heavy pail and carried it out her front door and down the steps.

Some women cleaned out their kitchen cupboards or rearranged their closets or had their hair done when they were feeling less than chipper. Her father's housekeeper had baked fattening desserts. Tiffany bought jewelry to cheer herself up. Ellen washed her car. Even in fifty degree weather.

There had been times when she still lived with her father that she'd washed every single automobile in the multicar garage. By the time she'd finished washing his four luxury cars, she was usually too tired to dwell on whatever had been bothering her before. Unfortunately, doing such a menial task herself rather than have the servants do it had irritated her father even more than the simple fact of her very existence. The uncomplicated process of cleaning large vehicles had worked as a sort of therapy with the added benefit of turning inward anger and hurt into outward energy. Removing dirt and grime helped alleviate her frustrations, clarifying a situation or a problem so she could see it more clearly. Plus it was better than batting her head against a brick wall, which basically described any dealing she ever had with her father.

Luckily, the manager of her apartment house allowed the tenants to use the alley alongside the complex to wash their cars or to park recreational vehicles. Ellen and the other tenants knew they owed this privilege to the fact Mr. Pomeroy had a classic Thunderbird and a small travel trailer he kept in the alley, both of which he kept spotlessly clean.

After Ellen uncurled the hose from its coil, she turned on the water and proceeded to rinse off her car and suds it down. By the time she was halfway through, her fingers were chilled to the bone, but she didn't stop.

Because she was concentrating on rinsing off the soaped side of the car, she didn't see the gray Jaguar as it pulled into the alley. She was also blissfully unaware of the reaction of the man sitting behind the wheel when he saw how snugly her jeans hugged her bottom as she bent over to direct the spray from the hose on one of the hubcaps.

The first indication she had that she was no longer alone was when the hose was taken out of her hand.

She jerked her head around and saw Rudd holding the spray nozzle so it wouldn't hit either one of them. She glared at him. "What are you doing?"

"What does it look like I'm doing?" he muttered as he directed the spray toward the soapy car, inadvertently getting her wetter when some of the water splashed off the car and onto her legs.

"It looks like you're getting me wet."

"You're already wet."

Ellen stood back and studied him. It didn't take a genius to figure out that he was angry. She wasn't too pleased to see him, either. She'd been evading him all week by ignoring the messages he'd left on her answering machine several times. The last couple of days there hadn't been any calls from him so she thought he'd given up on her. She probably should have expected him to contact her again before he left for Nantucket that morning, but she hadn't expected him to show up in person.

As she bent down to take the sponge out of the water to continue washing her car, she smiled to herself. Maybe Rudd Lomax needed a little occupational therapy this morning, too. In his case, to work off some of his angry impatience.

Before she could wring out the sponge, it was taken out of her hand. Protesting, she tried to take it back. "I need that. I'm not finished."

"Yes, you are." He turned her reddened hand over and held it up practically in her face. "Your hands are almost frozen now."

He brought her hands together and began to rub them to try to bring some warmth back into them. Ellen protested, "Ouch! That hurts."

He looked at her for a few seconds, then dropped her hands and stepped over to turn off the water faucet. Coming back to her, he took one of her icy hands and started to walk toward the entrance of her apartment building.

Pulling back, Ellen said, "I want to finish washing my car."

"It's as clean as it's going to get. I don't know why you have this thing about wanting to turn into an icicle, but it's not going to happen while I'm around."

Even though it had been six months since he'd walked her to her door, he remembered which apartment was hers. When he stopped in front of her door, he held out his hand.

She looked down at his outstretched palm, a perplexed expression on her face. "Now what?"

"Your key."

She slid her hand into her back pocket and withdrew several keys on a key ring. He took it from her before she could slip it into the lock. When the door was open, he waited for her to proceed him.

Shutting the door behind him, Rudd ordered, "Take a hot shower and put on some dry clothes."

"Don't start with the bossy bit, Rudd. This happens to be my apartment, not yours."

"True, but you're wet, and I'm not." His gaze went to the front of her sweatshirt, lingering over the damp patches clinging to her breasts. "You're the craziest woman I've ever met, you know that? What in hell possessed you to wash your car on a cold day like this?''

Ignoring his last question, she commented on his first statement. "You wouldn't want a crazy woman around your daughter, so why don't we call the whole thing off? Okay?''

"Nice try, but it won't work. Go change. I'm going to make some coffee.''

She could have argued the point, but she would have been talking to herself. Rudd evidently didn't believe in wasting any time or else he was dying for a cup of coffee. She didn't have to wonder how he found the kitchen. Her apartment didn't require a lot of steps to get from one room to the other, considering there were only three of them.

The aroma of coffee filled the air the moment she opened her bedroom door fifteen minutes later. The steaming shower had warmed her, leaving a rosy glow on her skin in place of the redness caused by the cold air and water. She had exchanged her damp, faded jeans for a pair of clean jeans and a white knit sweater with a wide neckline that slipped down one shoulder.

When she entered her kitchen, she found Rudd leaning against the counter near the sink, a cup of steaming coffee in his hand. He'd taken off his leather jacket and had hooked it over one of the chairs. He was also wearing jeans and a sweater, his a dark, rich red that accentuated his dark hair and tanned skin.

It was odd how different the kitchen seemed with Rudd occupying her familiar territory. Or how much space he occupied. The small, windowless kitchen had just enough room for a table and two wooden chairs at one end with enough space to move between the stove, refrigerator, and sink without needing to take more than two steps. Rudd's solid frame didn't leave much extra room.

A cup was sitting on the counter to one side of him, steam rising from the top. She crossed the linoleum floor and picked up the cup obviously meant for her before walking over to the small table and pulling out one of the chairs.

He had told himself that he'd come early to see her because he couldn't wait for her to call him. Now his impatience was taking another form as his gaze lingered over her bare shoulder exposed by her sweater's wide neckline. Knowing she wasn't wearing anything underneath the sweater was giving him problems remembering he had other reasons for being in her apartment other than wanting to take her into the bedroom.

"You have an interesting apartment," he said to break the silence and the direction his thoughts were going. "I can honestly say I've never seen a picnic table in a living room before."

She was relieved that anger no longer glittered in his eyes. "Really? Why is that?"

"I guess I don't get around much," he drawled. "Would you mind telling me why you would have one in your living room?"

"Not at all. I couldn't afford a proper drawing table when I was in school, but I found a picnic table at a garage sale that worked perfectly for what I needed. In fact, I found it was better than the regulation table once I covered it with a sheet of plywood."

"I remember reading an article in the local newspaper about your father bidding on an antique writing desk that supposedly belonged to Napoleon. If he could afford to pay half a million dollars for a desk, I would have thought he could have bought his daughter a drawing table."

"It proved to be a fake. He didn't take it very well, from what I heard."

Rudd had been looking around her tiny kitchen, but the dry tone of her voice brought his gaze back to her. "I don't imagine he would. You still haven't explained why your father buys expensive antique desks while his daughter buys picnic tables at a garage sale."

"My father and I have different priorities."

"Obviously. What about your mother? You never mention her."

Most people accepted her reticence in discussing her family. Rudd wasn't most people. "She left when I was young. Tiffany found out from her mother that there'd been quite a scandal when Paul Sheridan's wife ran off with his law partner."

She could have been talking about the weather, he thought. "Where is she now?"

"According to a newspaper clipping Tiffany showed me, my mother was killed in a car accident in Los Angeles." Her brow creased with thought. "That must have been about fifteen years ago, I guess."

Which meant she'd been fifteen when she'd found out her mother was dead. "Tiffany told you? Not your father?"

"Her name was never mentioned in my father's house from the day she left. I have the dubious distinction of looking like her, which doesn't exactly endear me to my father."

Rudd realized she'd just given him the reason her father treated her like dirt. "That must have been tough, growing up without a mother."

The emotion missing during her discussion about her mother was suddenly in her voice and glittering in her eyes. "Tiffany's mother, the sweetest woman God ever put on this earth, is blind because of a drunk driver. That's tougher than anything I've had to deal with."

Ellen frowned when he stared at her with an odd expression in his eyes. "Why are you looking at me like that?"

"You keep surprising me."

"I try to please."

"You manage to do that quite well." A corner of his mouth curved upward. "How long have you lived here?"

She wasn't at all pleased with the direction the conversation was going. No matter how she answered him, it would inevitably lead to more questions. "Quite a while."

"How long is 'quite a while'?"

"Does it matter?"

He took the time to sip his coffee, his gaze on her the whole time. Finally, he said, "Apparently, it does or you would simply answer the question."

She lifted her shoulders in a dismissive gesture. "I moved here before I started my freshman year of college. To save you from having to subtract, it was twelve years ago."

His gaze roamed around the tiny kitchen. "Did you sign a lifetime lease or something?"

She couldn't blame him for wondering why she would still be living in a dinky apartment when she could undoubtedly afford something bigger, not to mention nicer. He wasn't the only one who thought that, just the only one who put it so bluntly.

"I like it here."

"Obviously. That still doesn't explain why you've never moved into a bigger apartment."

"This is my home."

There was something poignant in the way she said "home" that affected him strangely. Considering where he lived, he was the last person to judge her choice of living quarters. Rudd waited until she'd taken one sip from her cup before he asked, "Have you come to a decision yet?"

She didn't need to ask about what. She leaned back in her chair. "I guess you couldn't wait for my phone call."

When she moved, her sweater had fallen an inch farther off her shoulder. His fingers tightened around the mug to keep from trailing them over the delicate curve of smooth, bare flesh. It took him a few seconds to remember what they were talking about.

"I couldn't take the chance that you might not call at all, especially since you haven't had the courtesy to return my calls this week."

Ellen hated knowing he had a right to be angry. Defensive, she answered, "I haven't made up my mind yet."

He reached into the breast pocket of his shirt and took out a photo. Handing it to her, he said, "Maybe this will help."

She didn't want to look at the picture, knowing instinctively who would be in the photo, but she had no choice. She had tried very hard all week not to think about his daughter. Now the little girl would become real.

Ellen studied the image of the child staring into the camera. The likeness to Rudd was remarkable. Dark hair, the same linear cheekbones, even a similar solemn, unsmiling expression. The haunting sadness in the girl's eyes tore at Ellen's heart.

Her voice shook slightly as she murmured, "This isn't fair, Rudd."

"I don't feel like being fair. It isn't fair that I can't make her understand that I want to do everything possible to make her be a happy, normal, little girl. I can say it over and over, but she doesn't understand what I'm trying to tell her."

Even though she resented the emotional blackmail he was inflicting by producing the photo of his daughter, Ellen couldn't fault his reasons for using whatever means at hand. Maybe he was finally realizing his duties as a parent and was willing to take them seriously.

Staring down at the image of the unsmiling child, Ellen bit her lip. She knew how alone Katie must be feeling right now. She'd been a year older than Katie when her own mother had left the house never to return. But there was a big difference between Katie's situation and her own. Katie had a father who seemed to finally want to become involved in his child's life.

It was for this reason that Ellen slowly placed the photo down on the table and faced Rudd, saying, "I've given this a great deal of thought, Rudd. I would really like to help you and your daughter, but there's one thing that makes me think I'm the wrong person to go to Nantucket with you."

"What is it?"

"Ever since we met again at the party the other night, you've spent half the time being angry with me for some reason or other. I'm not sure I want to spend time in the company of someone who's furious with me."

Something moved in his eyes as he stared at her. Then a corner of his mouth curved into a mocking smile. "It isn't you I've been angry at. It's me. I'm mad at myself because I can't fight the way you make me feel. I was attracted to you six months ago and that hasn't changed."

"And you don't want to be," she stated, needing what he was saying clarified.

"I didn't want to be," he answered, purposely changing her statement to the past tense. But that didn't seem to make a difference.

"So, it appears we have a problem."

He shook his head. "There's no problem. I want you to come to Nantucket. I can't promise I won't want to take you to bed, but I can promise I won't unless it's what you want, too."

At least now she knew where she stood, even if it was on shaky ground.

There was still the happiness of a small child to consider that had to take precedence over her bruised ego. She took a deep, steadying breath and said, "My Spanish might be a little rusty, but I'll go to Nantucket with you."

He lowered his head and stared down at the coffee mug he was holding tightly in his hand. After a few moments, he raised his head and met her gaze, the relief and flickering hope in his eyes laid bare for her to see.

"Thank you, Ellen."

She took a sip of coffee, more for something to do than because she wanted the coffee, deeply affected by the emotion in his eyes. "You're welcome," she replied.

"I should have mentioned this before. I'll pay you for whatever time you—"

Her coffee mug made a loud clunk on the table as she set it down next to the photo with more force than was necessary. "I wouldn't try it if I were you," she said tightly. "If you think I'm the type of woman to take money for helping a small child, then you don't know me at all."

She turned to leave the kitchen with the intention of opening the door so he would leave. It took him two strides to reach her and turn her around. He put his hands on her shoulders to keep her in front of him, aware of the delicate bones under his fingers. Proud and defiant, she lifted her chin and glared at him.

He'd never wanted a woman more.

Easing his hold, he clamped down on his raging hunger. "I don't mean to insult you, Ellen. Simply saying thanks doesn't seem enough, somehow. It isn't as though I can expect you to do me this favor out of friendship. I thought it might make you feel better about going with me if we kept this on a business basis."

That was clear enough, she thought. If he'd taken an ad out in *The New York Times,* it couldn't have been more obvious what Rudd thought of her agreement to help him.

She had her own point to make. "I'm not doing this for you. Your daughter must be feeling very alone right now. Her mother is dead and she has only her nanny to talk to, and now she's in a strange place away from everything that is familiar to her."

"I'm asking you for a hell of a lot when you're getting nothing back in return."

She could have argued that notion. She was getting a great deal. She was getting her ego battered free of charge by his distaste of the idea of becoming personally involved with her.

"I'm going because your daughter needs to know she has a father who wants to take care of her. You offer me money, and you'll have worse than a few scraped knuckles."

The last thing he thought he would be capable of doing at this moment would be to smile, but Rudd couldn't help it. Her heated response was much easier to deal with than her cool acceptance. A corner of his mouth lifted as he looked down at her.

"You really think you're one tough cookie, don't you?"

"You bet. Blackstrap molasses and hardtack. When would you want me?"

She watched in fascination as his eyes glittered with a heat that made the coffee she'd just sipped seem like ice water. She felt his fingers tighten on her shoulders, as if he were going to pull her into his arms. Then he dropped his hands abruptly as though touching her was burning his fingers, which was pretty close to the feeling he was experiencing.

He took up his former position leaning against the counter and calmly picked up the cup of coffee again. Ellen was irrationally pleased to see that his hand shook slightly. Maybe he wasn't as unaffected by her as he wanted her to believe. Or that she wanted to believe.

Stating her question a little differently, she asked, "When do you want me to come to Nantucket?"

A corner of his mouth curved upward before he glanced at the watch on his wrist. "How long would it take you to pack?"

Stunned, she stared at him, her eyes widening in disbelief. "You want me to leave with you now?"

He wished she would stop using the word *want*. It too accurately described how his body was responding to her. "I'm leaving now. You've just agreed to spend the weekend with me. What's the problem?" He paused a moment then said, "Unless you have other plans."

Her fingers clasped the coffee mug, wishing it held something stronger. "As a matter of fact, I do. I've made plans to have dinner with someone this evening."

"You have a date?"

She felt like throwing the cup into his face. He made it sound as though her having a date was as absurd as rain falling up instead of down. "Odd as that must seem to you, there are a few men who enjoy my company," she replied tartly.

He didn't find that odd at all. He just didn't like the thought of her being with another man. And he didn't like his jealousy any better.

Rudd's intent gaze never left her face. "I don't suppose you'd consider breaking the date?"

She shook her head. "No, I wouldn't."

"Who's the guy?"

"No one you would know."

"Is this guy going to raise any objections to you spending the weekend with me?"

"*I* might if you put it like that," she said dryly.

He rephrased the question. "Is it serious?"

She could have told him she was going over to Jack's house for dinner where they were going to work on a mural in a room he and Sonya were setting aside for a nursery, but she would rather he thought she was going out for a completely different reason.

"I take my friends very seriously."

He didn't know why he was pushing, but he had the sense to stop. Rudd turned and set the mug down beside the sink. With his back to her, he placed his hands on the edge of the counter, his head slightly bowed. "So this weekend is out. How about next weekend?"

She should tell him she'd changed her mind. "If you haven't found someone else in the meantime, I'll go next weekend."

He turned. "I won't be looking for anyone else to take your place. I'd like to leave around seven o'clock Saturday morning, if that's convenient."

His considerate tone was socially correct and impeccably polite. She hated it. "Saturday will be fine."

Nodding his head once, he grabbed his jacket and, hooking it on one finger, slung it over his shoulder. He paused briefly. "You aren't going to go back outside and continue washing your car, are you?"

"No," she stated. "It isn't necessary any longer."

He looked at her with an odd expression. "Good," was all he said.

Ellen walked him to the door. Standing in the doorway, Rudd looked at her as he shrugged into his jacket. He shoved his hands in his pockets and murmured, "I thought I knew all there was to know about chemistry, but I'll be damned if I know what this is between us."

Whether it was an experiment or a conclusion, his kiss was devastating. Whether it was on purpose or not, he didn't touch her except with his lips. Whether or not she wanted his tongue melding with hers, she allowed him in.

Desire rose to the surface, hot and steaming as he eased the pressure on her mouth and closed his teeth over her bottom lip, then stroked his tongue across it.

When she gasped, he took her mouth deeper, the heavy beat of arousal throbbing between them. His breathing was as ragged as hers when he raised his head and looked down at her.

Stunned, Ellen stared at him, seeing him smile faintly at her dazed expression. Then he turned away and closed the door quietly behind him, leaving her alone. For a few seconds, she leaned against the solid, wooden door. During the last few minutes, her world had tilted off its axis, and she was unable to regain her balance. It wasn't as easy as it should have been. She'd been kissed before, but she'd never felt the searing clench of need like this.

There was one consolation, she thought, remembering the heated look of arousal she'd seen in his eyes before he'd left. Rudd seemed as bewildered about the attraction between them as she was.

She stepped away from the door, idly repositioning the small figurine of a baby seal as she passed the table in the hall on her way back to the kitchen. Following a pattern she'd set early in life, she straightened her surroundings when her emotions were in a turmoil.

Entering the kitchen, she walked to the table and reached for her coffee mug with the intent of washing it. But she didn't pick up the cup. She picked up the photo beside it. Holding it in her hand, she glanced toward the door, her first thought was to rush out of her apartment to try to catch Rudd and return the photo.

Then she realized he'd left the photo on purpose. A form of insurance, a reminder that a child's happiness was at stake if she changed her mind.

Chapter Seven

Ellen changed her mind about going to Nantucket at least a dozen times. And that was only on Monday. She'd packed and unpacked her overnight bag so many times, she was going to have to wash the clothes if she moved everything back and forth from her closet to the case and back again once more. By noon on Tuesday when she met Tiffany for lunch, she was a borderline basket case just waiting to be carried off to the nearest happy farm.

Her friend, naturally, wasn't going to let Ellen get by with denying she was uptight about anything, no matter how many times she tried. They were sitting at one of the tables of a small restaurant in a shopping mall when Tiffany's patience with Ellen's evasive answers gave out.

"Don't give me any of that garbage about nothing being wrong, Ellen. I know you, remember? You don't get a case of the fidgets over nothing. I've seen you through enough minor and major crises to know the difference between a little wrinkle and a big ditch. What's up?''

After a moment's hesitation, Ellen opened her purse and took out the photo of Katie Lomax that Rudd had left on her kitchen table. She'd been carrying the photo around with her since Saturday and was almost as familiar with the little girl's face as she was her own. She handed it across the table, and Tiffany gave her a puzzled glance before she took it from her.

After she examined the child in the photo carefully, turned it over and discovered there was nothing written on the back, she asked, ''Am I supposed to know who this is?''

''Her name is Katie Lomax.''

An elegantly curved brow raised in silent appraisal. ''Lomax? As in Rudd Lomax, the attractive gate-crasher the night of your birthday party? The one who spirited you away although you won't tell me a thing about what happened after you left with him?''

''She's his daughter.'' In a few succinct sentences, Ellen told Tiffany about Rudd's ex-wife, how Rudd had ended up with his daughter, and his request for her services as an interpreter.

Tiffany studied the photo again. ''You agreed to help him, of course?''

Sighing heavily, Ellen played with the silverware beside her plate. ''Yes. Against my better judgment.''

Handing the picture back to Ellen, Tiffany asked, ''So what's causing those frown lines? It sounds pretty straightforward to me. Unless you left something out.''

''Well, there is one little thing,'' she admitted grudgingly.

Tiffany leaned forward, waiting for Ellen to continue. When she didn't Tiffany prodded, ''What little thing?''

"I sort of met Rudd six months ago and sort of had dinner with him."

Tiffany pursed her lips for a moment. "Gee, Ellen. This sounds really exciting. I've never 'sort of' met a man before and 'sort of' had dinner with him. Did you 'sort of' fall for the man?"

Ellen released the knife she'd been playing with and scowled at her friend. "I told you, I only saw him that once. Nothing ever came of it. He never called to ask to see me again. I didn't see him again until he showed up at the hotel the night of my birthday party. The reason he wanted to see me was because I was the only person he knew who spoke Spanish, not because he suddenly couldn't live without me."

Picking up her glass of water, Tiffany took a sip instead of making a comment right away. When she did, her voice was gentle, her gaze serious and concerned. "Sometimes it only takes one meeting, one glance, one touch to become infatuated, attracted, or even in love with someone. You aren't the type of woman who would hesitate to help a child, especially with your particular circumstances, unless you had a darn good reason. For you to even struggle with the idea of going away for a weekend with this man when a child's happiness is at stake means you are more deeply involved with this little girl's father than you're letting on."

Ellen shook her head. "I don't want to become involved with Rudd Lomax. That's why I'm not sure it's a good idea for me to spend time with him."

"Because he dropped you once before, and you don't want it to happen again?"

"Call me foolish, but I don't particularly like to walk into a situation knowing there is a chance of being rejected. Contrary to popular belief, lightning can strike twice in the same place. I'd just as soon not get burned again.''

"Understandable," agreed Tiffany. "But could you live with yourself if you didn't make a small child's life a little easier by helping make her relationship with her father better for both of them?''

"I can help with the language problem, but I can't do anything about making Rudd a father who cares about his daughter."

"But he does care. He looked you up when he realized he needed help," reasoned Tiffany, as she lifted a hand and gracefully gestured for the check when she spotted their wandering waiter. "I think you're more concerned about your own feelings for this man."

Ellen thought *concerned* was a tame word for the gut-wrenching fear knotting her stomach. "I could never be serious about a man who ignored his daughter's existence for the first four years of her life."

Dropping her light tone, Tiffany said, "You already are serious about him, Ellen. You wouldn't be putting yourself through all this agony of decision if you didn't care about him. You know, there could be a darn good reason why he didn't see his daughter all that time. Maybe he and his ex-wife didn't get along. There could have been legal problems. There could be a lot of different reasons. Perhaps after you spend some time with him this weekend, you'll understand."

Her friend's arguments were all valid, but Ellen always came back to one irrefutable fact. "I'll never understand someone who could ignore his own child for four years."

"And you can't turn your back on a small child. You know what it's like to have a father who has neglected you for most of your life. Even if there's a danger of Rudd

Lomax breaking your heart, you can't let that little child down when it's within your power to help her."

Looking down at the photo of Katie Lomax, Ellen said, "I guess I don't really have a choice, do I?"

"No. I don't think you do." Tiffany fumbled through her purse for some money to pay their bill. "What you need are some new clothes to take with you. We still have a little time left before you have to return to your office. We'll find something incredibly sexy to knock Rudd Lomax out of his socks."

Shaking her head in exasperation, Ellen said, "I'm not going to buy a new outfit. Rudd's socks are going to stay on his feet. Since you have the need to buy something for this trip, how about if we find a bookstore so we can find some books to help Katie learn English?"

Tossing some cash onto the table, Tiffany scoffed, "You're no fun. I'll compromise. We'll get the books and the sexy outfit."

Aside from ending up with some frothy underthings only she would ever see, Ellen had ended the battle with herself about the wisdom of spending the weekend with Rudd and his daughter. It was only for two days, and she would be helping a small child. Tiffany was right. Her conscience wouldn't allow her to do anything else. The rest of her would cope. She was going into this with her eyes wide open and her heart safely encased in caution. She didn't have a thing to worry about.

Wednesday evening, she had her arms full of two grocery bags, her art portfolio tucked under her arm, and the strap of her purse looped over her shoulder as she left the elevator in her apartment building. It would have made more sense for her to make two trips instead of trying to carry everything all at once, but she wasn't feeling particularly smart, just tired. It had been one of those days when the creative juices had dried up along with several jars of premixed colors of paint she needed to finish a design on time. It had required a little redesigning to get the job done, but it ended up working better than the original, so all had not been lost.

At her door, she fumbled with the flap of her purse while balancing one of the grocery bags on her hip. As she dug into her purse for the keys, she saw one of the apples at the top of the bag in her other arm start to move. There wasn't a darn thing she could do about it at the moment except watch it slowly fall over the side of the paper bag.

She waited for the soft thud of the apple hitting the carpeted floor. She had a long wait. There was no thud.

If she could have seen her feet, she would have looked for the stupid apple so she wouldn't step on it. But when the apple suddenly levitated in front of her face, she let out a small screech. Then she realized it was being held in the palm of a man's hand.

Jerking her head to the side, she gasped, "Rudd! What in the world are you doing here other than giving me a heart attack?"

"Playing left field." He stuck the apple back into the grocery bag before taking it away from her, grunting as he took the full weight of the sack. "Good Lord, Ellen. What have you got in here? A bowling ball?"

"How'd you guess?" she muttered, as she stuck her key into the lock. After opening the door, she stepped into her apartment and let the portfolio under her arm drop to the floor in the hallway.

Rudd followed her into the kitchen where she deposited her sack onto the counter, then turned to take the other one from Rudd. Instead of emptying the contents immediately as she would have done if she were alone, she turned to face him.

"Are you here to call off the weekend?"

He shook his head. "No way."

"But this is Wednesday, not Saturday."

"Thank you, Ellen," he said with mock gravity. "I occasionally know what day it is."

He reached around her and took the apple back out of the sack. "I wanted to make sure *you* haven't changed your mind."

What mind? She'd lost it days ago. "I usually keep my word when I say I'm going to do something." She watched as he bit into the apple. "Help yourself."

"Thanks," he said with a faint smile. "I think I will."

She caught a glimpse of a white shirt and tie under the trench coat he was wearing. Evidently, he'd come to her apartment directly from work. She thought briefly about making polite conversation about the weather or his work, but didn't. As before, he made her feel crowded in the small kitchen, not just physically, but emotionally, as though he were filling an empty space inside her just by being in the same room.

Because that realization made her wonder how empty she would feel when she was alone again, she brushed past him to walk into the living room. Kicking off her shoes, she shrugged off her suit jacket and draped it over the back of the couch. Rudd continued to munch on the apple as he leaned against the doorframe and watched her plump up one of the throw pillows and straighten a stack of magazines on the coffee table.

"Am I stopping you from doing something?"

"As you can see, I'm doing it."

"All I can see is you're finding things to do that really don't need doing. Why are you so nervous?"

"Good question," she murmured. Falling back on good manners, she asked, "Would you like something to drink to go along with the apple? I don't keep any beer or alcoholic beverages on hand, but I could make coffee."

He smiled faintly. "*Palmer's Etiquette Guide* again?"

"My impeccable upbringing. Do you want coffee or not?" she asked aggressively, making a mockery of her previous statement about good manners.

He shook his head. Finished with the apple, he turned back into the kitchen, then returned to the living room without the remnants of the fruit. He took up his stance in the doorway again, propping his shoulder against the wood frame, his hands shoved into the pockets of his trench coat.

"I owe you an explanation."

"About what?"

"About why I didn't call you or try to see you again after we met six months ago." He saw her begin to shake her head and the guarded expression returned to her eyes. "It's between us, and I want to get it out of the way. I don't want any misunderstandings clouding the issue this weekend."

"I think I've got it fairly straight," she said dryly. "Your daughter speaks Spanish, I translate it into English, you tell her something back, and I tell Katie in Spanish what you said."

"I'm not talking about Katie. I'm talking about us. You've been defensive with me ever since I saw you at the hotel. If we're going to be spending the weekend together, I would like to get a few things cleared up before we leave."

She half expected him to bring out a list and start reading from it. Crossing her arms across her chest, she said, "I'm all agog."

His expression could best be described as glowering. "You're not making this easy."

"Sorry," she murmured, sounding anything but sorry. "By all means, let me make it easy for you. Our previous meeting reads like a poorly written script for a soap opera. Two people meet, have dinner and a few laughs, a good night peck on the cheek, and a tidy exit. Then the curtain goes down. The end."

"We must have had two different sets of scripts. I don't recall kissing you on the cheek. I remember how soft you felt, how you moved against me, how your tongue stroking mine nearly made me go up in flames. If I hadn't stopped, we would have finished the kiss in your bedroom and not come out for days."

She couldn't look away from the heated awareness in his dark eyes. Her chest began to hurt, and she realized she'd been holding her breath. Her pride forced her to pull air into her lungs and answer, "I'll stick with my script."

His eyes narrowed. "So you would just as soon forget what happened between us six months ago?"

"I already have."

He didn't believe her. Slowly walking toward her, he murmured, "Let me refresh your memory."

When he dragged her into his arms, he felt her warm breath on his skin. Pleasure skimmed through him as he took her mouth with more force than he intended. Need rode him like an angry shadow. A fiery specter clawing at him, haunting him until he thought he would go crazy unless he could get it off his back.

Slanting his mouth over hers to give him more of her taste, he let her scent surround him, engulf him. He could tell himself he only wanted to show her she hadn't been able to forget the explosive embrace they'd shared at her door six months ago. He could, but it would be a lie. It wasn't his ego that was bruised. The pain came from knowing no matter how much he wanted Ellen, he wouldn't do anything about it until she showed him or told him she wanted him just as much.

His heart thudded painfully in his chest when he felt her hands clench his shirt and her tongue slide along his. Exhilaration flooded through him. She was as caught up in the magic between them as he was.

When he felt the edges of control thin out to a thread, he raised his head and looked down into her glazed, green eyes. Knowing she was aroused didn't make it easy for him to step away from her. When her gaze followed him, he saw confusion and hurt.

Running his hands restlessly through his hair, he said, "I didn't come here tonight to take you to bed."

"I didn't think you did, and we haven't."

This wasn't going at all the way he'd planned, but he charged ahead, anyway. "I failed at trying to make my marriage work. I don't want to fail with Katie or with you."

She waited for more of an explanation than he'd given her so far, but he didn't say anything else. Unsure what he was trying to tell her, she clasped her hands together so he wouldn't see how they were trembling. "Relationships don't come with guarantees and children don't, either."

"I don't like leaving things to chance."

If he thought that what he was saying made sense, he was wrong. If anything, she was getting more confused than ever.

"You can't control everything in your life, Rudd."

"Maybe not, but I can put my daughter's needs ahead of my own. I've missed four years of her life, and I'll do whatever I have to do to make up for that. I *have* to put her first. Do you understand?"

"Some things you have to let evolve into whatever they are supposed to be."

He glanced over at the picnic table that served as her drawing area. A large sheet of paper was tacked to a drawing board that had been propped up by several books at the two top corners. A colorful geometric design was in several stages of production. "Is that how you create your designs? Just let them evolve?"

"Sometimes."

"That's the difference between us. I can't operate that way. I like everything orderly and in place."

She had the feeling he had just revealed more than a character trait. It was the way he wanted things to be in his life, and it had nothing to do with his scientific background. What puzzled her was why he appeared to be uncomfortable with the fact that she didn't fit into any pattern he was familiar with. The one thing he had made clear was that he didn't want any type of relationship with her, so why was he having such a battle with himself? And why did he kiss her again?

Unable to keep looking at her when his body was aching, Rudd let his gaze roam around the room. His attention was caught by one particular painting in the group of seven framed pieces of artwork nearly covering one wall. The watercolor depicted a young girl standing alone in a field of wildflowers. A straw hat hid her face, except for a determined chin and a pensive mouth. The child's arms were full of flowers, her dress an old-fashioned pinafore.

There was something familiar about the little girl, and Rudd stepped closer to examine it. When he spotted the signature, he turned to look at Ellen. "*You* did this?"

With a rueful twist of her mouth, Ellen drawled, "I'm overwhelmed by your praise."

He smiled crookedly. "I'm sorry. I didn't mean to sound condescending. I'm just surprised. This type of painting is a long stretch from designing sheets and pillowcases."

She wondered if he realized he was steadily digging a deeper hole for himself. "Designing sheets, as you call it, pays the rent. Those paintings on the wall don't."

Rudd continued to study the painting without making any further comment. His silence was beginning to wear on her nerves. "What is it you want from me, Rudd? Do you want me to put it in writing that I don't expect anything to develop between us? I'll do it, if it will make you more comfortable with my presence this weekend."

He shoved his hands into the pockets of his trench coat. "That won't be necessary," he said with irritation. "I just want you to understand that I have to put my daughter first right now."

The more he explained, the less she understood. If he was worried because she'd responded when he'd kissed her, she didn't consider the kiss made a major commitment, for Pete's sake.

"It will be difficult, but I'll try to control myself this weekend. Your virtue will be safe with me." She got to her feet, feeling oddly humiliated that he felt he needed to make excuses not to become involved with her as if she were some pathetic, love-starved spinster. Walking in her stockinged feet to the door, she pulled it open. "Now, if you'll kindly leave, I'd like to change clothes and do some work I brought home with me."

He came toward her, stopping in front of her. "You make me sound foolish."

She shook her head, a hint of amusement glittering reluctantly in her eyes. "You're doing that all by yourself."

He smiled faintly. "I guess I am. You still want to take the chance of going to Nantucket with a crazy man?"

"I live for danger."

He shook his head in bemusement and did something that seemed to startle him as much as it did her. He lifted his hand and lightly touched her nose in an affectionate gesture. Something moved in his eyes when he lowered his gaze to her mouth. His mouth twisted ruefully as he dropped his hand.

"I'll see you Saturday."

She fought back the desire to put her arms around him and simply hold him. He seemed so sad and lonely even though she sensed sympathy was the last thing he would accept from her. He appeared to be fighting enough battles with himself. She supposed she should be flattered he considered her such a threat to his peace of mind, but that wasn't even close to the way he made her feel.

He seemed to be waiting for her to confirm the plans for Saturday so she nodded and said, "Seven o'clock."

After a brief hesitation, he gave her an abrupt nod of his head, then left.

Ellen slowly closed the door and leaned against it. What was that all about? she wondered. If he had come to make a point, she'd missed it altogether. She had known his reasons for wanting her to go to Nantucket. It wasn't necessary for him to beat her over the head with them.

Or to kiss her.

Chapter Eight

Rudd knocked on Ellen's door at exactly seven o'clock the following Saturday morning. When she opened the door, she didn't immediately move out of his way so he could enter her apartment. Even though she'd come to terms with her apprehensions, she still wasn't totally sure she was doing the right thing.

After raising her gaze to meet his, she slowly stepped back and made a gesture for him to come in. His gaze slid over her blue-and-white striped shirt and royal blue slacks, down to her rubber-soled loafers. His examination reminded her of a drill sergeant inspecting the troops.

He looked up and caught her studying him. "Are you ready?"

Now was the time to tell him she wasn't going. Instead, she found herself saying, "I'm as ready as I'll ever be."

"You'll need a coat. It's cold."

She took a red leather jacket from the hall closet. As she slipped the coat on, he stood in the entryway watching her without offering any assistance, much to her relief. She'd come to terms with the part she was to play that weekend. She would be able to do it without any difficulty as long as he didn't touch her.

By the time Rudd placed her suitcase next to his in the trunk of the car, the clock on the dashboard read a little after seven o'clock and the sun would have been shining by now if it had been that kind of day. For once the weatherman's prediction was right on the money. It was indeed an overcast day with a chance of rain. A very good chance.

While Rudd waited for her to fasten her seat belt, he said, "I hope you don't mind a long ride. It'll be a couple of hours before we reach the marina."

She jerked her head around. "Marina?" she repeated, hoping she hadn't heard him correctly. "What marina?"

"I have a boat in Cape Cod we'll be taking across Nantucket Sound to the island."

It hadn't occurred to her that the only way to get to Nantucket was over water. It should have. Nantucket is an island which means to anyone with half a brain that it is surrounded by water. Which means they have to go across water to get to it. All simple deduction. It was just a shame she'd never thought of that before now, when she could have semigracefully bowed out of the expedition.

She closed her eyes to shut out the thought of dark, icy water closing over her. It didn't work. She rubbed her arms as though she could erase the sensation of exhausted muscles and chilled skin. Even though the memories were years old, they were still all too vivid. She remembered the feeling of trying to stay afloat, water stinging her eyes, and fear clutching her stomach as though it had happened yesterday.

Feeling ridiculous, Ellen dropped her hands back into her lap. This wasn't even close to the same situation as before. She was going on a boat of her own free will. There was no reason for her to go overboard this time.

"Ellen?"

Startled, she jerked her head around to meet his puzzled gaze. A little too loudly, she barked, "What?"

"What's wrong? We're only going to Nantucket, not to the Himalayan mountains. Why are you so jumpy?"

"Is there any other way of getting to the island than by boat?"

"We could take a plane or a helicopter, but that's not really necessary when I have a perfectly good boat."

She bit her lip, then decided she might as well be honest up front rather than have him discover the truth the hard way. Like when she clung to the dock like a barnacle rather than get on the boat.

"During our one and only long conversation over dinner, did I mention I'm not exactly a world-class sailor?"

He smiled faintly as he leaned forward and turned the key in the ignition. "You'll be fine."

It was easy for him to say, she thought irritably. He was probably as much at ease on a boat as he was behind the wheel of a car.

Staring out the windshield, she murmured, "Don't say I didn't warn you."

As they left the city limits, Ellen used a trick she'd learned during the long hours of isolation when she'd been kidnapped. She chose a word and began to see how many other words she could make with the letters contained in the original. Orange: ran, groan, gone, roan, nag. When she couldn't find any more, she went on to another word. One advantage in being older was that she had a larger vocabulary to choose from now than she did when she was six, she reflected after she came up with the word *chartreuse*.

She had no idea how much time had gone by when she became tired of playing the word game. The heater had taken the chill out of the air, and music played softly from the radio. Occasionally there were signs along the freeway stating how many miles were left before they reached Cape Cod.

She stared at the rear of the vehicle some distance ahead of them, finding the sight of another car oddly comforting. With Rudd only a few feet away, she wasn't alone, but she felt alone with her tortuous thoughts that she couldn't share with him.

To keep from dredging up any more memories, she asked, "How long have you had a place on Nantucket?"

"It's been in the family for as long as I can remember. The lodge originally belonged to my grandparents, then my parents took it over. When my father died seven years ago, my mother asked me to use Serenity Lodge because it held too many memories for her."

"Does your mother live in Boston, too?"

"She has an apartment in the city, but she's rarely there. She needed something to do after losing my father so she opened up a travel agency. Right now she's on a cruise in the Bahamas with some friends, combining business and pleasure."

"How does she feel about being a grandmother?"

Even though he kept his gaze on the road, she detected a softening around his mouth when he answered, "When I told her I was bringing her granddaughter to the summer house, she reacted as though Christmas had come early this year. She is anxious to meet her granddaughter."

"Your mother hasn't seen Katie yet?"

''My mother had already left on her cruise before Katie came to the States. She'll see her when she gets back next month.''

Ellen couldn't understand Rudd and his mother's cavalier attitude about Katie. His mother could go on a long cruise but couldn't be bothered to go to Spain to see her granddaughter? If Ellen hadn't seen the concern in Rudd's eyes when he'd asked her to go to Nantucket, she would have come to the conclusion he didn't care at all about his daughter. He'd gone to the trouble of looking her up to act as an interpreter and apparently cared for the child's welfare. But she was still having trouble reconciling his neglect since Katie was born. It was like out of sight, out of mind.

When she didn't come up with any more questions, the conversation died. Rudd kept his attention on the road and traffic without making any effort to fill the silence.

To get her thoughts off of the upcoming boat ride, she filled her mind with designs and colors, working out a pattern in her mind she could later transpose onto paper. When the images blurred, she tried making a mental grocery list to replenish the meager supply of food in her apartment. She leaned her head back against the seat and closed her eyes, hoping to shut out the fear of the voyage ahead of her.

Rudd was aware of the moment Ellen fell asleep. He shifted a brief glance in her direction to make sure. Her skin was pale, her long lashes resting on her cheeks. Her lips were slightly parted, her breathing slow and deep. The light color of her shirt showed through the open front of her jacket, her breasts gently rising and falling with each breath she took.

The thought of running his hands over the cotton fabric covering her breasts had his fingers tightening around the wheel. He swore under his breath when he felt the surge of hunger in his loins. Ellen was sound asleep, her charming smile absent, her sassy mouth silent, yet he was aching with desire. Even after he'd brought Katie back from Spain, thoughts of Ellen had crept into his mind.

He heard her sigh softly in her sleep, the sound vibrating through him. It felt right to have her beside him. She completed him somehow, made him feel whole. He didn't understand it, but he couldn't deny the feeling.

He slowed the car as he saw the exit coming up that would take him to the marina. He allowed himself another glance at Ellen. This was going to be an interesting weekend, he thought with anticipation. A beginning. They had some distance to cover, but he was in for the long haul.

When he finally stopped the car at the marina, Rudd let Ellen sleep while he unloaded the trunk and stored the supplies he'd brought onto his boat. It took him two trips before everything was secured on board. During his last trip, he'd put on a heavy, navy-style pea jacket over his jeans and black pullover sweater. The wind was cold off the water.

When he returned to the car, he walked around to the passenger side and opened the door.

Instead of waking her, he allowed himself a few moments to soak up the pleasure of simply looking at her. She appeared so defenseless and vulnerable while she was asleep. He smiled slowly as he remembered the way she'd confronted him earlier. Like a multifaceted diamond, Ellen Sheridan had many sides, and he was becoming fascinated by each and every one.

Rudd gave in to the temptation to touch her while she slept. He ran the back of one finger down her cheek, feeling the cool silk of her skin, watching her eyelashes flutter as his touch disturbed her sleep.

"Ellen," he said gently. "Open those beautiful green eyes. We're here."

In the time it took her to focus her eyes, she became aware of Rudd's shadowy face close to hers. Her voice was husky with sleep. "Where is here?"

Taking her arm, he drew her out of the car. "At a marina in Cape Cod."

So it hadn't all been a bad dream, she thought wearily. Her stiff muscles protested a little as she got out of the car. The wind off the Sound whipped around her as she stood beside him, tearing some of her hair out of the fastener at the nape of her neck. Her body shuddered, but it wasn't solely due to the cold air.

Rudd's breath caught when he saw the expression in her eyes. He'd expected to see resignation, irritation, maybe impatience, but not fear. Soul deep, agonizing fear. As he stood stiffly in front of her, he saw her struggle to combat her terror until she was in control. The tough cookie looked as though she could crumble any moment.

"Ellen? What's wrong?"

She made a dismissive gesture with her hand. "Nothing. Why?"

"You look like someone who's about to face a firing squad. Having second thoughts?"

"No."

He didn't believe her. "You were serious about not being a good sailor, weren't you?"

"Oh, yes." She sighed. "I was perfectly serious. But I'll survive. Let's get this over with."

"All right. Come on."

She saw the outline of boats tied up to slips ahead as he drew her toward the thickly populated marina. There was a muted sound of water slapping gently against fiberglass and wood hulls. Tall masts were weaving slightly as the sailboats swayed with the movement of the water. Sunlight shimmered on the black surface of the Sound before being eclipsed by a dark cloud.

Her gaze remained locked on the boats instead of watching where she was going. When one of her heels struck a loose rock, she stumbled and Rudd grabbed her arm.

He stopped walking. "You're not fully awake yet. It's only a little farther. Do you want me to carry you?"

"No!" she said with a quaver in her voice, hating the memories she thought she'd conquered. She'd been carried aboard the other boat, slung over a man's shoulder like a bag of potatoes.

Under his hand, Rudd felt the tremors in her slender frame and misunderstood their cause. He took the lapels of her jacket and brought them together in front of her to try to give her more protection from the cold sea air.

"You'll be warmer in the cabin out of this cold wind."

In an attempt to put off the time she would have to stand on the rocking deck of a boat, she admitted, "I'm not looking forward to this."

"Unfortunately, it's the only way for us to get to the island," he murmured, wishing this wasn't the way things had to be. She obviously didn't want to take the boat across the Sound, but it was too late to make other arrangements.

She sighed. "I know. Don't pay any attention to me. I should never have seen that movie about the *Titanic*."

As they walked out onto the dock, Ellen felt the wind tug at her hair. In the distance, she could hear the low rumble of thunder. "Is it going to rain?"

"I checked the weather before I picked you up. It's a little windy." He chuckled when she rolled her eyes as though he'd made a colossal understatement. "There are no gale warnings posted. Don't worry. I wouldn't take the boat out if I thought it was going to be dangerous."

She concentrated on each step she took, trying not to let her shoes catch in the cracks between the rough boards. The water would be cold and deep if she lost her balance and fell in. Cold and merciless, dragging her down into the chilling darkness.

She bit her lip as she tried to conquer the past.

Feeling foolish, she hoped she could hide her reactions from Rudd. The last thing she wanted to do was to explain her fear without what little self-control she had. She never talked about the kidnapping, much less thought about it for years, having put it away in her mind where she had wanted it to stay.

Rudd finally stopped at one of the boats. He dropped his hands to her waist. "Put your hands on my shoulders to brace yourself. I'm going to lift you aboard."

She did as he ordered. It was either that or go running down the dock like a complete idiot. When she placed her hands on his shoulders, she felt his fingers tighten on her waist just before she was hoisted off her feet.

When her face was level with his, he saw the drop of blood on her bottom lip where her teeth had broken the skin. The sight of it made him furious; with himself, the situation, and Ellen for making him feel guilty.

Chapter Nine

A gusty breeze whipped a lock of her hair across his cheek when he brought her up closer to his face until she was only inches away. "Dammit, Ellen. Why are you acting like I'm going to take you out into the Sound and throw you overboard?"

Ellen sucked in her breath. His question was too close to the past, but he had no way of knowing that. She had to prove to herself she could overcome her fears.

She ran her tongue over her dry lips, tasting salt from her cut lip. "You said you were going to lift me aboard the boat."

Rudd stared at her, puzzled by her quiet determination when he could see she was badly frightened. He should be glad she was making it easy for him by not struggling or whining, but for some reason, her chin up courage was harder to face than tears would have been.

Because there was nothing else he could do, he lifted her onto the deck of the forty-foot boat, climbing aboard himself a few seconds later.

When she was standing on the deck, he gestured toward the vertical hatch cover that had been drawn back. "I put your case on one of the bunks in the cabin. There's a thermos of hot coffee in the galley. You'll be warmer down below than up on deck. There's a light switch on the right as you go down the steps."

Ellen turned and walked carefully across the deck as though she were walking on eggs and stepped down into the cabin.

Rudd stood on the deck with his legs apart for balance, his gaze on the dark cabin Ellen had disappeared into. He waited to see the light go on before he went to the bridge to start the engine.

Several minutes later, he was still waiting.

The light didn't come on. He frowned. Ellen wasn't familiar with the boat so it was hard to imagine her finding her suitcase or anything else in the dark interior. Maybe she hadn't heard him when he'd told her where the light switch was located. As impatient as he was to get underway, he couldn't let her fumble around in the dark the whole trip.

He stepped over to the hatch. Cursing himself for neglecting to leave the light on when he'd carried supplies to the boat earlier, he called out, "Ellen? Can't you find the light switch?"

When he didn't receive an answer, he started down the stairs, stopping on the second step to listen for any sound that would indicate where she could be or what she could be doing.

"Ellen? Dammit, where are you?"

All he heard were the waves slapping against the hull and the clatter of the rigging lines on the masts of the boats nearby. Running his hand along the bulkhead on his right, he found the light switch and flicked it on.

His hand froze on the switch when he saw Ellen only a foot away from him. She was standing with her back pressed against the starboard bulkhead. The palms of her hands were pressed against the hard surface behind her. Her eyes were tightly closed, her face a frozen, pale mask. She was panting as though she'd just run a race.

His chest tightened painfully. He'd been wrong when he thought witnessing the courageous way she was facing the situation was difficult. The sight of a single tear leaving a glistening trail down her cheek was much worse.

He spoke her name softly and reached out to touch her with the intent to comfort her, but he drew his hand back quickly when she made a sound of distress and jerked away from him. Her eyes snapped open, her expression one of blind distress and mindless fear.

"Ellen?" he murmured quietly. "It's Rudd. You're all right." When he heard her take a deep, ragged breath, he asked gently, "What's wrong? Couldn't you find the light switch?"

He could tell the minute she realized who he was and where she was. A great shudder shook her entire body, and she took another deep, hoarse breath before she met his concerned gaze.

Her voice was oddly hollow. "I did try to warn you I wasn't a very good sailor."

Rudd's gaze went to her mouth, and he watched in fascination as her pink tongue slid over her dry bottom lip. She was recovering from whatever fright she'd had, yet he hesitated questioning her about the cause of her distress. But he needed to know what was frightening her.

He took a step toward her and she backed away from him.

She quickly glanced around the galley as though searching for something, then looked beyond where the sleeping quarters could be seen. "I'm going to put on another sweater. You were right. It is cold. Don't you have some boat stuff to do so we can get to Nantucket?"

Rudd's eyes never left her as she turned away to walk toward the bunks. Her movements were stiff, oddly uncoordinated, which wasn't the way she usually moved. She stopped in front of the satchel he'd placed on the bunk. Then she turned her head and looked at him, her expression withdrawn as she silently challenged him with her gaze, daring him to argue with her.

He met her challenge with one of his own. "I'm taking you back to Boston."

"No!" she said forcefully. "I have to do this."

"No, you don't," he argued, willing to do anything to wipe that haunted look from her eyes. "You don't have to prove anything. Nothing is worth putting yourself through this."

She lifted her chin as though daring him. "I'm going. Let's get this over with."

He could be as stubborn as she was. "I'll figure out another way at another time."

She was tempted to take his offer, but her pride kept her from accepting it. "It would waste too much time to change our plans now." Feeling as though he deserved an explanation for her strange behavior, she said offhandedly, "I had a bad experience on a boat a long time ago, and it caught up with me for a few minutes."

He'd figured that out for himself when he realized she wasn't suffering from a simple case of seasickness. "What happened?"

"It doesn't matter."

"Dammit, Ellen. Talk to me. Maybe I can help."

She gave him a completely baffled look as though what he offered was a foreign concept.

He continued to study her expression, still not convinced but torn with the decision that had to be made. "I've handled boats since I was fourteen, Ellen. I won't let anything happen to you."

She made a shrugging motion with her shoulders, the movement stiff and jerky rather than casual. "You go do whatever you have to do to get this tub to Nantucket."

Following her lead, he kept his voice light. "This tub, as you call it, has all the conveniences of home. A galley where you can find food if you're hungry. A head, or as you landlubbers call it, a bathroom. There are bunks if you want to lie down." He gestured toward a control panel set into the bulkhead to her right. "The blue button is for the intercom system if you need to reach me on the bridge."

She gave him a mock salute. "Aye, aye, captain. I'll be shipshape or whatever it's called down here."

For a moment, he simply stared at her. Then he said quietly, "I'm sorry to put you through this, Ellen. I had no idea taking the boat across the Sound would be a problem."

She saw the concern in his eyes, and baffled confusion. She had to change that. She wasn't ready to answer any questions right now. She still had to get through the boat trip. "It's not a problem as long as you keep the boat riding on top of the water and not under it."

Smiling faintly, he drawled, "I'll see what I can do."

When he still hesitated, she pointed toward the hatch and said aggressively, "Go! The sooner we get out on the briny deep—" She couldn't stop the shudder that went through her. "Never mind," she said with a mocking tilt to her mouth. "I think I'll reserve my colorful descriptions for providing inspiration for my artwork."

He couldn't accept her unspoken invitation to join her in making fun of her fear. "It's still not too late. We don't have to take the trip now."

She bit her lip and shook her head. "I have to do this."

Rudd finally accepted her decision and went topside. The cold air hit him in the face, but he didn't even feel it. His thoughts were preoccupied with the woman in the cabin. Her act hadn't fooled him one bit. She might have her fear under control at the moment, but it was very real and very overwhelming for her.

In all his imaginings of how he would play out this weekend, none of them had included Ellen being scared out of her wits.

As he began to cast off, Rudd resolved to find out what had happened to Ellen to put that gut-wrenching fear in her. She didn't trust him enough yet, but she would.

Once she was alone, Ellen turned on all the lights she could find, unconcerned about wearing down any battery or whatever furnished the electricity. She pulled back the curtains covering the small rectangular window. It wasn't dark outside, but the overcast sky wasn't doing much to illuminate the interior of the cabin. Light was the opposite of dark, and that was reason enough for her to try to make her surroundings brighter.

She sat on the bunk and took the deep, steadying breaths she'd been taught as a method of easing stress. Her mouth twisted in an expression of self-mockery. She thought she'd mastered her fear of water and dark places a long time ago. Obviously, she was wrong. Avoiding the occasions when she would be exposed to either one had eliminated the cause, not the fears. Just because the nightmares had disappeared didn't mean the memories had vanished.

After the breathing exercises, she remembered another of the therapy lessons, to concentrate on something else rather than dwell on things that upset her.

It wasn't difficult to come up with a subject. She thought about Rudd.

What was it about him that affected her so strongly? she wondered, not for the first time. She could tell herself it was simply infatuation for an attractive man. She could try to convince herself she was merely intrigued. There were any number of reasons she could give herself for the attraction she'd felt since she first met him.

It didn't matter that she couldn't put a name to the emotions he stirred within her. Lord knows, she hadn't come up with one, yet. She wasn't that familiar with love to use it as an explanation for the way Rudd made her feel. She was more comfortable with the term physical attraction, even though she knew it didn't completely cover all the feelings she experienced when she was with Rudd. It was certainly easier to accept than any other tag she could think of.

There hadn't been that many people in her life whom she loved or who loved her back. Certainly no one in her immediate family. Her mother had left when she was too young to really know her, and her father had always been a remote, cold fixture in her life for as long as she could remember. Her relationship with Tiffany was as close as she'd ever come to caring for someone other than her father's housekeeper, Mercedes, to trusting another person and having those feelings returned.

Leaving the bunk, she walked over to the sink in the galley. She found a plastic glass in one of the cupboards and filled it with water from the tap. As she brought it up to her mouth, the deck under her feet sloped suddenly as the boat rocked unexpectedly. When she tried to find her balance, most of the water in the glass spilled down the front of her shirt and down past the waistband of her slacks.

Muttering under her breath, Ellen held the wet material away from her body after she put the glass in the sink. Dabbing at the moisture with a hand towel didn't help. The soaked fabric and cool air in the cabin didn't mix well against her skin. She was going to have to change her clothes.

As she stepped over to the bunk where Rudd had placed her case, a crack of thunder made the air vibrate around her with rumbling intensity.

"Just what I need," she muttered under her breath. "Sound effects."

Unzipping her case, she took out a royal blue cotton sweater and a pair of white denim jeans and laid them on the bunk. After she unbuttoned her shirt, she let it fall to the floor before unfastening the waistband of her slacks and sliding them down over her hips. The cool air in the cabin made her move a little faster to slip the sweater over her head.

She was reaching for the jeans when she was suddenly aware she was no longer alone. Turning her head around, she saw Rudd standing on the bottom step, his gaze on her bare legs. When he raised his gaze to meet hers, she forgot what she was supposed to do with the jeans she held in her hands. His eyes were dark with arousal, and she felt her breath stop in her lungs. A small part of her mind registered the fact he was wearing a yellow rain slicker that glistened with salt spray.

A current of attraction arced across the space separating them, as powerful and as elemental as the storm brewing outside.

Ellen looked away, unable to meet his intense gaze a second longer without giving in to the desire to throw herself into his arms. She stepped into the jeans, aware he was watching every move she made. It required a ridiculous amount of concentration for her to perform the simple act of zipping up the front closing, something that she'd done hundreds of times before without any trouble.

Tugging the sweater down over her hips, she raised her head and looked at him. "I spilled water on my clothes," she explained. "Is there something you wanted?"

"Talk about a loaded question," he murmured.

He leaned against the bulkhead with one leg higher than the other on the steps. His stance made her wonder if he was coming down or going up. "I'm ready to cast off. The weather's going to be a bit rougher than I expected, but I checked with the weather service and there are no small craft warnings posted. I thought you might feel safer if you were wearing a life jacket."

The only time she would feel safe was when solid ground was under her feet again. Her mouth twisted in a mocking smile. "I wouldn't mind knowing where one is."

He came down the steps and walked over to a bench built into the port side of the cabin. Bending down, he drew out a drawer concealed underneath and lifted out a life jacket. Straightening, he tossed it onto the bench. "I'm putting one on as soon as I'm topside. I'll also have a lifeline attached so you don't need to worry that I'll be washed overboard."

"I wasn't worried."

He smiled faintly. "Of course, you weren't. I don't know why I thought you might be." He glanced briefly at the small lamp hanging over the table. It was swaying back and forth. "As you can see, the water is getting rougher. If you want some coffee, there's some in a thermos in the box. Don't light the stove. Don't leave anything out on the counter that could roll off. The sea is getting a little choppy, but it's nothing to worry about. Okay?''

"Aye, aye, sir."

His gaze rested on the shadows under her eyes. "Why don't you try to get some rest? It will make the trip shorter for you."

Knowing herself she was a coward was one thing, Rudd being aware of it was quite another. She came forward, stopping near the cardboard box of supplies he'd placed earlier on the table.

In the same matter-of-fact tone he'd used, she said, "I'll put these things away. I'd offer to help you do whatever it is you have to do to get this thing moving, but I would be more hindrance than help."

"I'll manage." He studied her expression for a moment. "Are you ready to tell me why you're so frightened by being on a boat?"

She slowly shook her head.

His gaze dwelled on her face for a few seconds longer. He wasn't surprised she hadn't answered him. What did surprise him was how disappointed he was that she didn't trust him enough. He turned to retrace his steps back topside. The quicker he got under way, the faster they would get to Nantucket Island, and the sooner Ellen would meet Katie.

Two hours later, Rudd tugged the thick rope over the deck clamp to secure the bowline to the dock in Nantucket. His fingers were stiff with cold, his eyes burning from salt spray. The muscles in his arms were aching from wrestling with the wheel. He was in the mood to tell the marine weather service what they could do with their predictions.

He'd enjoyed the exhilaration of mastering the difficult swells he'd had to navigate, but now he had to think about how his passenger had managed to deal with the rough ride. Even the hardiest of sailors would have been tightening the straps on their life vests.

Once the boat was securely tied up to the dock at the marina in Nantucket, he slid back the hatch and stepped down into the cabin. He blinked several times. All the lights were on. Looking around, he noticed the supplies had all been put away and the box shoved under the table out of the way. Ellen's case was closed and tucked in a corner of the bunk. The life jacket was laying on the couch.

There was only one thing missing. Ellen.

He searched the sleeping area in the bow of the boat, but Ellen wasn't there, either. A flicker of fear tightened his stomach. Where in the hell was she?

The only place he hadn't checked was the head, the nautical equivalent to a bathroom. It was possible she could be seasick, considering how rough the seas had been. He didn't bother knocking but opened the door. When he saw her, he could only stand in the doorway staring at her.

Her legs were spread apart for balance, a tube of lipstick in her hand. Her hair was arranged in an intricate French braid, and she had freshened her makeup. In spite of her attempts to camouflage her pallor, he could see her skin was white and not tinged with the telltale green some people acquired when they were seasick.

There were a lot of questions he wanted to ask. He settled for the obvious one. "What are you doing?"

Instead of turning her head to look at him, she met his gaze in the mirror. "What does it look like I'm doing? I'm trying to find my mouth with this tube of lipstick. It's not as easy as it sounds."

Finding her mouth would be a snap. He would have been able to find her lips with his eyes closed in a darkened room.

He leaned against the doorframe, his arms crossed over his chest. He took in the way her fingers were gripping the tube of lipstick, noting the slight tremor in her hand that had nothing to do with the rocking motion of the boat.

"I thought I'd find you cowering under one of the bunks and here you are putting on war paint."

"I was trying out one of Tiffany's theories. She swears that nothing can ever be too awful if she looks good." Rather than smear a streak of lipstick across her cheek or her chin, Ellen recapped the tube and dropped it into her makeup case. "I give up. I'll end up with lipstick on my forehead."

Smiling faintly, he suggested, "If you're finished gilding the lily, we can leave the boat."

Her eyes widened in excitement. "We're tied up to a dock that's attached to solid ground?"

"Last time I looked. Do you want to get off or have you had a change of heart about boats?"

Tossing her cosmetics into her bag, she started to squirm around in the tight compartment so she could face the door. "You've got to be kidding. I'll take land over water any day of the week. Are we going to see Katie right away?"

He moved back out of the doorway. "I need to call the house first to make sure the nanny won't take Katie out, which she's done before even though she knows I come to see Katie every weekend. While I phone the house, you can relax for a little while. Maybe have something to eat before we go see Katie."

She stopped in the doorway. As anxious as she was to get off the boat, something he said was puzzling. "You have a phone on the boat?"

"A radio but no phone," he explained. "I'll call from the place where I'm staying."

She should be asking where that was, but at the moment the only thing she cared about was getting off the darn boat. She had taken it for granted they would be going to his summer home immediately. Evidently, that wasn't how it was going to be. After the harrowing trip across the Sound, she didn't care where they were going as long as it was on land.

After Rudd had all the lights turned off and their cases up on deck, he helped her on with her jacket. Turning her to face him, he held on to her lapels to keep her from turning away from him.

"I'm giving you notice. Before the weekend is over, I'm going to know what happened to you on a boat."

"That's not part of our agreement."

"I just added it." His gaze slid down to her lips, which were set in a rebellious line. "It'll be interesting to see what else develops this weekend."

"You'd have a hard time beating that boat ride for thrills and excitement."

Taking her hand, he drew her toward the steps and dry land. "I love a challenge."

Chapter Ten

The dark clouds were thinning out. It was as though Mother Nature had adjusted a dimmer switch to allow more illumination for the inhabitants of the island. Ellen leaned forward as a structure became visible at the end of the road they were traveling on. She blinked once, then again, finding it difficult to believe what her eyes were telling her she was seeing.

The silhouette of the unusual building was unmistakable. It was a windmill.

Ellen stared in fascination. The wide canvas-covered blades weren't revolving, which was odd considering the wind was buffeting the trees alongside the road. Even though Ellen couldn't see any other buildings along the gravel road, she still couldn't believe it was their final destination until Rudd parked the car in front of the weathered, slightly dilapidated building.

"Shades of Don Quixote," she murmured to no one in particular. It seemed appropriate somehow. She felt as though she'd been tilting at windmills ever since she first looked up and saw Rudd standing in front of her at the hotel.

With her gaze remaining on the unique building in front of her, Ellen opened the door of the car Rudd had driven away from the parking lot adjacent to the marina. A blast of strong, gusty wind nearly knocked her off her feet, and she was thankful for Rudd's strong grip on her hand as he drew her away from the car toward the windmill. He seemed to be forming the habit of taking her hand whenever they went from one place to another. She really should tell him she could manage just fine on her own, but she liked the feel of her hand in his.

She could hear the distant sound of waves crashing against the shore, giving her the impression the windmill was situated near the coast of the island. From where she was standing, she couldn't see any water. She wasn't familiar enough with the island to know whether they were on the side facing the Sound or the ocean. There were clusters of shrubbery between the windmill and the direction the sound was coming from, but it was obviously close.

Tall weeds growing in profusion on either side of the cement walkway were bent over by the strong winds. Clumps of grass were growing between the cracks of the sidewalk, adding to the neglected feel of the place.

A dark cloud passed overhead. The wind made the wooden blades of the windmill creak ominously, as though it were protesting not being able to whirl around like it had been built to do.

Glancing around, Ellen murmured, "I've got to stop watching those late night scary movies on television."

Rudd looked around, amused by her reaction. "I guess it is sort of *Wuthering Heights*ish, isn't it? There are a number of unique buildings on the island. It has an interesting history."

"Like pirates and smugglers?"

"There were a few of those. Some respectable historical events happened here, too. For example, Benjamin Franklin's mother, Abiah Folger, was born on the island."

"Here?" she asked.

Rudd chuckled. "No, not here. Cheer up. It's better inside."

"What are we doing here?" She jerked her head around. "This isn't your summer house, is it?"

He reached above the door and took down a key. "This place belongs to a friend of my mother. I've been using it since I brought Katie back from Spain. My summer house is about a mile away."

The windmill wasn't the only thing that was odd. Before she could stop herself, she asked frankly, "Why aren't you staying at your own house with your daughter?"

Rudd frowned as he unlocked the door. She asked more questions than Walter Cronkite. "I visit Katie a couple of hours at a time. A few hours in the morning, then some more in the afternoon."

Unsatisfied by his answer, she persisted, "Why not spend the complete weekend with her?"

"I thought it would be better if she gradually gets used to me."

Ellen didn't understand his reasoning. If she had been in the same circumstances, she would have wanted to spend every minute of every day with her child. But then, she wouldn't have ignored her child for the first four years of her life, either.

The door squeaked loudly when Rudd pushed it open. As a stream of light illuminated the floor in front of them, Ellen realized Rudd had brought a flashlight with him. She wondered why he didn't just turn on a light switch.

Rudd walked directly to a round table, laying the flashlight down on the wood surface before striking a match to light a kerosene lamp. Once the lamp was glowing, Rudd went over to a small window and folded back the wooden shutters, which allowed the light—such as it was—to come in from outside. Rain-filled clouds had returned overhead. After doing the same to the other window, he said, "I'll be back in a minute with our cases."

With the additional light, Ellen was better able to see the interior of the windmill. Her gaze was immediately drawn to one unique, very large feature in the middle of the windmill that took up an astonishing amount of space. At one time, the windmill had apparently been used to grind grain, and for some reason, the wooden gears and grinding stone hadn't been removed. A large, circular cement stone lay on its side above a shallow trough, both located in the center of the octagon-shaped room along with assorted gears and pulleys and other mechanisms. An attempt had been made to convert the rest of the space into a living area. On the side of the mill where she was standing, she saw a small, apartment-size refrigerator and a hot plate on a counter built around a small sink. Instead of faucets, there was a hand-crank water pump. A couch with sagging springs had been pushed against one of the walls. Draped over the back, a crocheted afghan made in the granny square pattern partially covered the faded cushions. A wood stove was nearby. The only other piece of furniture was an antique rocking chair with a cane seat.

Despite the primitive conditions, Ellen found the windmill had a rustic serenity that appealed to her artistic nature. It made no pretense of fashion or style, its purpose, one of unsophisticated comfort. Take it or leave it.

There was one exception to the bucolic furnishings. Paintings covered the walls from floor to ceiling. The light from the lantern wasn't enough for her to be able to see them clearly. Ellen aimed the flashlight at one of the paintings, astonished when she recognized the work of the artist. Shining the light on the one next to it, she saw that painting was by the same artist. So were all the others.

Ellen directed the flashlight to the other side of the grinding wheel. Considering they were apparently going to be spending the night here, she was interested to see whether she was going to have a bed to sleep in or be expected to bunk down on the lumpy couch.

The yellow beam of the flashlight picked out the sparse furnishings in the area that served as a bedroom of sorts. There was a scarred wooden dresser with a speckled, oval mirror above it. Farther along the wall was an iron bedstead with a mattress that had a definite slump in the middle. The bed was covered with an antique quilt that had been washed so often, the various prints blended together in a faded patchwork of indiscriminate design.

The only fault she could find with the bed, other than the less than firm mattress, was the fact there was only one.

Ellen retraced her steps to the other side of the mill to discover Rudd had returned. He was kneeling in front of the wood stove, crumpling up several sheets of newspaper and shoving them into the open cavity of the fat-bellied stove. Then he arranged some kindling and a couple of medium-size logs inside. The precise way he laid the first gave her the impression this wasn't the first time he'd done this.

Her gaze was drawn away from the stove to a sight that created a heat of its own within her. The denim material of his jeans was stretched tightly over his firm thighs as he knelt on the floor. His long fingers were splayed out on each thigh as he stared into the fire to make sure the wood was catching. For a few seconds, Ellen stared at his hands, remembering how she felt whenever he'd touched her. Wanting him to touch her again.

She looked away. Wishing for what she couldn't have was a waste of time and would only lead to disappointment.

She needed to break the silence. "Nice place."

Rudd stared at the flames licking at the pieces of kindling. "Sarcasm isn't really necessary, Ellen. It's clean, it's dry, and it's not a boat. That's about all you can say about this place."

"I wasn't being sarcastic. I sincerely meant what I said. This is a nice place. A little unusual, but that's what makes it so charming."

He turned his head and looked at her over his shoulder, an odd expression entering his eyes. "You're serious, aren't you?"

Instead of answering his question, she asked one of her own. "Why do you find that hard to believe?"

He realized he'd expected her reaction to be the same as his ex-wife's. Cynthia had had only disparaging remarks to make after he'd brought her to the windmill to meet Willa.

A corner of his mouth lifted slowly. "I guess it isn't that hard to believe you would like it here. A woman who has a picnic table in an apartment she keeps for sentimental reasons would be able to take an antiquated windmill in stride."

She listened for a note of censure in his voice, but didn't hear one. "I have simple tastes."

"It makes for an interesting combination."

"What does?"

"A complicated woman with simple tastes." Glancing around, he then brought his gaze back to her. "I didn't think about the living conditions until I had to light the kerosene lamp. I haven't given much thought to your comfort since I picked you up at your apartment, have I? First you take a boat ride from hell, then I bring you to a drafty windmill that has furnishings the Salvation Army wouldn't accept."

After shedding her jacket, she sat down on the couch at the end nearest the stove. Her intention had been to get closer to the fire. In doing so, she was also much closer to Rudd. An added benefit.

"I admit I wasn't wild about the boat ride, but that wasn't your fault."

Even though she was attempting to maintain a cool facade, he saw through it. "Do you want to talk about it?"

"About what?"

"About what happened to put you off boats. You said you had a bad experience on a boat at one time, but you didn't say what it was."

She shrugged. "It was just one of those things that happen when you're a child that gets all blown out of proportion in your mind over the years." In case he wasn't satisfied with her limp explanation, she changed the subject. "I noticed all the paintings on the wall are by Willa Chase. Your mother's friend must be a fan of her work."

He recognized a red herring when he saw it. Remembering Tiffany's statement about why Ellen changes the subject during a discussion, he let her get away with it. "The artist who owns this place *is* Willa Chase." Rudd's eyes glittered with amusement when he saw her mouth drop open. "Close your mouth, Ellen. A fly might pop in."

"It's too cold for any self-respecting insect to be out and about. You're serious, aren't you? This place belongs to Willa Chase?"

Grinning now, he said, "Cross my heart. She usually spends her summers here."

"I've admired her work since I was in art school. I bought one of her prints when I was a freshman and on a tight budget. I gave up groceries for a week in order to buy it. Living on macaroni and cheese dinners was a small sacrifice to make to possess something so beautiful."

"I didn't see a Chase print in your apartment."

"That's because I have it hanging in my bedroom."

The one room he hadn't been in. "Why didn't you just ask your father to buy the artwork for you? I would think the price of a Willa Chase print would be chicken feed to him."

"I pay for my own extravagances. To me, it was more important to feed the inner soul than the outer woman," she quipped. She looked around at her surroundings, then at the paintings on the wall behind her. "Why am I having trouble associating the woman who paints delicate flower studies with the person who lives in a place without electricity and running water?"

Smiling slowly, Rudd asked, "How did you picture her? As a frail, white-haired grandmother-type woman with her hair knotted into a tidy bun and a cup of Darjeeling tea nearby while she painted?"

"Something like that," conceded Ellen with a faint smile. "So tell me how far off I am."

"The last time I saw her two months ago, she had just had her red hair done into something she called a beehive. The red silk rose stuck in her hair matched the color of the dinner plate-size roses that were splattered all over her black silk dress. If I remember correctly, it wasn't a cup of tea she ordered. She had two Bloody Marys with lunch, which consisted of clam chowder and apple pie à la mode. She also told the waiter he should think about modeling as a career, although she suggested he should get his teeth capped first and wear tighter pants.''

Ellen's face reflected her surprise, then her amusement. ''Another preconceived notion shot to pieces. Obviously, you know her well since she's allowing you to stay on her property. I can't help wondering how you became friends with her.''

''Why? Because you think I'm a stodgy chemist? Don't you think I could possibly be the type to find an eccentric woman interesting? I'm with you, aren't I?''

His questions reminded her that she didn't really know him. And why she didn't know him very well. It's almost impossible to get to know another person after only several hours of conversation over dinner. She'd be better off remembering she was on Nantucket for the daughter, not the father.

Drawing back, she said, ''You're right. I'm making a judgment call when I have nothing on which to base my opinion. It's none of my business.''

''Ellen,'' he said gently. ''I was teasing.''

She stood up. ''I'd like to clean up a little before I meet your daughter. Where would the bathroom facilities be located? If there is such a thing.''

The sudden change of subject and the tone of her voice had him staring at her for a few seconds without responding. Before she turned away, he thought he saw a hurt expression in her eyes. In one smooth motion, he surged to his feet and turned her around by putting a hand on her shoulder.

''Dammit, don't look at me as though I've just slapped you. First on the boat, and now. You make me feel as though I should be crawling around on the floor with the rest of the lowlife.''

She blinked. ''What are you talking about? All I did was ask where the bathroom was located.''

''This is going to be one hell of a long weekend if I have to watch every word I say so you don't duck behind that wall you put up faster than a flash fire. Why don't you make a list of the topics I can talk about and those I can't. It would save a lot of headaches.''

Instead of getting angry, Ellen blew a silent whistle with pursed lips. ''Boy, you have a humdinger of a temper.''

A choking sound came from deep in his throat as he stared at her glittering eyes and wide smile. His temper fizzled out like a wet firecracker.

Shaking his head in bemusement, he did the only thing a mere male could do when faced with a perplexing female. He gave up. Then he pulled her into his arms and hugged her.

Ellen slid her arms around his waist and hugged him back. As much as she was enjoying the feel of his solid body pressed against hers, she knew she had to respond to his accusations.

When she reluctantly withdrew her arms from around him, Rudd made a sound of protest but eased his hold on her. Still keeping her trapped in his arms, he looked down at her hands, which she'd placed on his chest, then met her gaze when she began to speak.

''You should have believed Tiffany when she said I change the subject when I'm losing an argument. I also change the subject or get quiet when someone says something I don't like.''

''Wouldn't it be easier to simply get mad, blow off steam, then make up?''

''You'd think so, but I can't.''

"You can't get angry?"

"Oh, I get angry," she admitted as she moved several steps away. "It's the blowing off steam that I can't master."

Rudd ignored how empty his arms felt without her and concentrated on her confession. That might not be the word she would have used, but it fit. Aside from being surprised that she would confide in him, he was astonished by her admission. After hearing the few things she'd said about her childhood, it wasn't all that difficult to understand. Alienated all her life by her father, she couldn't alienate anyone else by having a knockdown, dragged-out argument.

Smiling, he asked, "How about kissing and making up? I think you'd be a natural at that."

Tilting her head to one side, she gave him a melting smile. "You do, do you? But I'm not the one who was mad a minute ago. That was you."

"Works for me," he said slowly, his eyes darkening with arousal.

"I'll pass, thanks. You don't seem to be angry any longer."

"I could work up to it again if that's what it'll take," he offered, stepping toward her.

Shifting to one side, she dodged his hand. "I have a better idea. Why don't you tell me if this place has a potty."

As an evasion, it was a darn good one. "You have that down to a fine art."

She blinked, then frowned. "What?"

"Changing the temperature from hot to cold." He raised his hand and gestured toward a door behind her. "Willa has her limits when it comes to roughing it. There's a bathroom on the other side of that door. Running water, all the modern conveniences."

"I knew I couldn't have been totally wrong about her."

Rudd drawled, "Did anybody ever point out to you that you have an unusual fondness for bathrooms?"

"I think you're the first." Taking two steps away, she paused, looking back at Rudd over her shoulder. "Are you aware there's only one bed here?"

"Since I usually sleep in it, yes, I'm aware there is only one bed."

"Isn't that going to be a problem?"

He met her gaze squarely. "It doesn't have to be."

A frisson of heat flowed through her veins at the thought of lying beside him on the quilt-covered bed. He would be warm, his arms strong and secure around her, his body hard and firm against hers. The idea was tempting. Lord knows she was attracted to him more than was sane, but she also still had a healthy degree of self-preservation alive and well inside her.

"There's also the couch or the floor," she said with false bravado. "Right now, I don't care where I sleep as long as it's on a solid foundation and not on the boat. And alone."

If he hadn't seen the flicker of arousal in her eyes before she lowered her lashes, he would have accepted her breezy response as a polite refusal. The fact she was as attracted to him as he was to her only made the situation more flammable. But she wasn't ready to move on to the next step in their relationship. He could only hope he could wait until she was.

Bringing his gaze back to the fire in the wood stove, he said, "You can relax. I plan to spend the night on the couch. You can have the bed."

Ellen was aware that the invisible door between them was being slammed shut again. He was very good at that, she acknowledged silently as she walked to the door he'd indicated. What she had to learn to do better was step out of the way when he was shutting her out so she didn't keep getting squashed.

When she came back ten minutes later, she immediately headed for the warmth emanating from the wood stove. Willa Chase had made the concession of having modern plumbing installed in a small room attached to the windmill, but had neglected to include any type of heating. Her estimation of the elderly artist went up a notch or two. The woman had to have the constitution of an Eskimo.

As Ellen rubbed her hands together and held them close to the stove, she glanced around. At first she thought Rudd had left the windmill until she heard the sound of a drawer being opened and shut on the other side of the partition formed by the grinding wheel.

A few seconds later, Rudd appeared around the stone. When she saw his gaze go to her hands near the stove, she explained, "I think I've lost the feeling in my fingers. You forgot to mention that I should have worn my jacket. Or a parka."

"Sorry," he murmured, the amused expression in his eyes contradicting his words. "I guess I haven't thought much about my surroundings. It's been a place to stay. That's about it."

"Your mind has been on your daughter," she added when he didn't. "Since she is why I'm here, shouldn't we be on our way to see her?"

He flicked a glance at his watch. "We've got a little time. I told Señora Santana we'd be there around eleven. I phoned her while you were freezing your—hands."

Once she could feel her fingers again, she moved away from the stove to sit down on the couch. "Tell me about her, Rudd. What's Katie like?"

He didn't say anything until he'd added another small piece of wood into the belly of the stove, then sat down in the rocking chair several feet away. "That's not an easy question to answer. I could describe what she looked like, but you've already seen her picture. I could find her in a crowd of other four-year-olds, but I don't know how she thinks, what she likes or dislikes. I've never heard her laugh or even seen her smile. I don't know if she likes spinach, Mickey Mouse, or sleeps with a teddy bear." His mouth twisted. "Some father, aren't I?"

She heard the frustration and impatience in his voice and responded to it. "That will all take time, Rudd. She's a stranger to you, but you're also a stranger to her. You both need time to learn about each other. You want to get to know her, and she has a right to get to know you, too. Communication is a two-way street. I can translate everything you say to her and if she says anything to you, but that doesn't really solve the problem."

Before he knew what she was going to do, Rudd ended up staring after her as she sprang off the couch and darted around the partition. "Ellen," he said irritably. "If you'll stay put, we could—" She was back before he finished what he was going to say and was handing him a book. He looked at it. "What's this?"

She sat back down on the couch, tucking her legs under her. "You're a college graduate, Rudd. Don't tell me you've never seen a book before."

He gave her a pained grimace. "I know it's a book."

"Give the man a cigar. He recognizes a book. Now read the title."

Turning the book so he could see the front cover, he let his gaze scan the two words that comprised the only writing on the brightly colored title.

Ellen made a soft sound of exasperation. "Aloud."

"It's in Spanish. If I knew how to read Spanish, I wouldn't need you here."

She wasn't sure whether his anger was directed at her or himself or the situation. "We're going to change that."

"Maybe I haven't made myself clear, Ellen. I asked you here to help me communicate with my daughter, not to teach me Spanish."

"I know why I'm here, Rudd," she murmured dryly. "That is a beginner's book of instruction which will help you learn some basic words and phrases so you will begin to be able to talk to her yourself. We'll have to work with Katie to help her learn English. I have some picture books for her. Between the two methods, we'll get some communication going."

He fingered the book, then leafed through some of the pages. *"Se habla espanol,"* he read out, following that with the translation. "Spanish spoken here."*

She corrected his pronunciation automatically, then smiled with approval when he repeated the words correctly. "Very good. There are some other books you can get that will help you learn more if you're interested, but I suggest you find an English tutor for Katie as soon as possible. The quicker she learns to speak English, the easier it will be for her when she starts school."

"You could teach her."

When she raised her gaze from the book he held in his hand to meet his eyes, she thought she saw surprise in his expression. *He* was surprised? What about her? It wasn't at all what she expected.

Along with being astonished, she was also practical, which apparently he wasn't. "I'm not a qualified teacher, Rudd. Katie needs a professional instructor."

"I remember you said you had a Spanish housekeeper, which is how you learned to speak Spanish. How did you learn from her?"

"Mercedes came to work for my father when I was very young. I picked up the language because she usually spoke Spanish when we were alone."

"You must have spent a lot of time with her."

Shrugging her slender shoulders, Ellen said, "It was a big house but I was only allowed in the kitchen and my bedroom. My father didn't want me to contaminate the rooms where he kept his priceless antiques. I gravitated toward the kitchen area where there was some noise, even if it was a foreign language. I somehow understood what Mercedes was saying and started speaking to her in her own language, and we sort of kept going on from there. It made her feel less homesick if she could speak the language of her heart, and it made me feel special, as though we had our own private language."

Rudd didn't detect any bitterness in her voice. She told him about the cold way her father treated her in a matter-of-fact tone, as though it were nothing remarkable or cruel.

"Maybe that method would work with Katie. She spends most of her time with her nanny, who only speaks Spanish to her. The little time I spend with Katie doesn't seem to have made much difference."

"Maybe that's part of the problem."

"What is?"

Ellen pursed her lips while she debated whether or not to interfere any more than she already had. She'd been invited to help him communicate with his daughter this weekend, but that didn't necessarily mean she had the right to tell him how to deal with his private life.

The sight of her pouting mouth was having an invigorating effect on his system. In an attempt to get his thoughts away from the desire to cover those lips with his own, he said, "Don't pull your punches now, Ellen. What's part of the problem?"

"You just said the little time you spend with Katie doesn't seem to have made much difference. Then maybe you should change that. As it stands now, you're a stranger who pops in and out of her life for a few hours on weekends. A child needs more than an occasional parent."

He looked away, his gaze going to the flames he could see through the vents in the door of the wood stove. "I told you why I brought her here instead of taking her to my place in Boston. I thought it would be easier for her to adjust slowly into a new environment."

"Or for you to adjust to her?"

He jerked his head around and his gaze slammed into hers. "You don't know what you're talking about."

Ellen made a scoffing sound deep in her throat. "You're wrong. I know exactly what I'm talking about. I'm an expert on having an absent father, and he didn't have your excuse. He and I both speak English, although we've never spoken the same language."

A muscle in his jaw clenched as his hands tightened on the book he still held in his lap. "You make it sound as though I don't want to get close to my daughter. You couldn't be more wrong. I would give anything to be a good father to her." He held up the book. "Did you happen to find a book on how I can do that?"

"I think it's like learning how to bowl or fish. Reading an instruction book could give you a list of the equipment you need, but you have to actually throw a bowling ball or dip a hook into the water more than once before you become an expert." She tilted her head to one side as she met his gaze. "You have the most important tool you need to be a good parent."

"That's encouraging," he drawled cynically. "What tool is that?"

She had the feeling he was just humoring her. Considering she also sensed that he was as mad as a hornet at her for interfering, it was a remarkable reaction for him to have. Since she'd gone this far, she might as well go the extra mile.

"You care about her, Rudd. You can't get that out of any book or buy that in any store."

The book fell to the floor when he stood up abruptly and took several steps away. Since the room was so small, he had to stop before he ran into the grinding wheel. He turned around slowly, his gaze veering across the room to land on the woman on the couch.

He didn't deny her statement or agree with it. "The way I feel about my daughter isn't the problem."

"It's the solution."

He stared at her for a long moment. Then his mouth twisted in a poor imitation of a smile. "You make it sound so easy."

"I doubt if loving someone is ever easy, but I would think it's better than feeling nothing."

He examined her face closely. She made it sound as though she'd never loved anyone before. Or had never been loved. He found either one hard to believe. Ellen chose that moment to meet his gaze for a brief moment, then looked away, unaware of the haunted sadness he'd seen in her eyes.

Uncurling her legs from under her, she got to her feet. "I need to get something out of my case, then I'll be ready to go."

Rudd's gaze followed her as she walked past him to go into the bedroom area. He was puzzled by the flat tone of her voice when she'd talked about loving not being easy. It made him wonder if she'd been hurt by some man in the past. Some man other than her father. If so, by whom? The thought of someone hurting her made him want to go to her and hold her in his arms until that sad expression left her eyes.

The questions flew out of his head when he saw what Ellen had tucked in her arm when she returned. He stared at the doll. Before he could ask her why she'd brought a doll, she walked over to him and shoved it into his hands.

"Hold her for a minute while I put my jacket on. Not like a football," she admonished. "Like this." She folded his arm and fit the doll into the curve. She glanced around. "Where did I put it?" she asked herself as her gaze searched the room. Spying the garment hanging over the back of the couch where she'd flung it, she said, "Ah, there it is."

While she slipped her jacket on, he glanced down at the toy. The red ribbon tied around the blond hair made of yarn was as bedraggled as the rest of the cloth doll, from its embroidered face to its faded yellow dress. The years hadn't been kind to the obviously well-loved doll, yet strangely enough, time hadn't taken away its charm. Rudd didn't need to ask her whose doll it was. He'd seen the way Ellen had held it a few minutes ago.

Returning it to her when she held out her hand for it, he murmured, "Do you usually travel with your own dolly?"

"Only when I go visit four-year-old little girls," she replied with a sweet smile.

"I've bought her several beautiful dolls. She hasn't even touched them, at least not while I've been around her."

"This one is different. Speaking of four-year-old little girls, I'm ready to meet yours. Are you coming with me or are you going to stand there the rest of the day making fun of Annabel?"

"Annabel?"

She lifted her chin. "What's wrong with the name, Annabel?"

He held up a hand to ward off the edge of indignation he heard in her voice. "Nothing. Absolutely nothing. It's a terrific name," he drawled as he reached for his own jacket. "For a cow."

He ducked as she swung her arm as though to hit him, and he suddenly laughed.

Ellen stopped in midswing and stared at him. The sound was magical and held her spellbound. Perhaps his laughter was a little rusty, as though from disuse, but it thrilled her.

Still chuckling, he took her arm and brought her into his arms. For the first few seconds, she was too surprised to feel his mouth over hers to respond. Then he deepened the kiss. Her fingers clenched into the material of his shirt as she felt the earth rock under her feet.

All too soon, he raised his head.

Breathless, she asked, "Why did you do that?"

"I had to, or go crazy."

"But you don't want—"

"I definitely *do* want, but I'm not going to do anything about it. At least not at the moment."

She was still in his arms, his body hard and firm and vibrant against hers. "Or ever. You are the one who didn't want to get involved, remember?"

His hands slid down over her back and hips. "I might have to reconsider my earlier stupid statement. At the moment, I'd say we are definitely involved."

Before she began to believe him, she broke away from his hold. ''With your daughter, not each other.''

His gaze lingered on her mouth, then raised to meet her eyes. ''We might have to reconsider the ground rules. But not right now. Let's go see Katie.''

Ellen allowed herself to be drawn toward the door, feeling as though she were being pulled in too many directions at once. The conflicts between her heart and her head were becoming more and more difficult to separate. Her body still vibrated with the sensations caused by his kiss.

He brought her along with him as he walked toward the door, a strange smile shaping his mouth.

It gave her an incredibly satisfying feeling to be responsible for making him laugh, she thought. Even if it took a near body blow to do it.

Chapter Eleven

When Ellen saw the place Rudd had casually called his summer home, she realized she had to stop making assumptions about him. She'd expected to see a small cottage, not the sprawling three-story house set among towering pine trees. A large, wide, screened-in porch stretched across the front and around each side of the white clapboard house. Carefully manicured shrubs clung to the front and around the sides.

Ellen thought it was an incredibly large house for one small girl and her Spanish nanny. It could easily hold a dozen active children without them bumping into each other. She hadn't asked, but now Ellen wondered if Rudd had household help. From what he'd said about the nanny, she didn't sound as though she would be very cooperative about acting as a cleaning crew and a cook other than for her own and the child's needs.

After he parked the car, Rudd didn't make any move to open his door. Ellen turned her head to look at him, finding his gaze stuck on the house, his expression oddly haunted and bleak.

He's afraid to see his daughter, she realized, wondering why it had never occurred to her before this. As badly as he wanted to become better acquainted with his daughter, he was apparently apprehensive about his new role as a father.

Ellen wondered if she had been brought to Nantucket to be more than just an interpreter. Whether Rudd had done it intentionally or not, she had no way of knowing, but she thought perhaps he'd wanted someone to act as an intermediary between them, like a third person who was called in to officiate a dispute between two battling factions. But this wasn't a war, she wanted to tell him. This was a small, defenseless child, and he was supposed to be a responsible adult.

She tried to place herself in Rudd's position and understand his feelings. It was undoubtedly a daunting situation to be in—somewhat like suddenly being handed a ball and then expected to pitch a championship game without any prior experience. At least baseball had a set of rules. She didn't know of any rule book Rudd could follow to guide him along the way, other than his own instincts. Her experiences with her own father had shown her examples of what *not* to do as a parent, so she might not be the best person to guide Rudd along the parenthood path.

But she was going to try.

There was nothing she could do about her own family circumstances, but just maybe she could do something about Rudd's.

"Are we waiting for a signal or something before we go in?" she asked gently.

She saw the tightness around his mouth soften as he smiled faintly, his gaze still on the house. "Not exactly. Each time I come to see Katie, it gets harder, not easier. It's like a painful ritual she has to sit through when I come to visit her. No matter how many times I talk to her, I get no response after Señora Santana translates what I've said. Half the time, Katie doesn't even look at me."

Placing her hand on the door latch, Ellen said, "Let's see if we can change that. Annabel might make the difference."

He turned to look at the doll she was holding, then raised his gaze to meet hers. "You're putting a lot of faith in an old doll."

"She's a very special doll. Fancy dolls with stiff hair and crisp dresses are pretty to look at, but they aren't very lovable. It's like trying to eat cotton candy. A second of pleasure, but there's no substance. Katie can hug Annabel without being afraid she'll muss her up."

"Even though you have no children, you seem to be an authority on little girls."

"I was one once. That's all the knowledge I have, but my money's still on Annabel."

"I'm willing to try anything at this point."

"Then let's go inside and introduce them."

The click of the latch seemed obscenely loud in the silence of the car when she opened her door, drawing Rudd's gaze to her as she started to swing her legs to the ground. Taking a deep breath, he followed suit and opened his own door.

Considering it was his house, it was odd that she was the one leading the way to the front door instead of Rudd. Someone had to, and he didn't seem to be making the effort. That was all right with her. She'd been opening her own doors, literally and figuratively, for most of her life.

A small, painted plaque hung above the door with Serenity Lodge printed on it in Gothic script. It was too early for her to tell if the name was appropriate or not.

Holding Annabel tucked into her waist with one arm, Ellen pulled open the screen door, then proceeded up the steps. She felt the door give under her hand as Rudd opened it even more widely behind her. She approached the white double doors, admiring the stained glass that made up the top half of each door, then stopped. Even her charge-ahead attitude had its limits when it came to trespassing on someone else's territory.

To her astonishment, Rudd rapped his knuckles on the door instead of walking into his own house.

A shadowy figure appeared through the stained glass. Then the doors were pulled inward. Yanked would have been a better description of the action taken by the woman who had come to the door. Ellen's first impression of Señora Santana was of a tall, lean, severe woman, both in her expression and in her clothing. There didn't seem to be anything soft about the nanny, either in her dress or her manner. Dressed all in black, with salt-and-pepper hair pulled severely back in a tight, ruthless knot behind her head, all she was missing to complete the picture of the Wicked Witch from *The Wizard of Oz* was a peaked, black hat and a broom. Her dark eyes were piercing and unwelcoming as she stood solidly in the doorway as though barring the way for Rudd to enter.

The woman's accent was as heavy as her tone as she said accusingly, "You are early, Señor Lomax."

"Only by a few minutes. I told you when I would be here, *señora,* and that I would have someone with me to meet Katie. Would you bring her into the living room, please?"

Ellen expected the woman to respond to the hint of command in Rudd's voice. He might as well have been speaking to himself. When the older woman flicked a dismissing glance in her direction, Ellen felt her irritation growing. The *señora* had all the charm of a poisonous mushroom.

A choice Spanish phrase she'd heard Mercedes use more than once when she was displeased came to mind, but Ellen didn't want Katie's nanny to be aware she understood her language just yet. If Señora Santana was undermining Rudd in front of his daughter, she would be more likely to do it in front of them if she didn't think either one of them could understand what she was saying to Katie. Having met Katie's nanny, Ellen thought of how easily Señora Santana could intimidate a small child with just one look. Ellen had been expecting someone a little closer to Mary Poppins, instead, she met the Dragon Lady.

When the woman made no move to respond to Rudd's request, he said, "This is Ms. Sheridan, *señora*. I've brought her here to meet my daughter."

No response. She didn't acknowledge Ellen either by looking at her or speaking to her.

Rudd's voice was bitingly but borderline polite. "Would you get my daughter, *señora?*"

The woman's expression spoke volumes. Resentment, anger, and irritation were apparent as she stiffly moved out of the way to allow them into the house.

Entering behind Ellen, Rudd asked, "Where's Mrs. Holloway, *señora?*"

"*En la cocina.*"

Rudd frowned as the severe woman walked away toward the stairs and ascended them with all the majesty of royalty.

Tearing his gaze away from the retreating woman, he turned to Ellen. "Why don't you wait in the living room? I want to find the housekeeper."

"Señora Santana said your housekeeper is in the kitchen."

For the first time since they arrived, Rudd smiled. It wasn't much of a smile, but better than the somber expression he'd had on his face since they'd left the windmill. "I knew I'd done the right thing by bringing you with me. You've saved me from chasing all over the house."

"Is Katie's nanny usually this charming?"

"Afraid so. At least she's talking. At first, she refused to even speak to me." Gesturing toward the doorway at his left, he added, "Make yourself comfortable. I want to make sure Mrs. Holloway has set another place for lunch."

He walked in the opposite direction toward another doorway, the sound of his footsteps the only sound Ellen could hear in the large house. She had never thought silence could be so loud, but in this house it was. It was an oppressive, smothering quiet. Ellen followed the direction Rudd had indicated a moment ago and walked into the living room, hoping to find a more congenial atmosphere. The artist within her had always been deeply affected by her environment, the mood of her surroundings and the people around her influencing her more than was comfortable at times. Like when she'd lived in her father's house. Like now.

It had nothing to do with the physical aspect of the house. The living room had been furnished with emphasis on comfort rather than show. Another difference between her father's house and Rudd's, she thought ruefully. Cream upholstery with light blue stripes, mahogany furniture in Queen Anne style, grayish blue carpet, a large painting by Willa Chase on the wall that faced the multipaned French doors. Spotting an assortment of photos in small, silver frames in a variety of sizes on the fireplace mantel, she stepped closer to examine them. Several of the pictures in the front were of Rudd's parents, at least she guessed that's who the two people were, especially when she saw one with Rudd standing between them. She had to pick up the ones in the back in order to see them better. There were, apparently, other family members as well. When she reached the end of the display, she realized there weren't any pictures of Rudd and his ex-wife. Certainly none of Rudd's daughter.

Glancing back at the room, she noticed there was something else missing. As in the entrance hall, there didn't seem to be any sign of a small child occupying this house. No pictures of her, no toys or children's books, no little fingerprints marring any of the shiny surfaces. In that aspect, Serenity Lodge resembled her father's house. Toys had been considered frivolous extravagances. She found this to be an odd idea for a man who spent thousands of dollars on various antiques that he locked away.

The only means at her disposal to change the appearance of the room was the rag doll she had brought with her. She stepped over to the sofa and placed Annabel on one of the cushions. It was a start.

She sat down on one of the upholstered chairs that faced the sofa, her thoughts on Rudd and his daughter. Maybe she was judging the situation unfairly, having only just arrived on the scene, but in her estimation, Katie was being kept in a pigeonhole, in the house and in Rudd's life. She couldn't help thinking he was keeping Katie isolated on Nantucket for his sake, not necessarily for Katie's sake.

The sound of footsteps had her gaze going toward the doorway. Two sets of steps, one of the sturdy-heeled shoes of the woman who'd answered the door and the other a faint, quicker stride.

A few seconds later, Señora Santana appeared in the doorway with a small girl standing slightly behind her. Ellen couldn't see Katie's face very clearly since she was looking down at the floor. The girl was dressed in a plain white shirt tucked into the waistband of a dark green skirt that hung loosely below her knees, black knee socks, and black shoes. The sides of her black hair were pulled severely back with a wide, black bow, the rest of the hair hanging down to her shoulders.

Ellen wished she had the right to insist on more cheerful clothing for the child. She wouldn't smile, either, if she had to appear dressed like she was in mourning.

Wanting to see Rudd's daughter's face, Ellen spoke to Katie in English rather than in Spanish. Even if Katie didn't understand her, maybe the sound of her voice would get her attention. She couldn't explain why she still felt she didn't want Señora Santana to know she spoke their language, but she went with her instincts.

"Hello, Katie. My name is Ellen."

Katie raised her head, lowering it again when Señora Santana spoke sharply to her in Spanish. Ellen stiffened with anger when she heard the older woman instruct the child to ignore her father's guest.

It was an effort to speak with some measure of politeness. Rudd hadn't exaggerated the woman's animosity. "Would you introduce me to Katie, please, *señora?*"

Ignoring her request, she heard the Spanish woman tell Katie that if she was real good and stood still for a few more minutes, she wouldn't have to sit in the hard chair again today.

That did it for Ellen. In Spanish, Ellen spoke to the little girl. "You can talk to me, Katie. You won't have to sit on any hard chair if you do.'' She glared at the woman beside Katie, daring the woman to contradict her. Señora Santana was too shocked to say anything.

Turning her attention back to Rudd's daughter, Ellen said, ''I've brought a friend of mine to see you, but you'll have to come over to her. She can't come to you.''

Ignoring Señora Santana's shocked expression, Ellen kept her gaze on Katie, who slowly raised her head and looked up. The woeful expression in Katie's eyes tore at her heart. It took everything she had to restrain herself from going to Rudd's daughter to take her in her arms.

Refusing to order the child around like Señora Santana did, Ellen gestured behind her and said in Spanish, ''My friend is here on the sofa. Why don't you come and say hello to her?''

Instead of complying with Ellen's invitation, Katie raised her gaze to the woman beside her, who scowled down at her. It wasn't necessary for Señora Santana to say a word. Her hard expression was enough. Katie dropped her head again and took a step backward.

Ellen slowly crossed the soft carpet to stand in front of the child's overbearing nanny. Looking the woman straight in the eye, she spoke softly in Spanish in a tone of voice she'd often heard her father use. Cold steel, laced with icicles.

The woman's head snapped up, her dark eyes widening with shock. Then she dropped her gaze, muttering a brief apology before backing away from the doorway. The nanny made a startled sound when she bumped into Rudd, who had been standing behind her. She excused herself, gathered the front of her skirt in her hands and hurried up the stairs as though the devil himself were nipping at her heels.

Ellen dropped her gaze to Katie to see if she would follow after her nanny, but the child didn't move. She had raised her head, though, and was looking at Ellen with wide eyes as if she'd just witnessed a miracle.

Clearly baffled by the cowed behavior of the usually belligerent nanny, Rudd's voice was a mixture of awe and admiration. "What did you say to her?"

"It doesn't translate all that well," she said evasively.

"Try. I could use a few pointers on how to deal with that woman."

Lowering her gaze to the child, Ellen thought she detected a small smile shaping the child's mouth before Katie again turned her attention back to the floor. Ellen was tempted to test the suspicion growing in her mind, but she waited.

Responding to Rudd's request, she answered, "Mercedes used to have a running feud with the gardener. She would use a few colorful phrases whenever he tracked mud through the kitchen or snitched cookies out of the cookie jar. I thought I'd give one of them a try."

He came forward, stopping when he was standing beside Katie. "Give me the gist of what you said. It worked like magic."

"Basically, I reminded her she was being paid a salary, not self-employed, which I suggested could be changed with very little trouble."

Out of the corner of her eye, she saw Katie frown and jerk her head up, a confused expression in the little girl's blue eyes. Ellen didn't think it was the look of someone who wished she knew what was being said. It was more like the child had been surprised by Ellen's answer, as though Katie knew her English explanation wasn't the same as the dialogue she'd actually had with the woman in Spanish.

The literal translation had more to do with boiling in oil and chicken entrails. Mercedes was a very earthy woman.

Rudd tilted his head to one side and stared at Ellen. "Now, why am I having trouble believing that was what you said?"

She shrugged. "It must be your scientific mind. You need everything documented and tested thoroughly before you'll believe it."

Thinking about his reaction to her, he commented, "Not everything has an explanation."

She looked away when his gaze lowered to her mouth. When she brought her attention back to Katie, Ellen caught the startled look in the child's eyes.

Turning around, Ellen retraced her steps and sat down in the chair she'd occupied previously. Still using English, she said, "I think I'll eat a bowl of ice cream with a shovel while standing on my head."

The expressions on both Katie's and Rudd's faces were almost identical: Bewildered, open-mouthed, and wide-eyed. Understandable, considering what she'd said. Except for the fact that one of them wasn't supposed to be able to comprehend English.

Rudd looked down at his daughter, catching her wide-eyed expression. "I don't understand any better than you do," he said with amusement. "It seems she's lost her mind." His gaze shifted to Ellen. With a rueful twist to his mouth, he said, "I forgot she doesn't understand me."

Smiling widely, Ellen glanced at Katie. "She understands you perfectly, don't you, Katie?"

Father and daughter stared at her again. This was becoming a habit. Then Katie's expression changed. *"No comprendo, señorita."*

Ellen shook her head. "It's too late now, sweetie. I'm on to you," she said in English, as she got out of her chair and walked over to where Katie stood frozen in the doorway.

Rudd's reaction came a few seconds later. "Have you lost your mind?"

She scowled back at him. "I don't think so. I haven't lost my hearing, either. You don't need to shout."

Lowering his voice, he said, "Ellen, she doesn't speak English. Remember? That's why I asked you to come with me."

Ignoring him, Ellen debated what to do. She knew she was right. At least she hoped so. She didn't want to try to force Katie to speak English even though she knew the little girl understood. From what Ellen had observed a few minutes ago, the child had been intimidated enough by the Spanish woman. But somehow, she had to show Katie that it was all right for her to speak English.

Taking Katie's hand, she led her over to the sofa. "I told you earlier that I've brought a friend of mine to meet you. Why don't you come over and say hello to her?"

At first, Ellen thought Katie was going to pretend she didn't understand. After a slight hesitation, the little girl stepped forward, her gaze flicking to Ellen, then to the sofa. Ellen gestured toward the doll she'd brought with her.

"Katie, this is my friend. I brought her all the way from Boston to meet you."

Katie lifted her hand and extended it slowly, carefully toward the doll. She touched the doll's foot, then higher to stroke the yarn hair, as though it were made out of spun gold.

Ellen waited beside Katie, fully aware of Rudd standing rooted in the doorway, staring at the tableau in front of the sofa. She could only hope he wouldn't interfere. She was following her instincts, which had led her in this direction without any guarantee she was going the right way. It was hard enough for her to play this out. She could only imagine what Rudd was going through.

She chanced a glance in his direction, slowly shaking her head when he looked like he wanted to say something.

With her hand still touching the doll, Katie looked up at Ellen with a silent appeal in her eyes. Ellen smiled down at her. "You can hold her if you want to, Katie. She likes to be held."

Scooting up on the cushion next to Annabel, Katie gently picked up the doll and held it on her lap, her little arms cradling the soft figure as though it were a real baby. Then suddenly, Katie looked up at Ellen, horror widening her eyes as she started squirming to get off the couch.

Startled, Ellen said, "What's wrong, Katie?"

In Spanish, the little girl exclaimed, "I'm not allowed to be on the furniture."

It was just as well the nanny wasn't in the same room or Ellen would be tempted to throttle her. "Nonsense," she said gently. "You can sit any place you want to, Katie," she answered in English.

Still clutching the doll in her arms, Katie looked at Rudd, her expression wary and unsure. Regardless of all the other visits Rudd had made to see his daughter, Ellen could tell the little girl was still unsure of him. After having met Señora Santana, it was clear how the nanny had been undermining everything Rudd had tried to do to get closer to his daughter.

When Rudd looked at her with a baffled frown, Ellen realized he hadn't understood what Katie had said. "Rudd, is it all right for her to sit on the furniture?"

He blinked, then answered, "Of course."

"Why don't you tell her that?"

A variety of expressions crossed his face. Comprehension was the one that won out over the others. He still wasn't convinced his daughter would know what he was saying, but he was willing to try anything.

Stepping forward, Rudd came over to his daughter and bent down in front of her. As badly as he wanted to touch her, he refrained. Barely.

Keeping his voice low and gentle, he said, "This is your house, too, Katie. You can sit on the sofa or the chairs any time you want. It's all right."

His daughter stared at him for a long moment before she glanced nervously in the direction of the stairs. Rudd lifted his hand and gently put a crooked finger under Katie's chin to bring her gaze back to his. "Don't worry about Señora Santana, Katie. I'll deal with her."

Katie looked down at the doll she still held in her arms. In accented English, she asked, "What's her name?"

It was necessary for Rudd to clear his throat since it was suddenly difficult for him to speak. Taking his cue from Ellen, he answered her question as naturally as he could manage. "Her name is Annabel. Why don't you sit on the sofa with her while I talk to Ellen for a few minutes. Then we'll have some lunch."

He waited until Katie was settled with the doll on her lap before he stepped over to Ellen and took her elbow. He drew her along with him to the doorway where he stopped.

His gaze went from Ellen to his daughter, then back to Ellen. He felt as though the world had suddenly tilted under his feet, and it was taking him a few minutes to find his balance.

Lowering his voice, he asked, "How did you know?"

"That she could speak English?" When he nodded, she answered, "I had my suspicions before I even saw her. It seemed likely that your ex-wife would have taught Katie

English. I wasn't sure until I saw Katie's reaction when I told you what I said to Señora Santana in English what I had said in Spanish. Her expression gave her away."

He shook his head in disbelief. "You saw in one hour what I haven't seen in the last month."

"I wasn't as closely involved as you've been, Rudd. Because you don't speak Spanish, you didn't know what the *señora* was saying to Katie. There was no way you could have known she was threatening her."

"Threatening her?"

Ellen put her fingers over his lips. "Keep your voice down. Katie might understand why you're angry. It doesn't matter how we discovered she understands English. The important thing is that you can now talk to her without an interpreter." She grimaced. "We have a different problem now."

"What's that?"

"Señora Santana. She has to go, Rudd. She's doing more harm than good. Before she realized I spoke Spanish, she instructed Katie not to have anything to do with me. Lord knows what she's said to Katie about you. Now that you know Katie can speak English, you don't need the nanny. For that matter, you don't need me."

"You couldn't be more wrong. I need you now more than ever."

Chapter Twelve

Under the circumstances, Ellen chose to take his words at face value. She had no illusions to the part she was playing in this little drama.

"First things first," she declared matter-of-factly. "Do you agree the Spanish Inquisition should be given her walking papers?"

He held his hand up. "Not so fast. Give me some time to think about this."

"I don't know why you need to think about it. The woman is poison, and she is spreading it to your daughter. She needs to pack her bags and fly back to Spain. She probably won't even need a plane. She could use her broom."

Rudd realized with amazement that he was smiling. His neat, little house of cards had tumbled down around him, and he was grinning like an idiot. "Why, Ellen," he drawled. "I believe that was a catty remark."

"Which goes to show I've been around Tiffany too much. You're evading the issue. Why?"

"If Katie's nanny leaves, who's going to take care of Katie? Mrs. Holloway only comes during the day, and I doubt if she would be interested in changing her schedule to include twenty-four hour duty since she has an ailing husband at home. I don't want to leave Katie with a stranger during the week while I'm gone."

Ellen leaned against the doorframe and met his gaze squarely. "There is another option."

Somehow, he wasn't surprised she would come up with one. Folding his arms across his chest, he asked cautiously, "Which is?"

"You could take Katie to Boston, put her in a day-care center or hire someone to stay with her during the day while you cavort with the test tubes, then you could be with her at night. Thousands of single parents do it all the time."

He dropped his arms. "You make it sound so easy."

She shook her head. "The *decision* is easy. Carrying it out will probably be one of the hardest things you've ever done." She glanced at the little girl sitting on the sofa, then brought her gaze back to Rudd. "But she's your daughter, Rudd. That simple fact gives her the right to get to know her father, her grandmother, to become part of the Lomax family. It wouldn't be right not to give her that chance."

Rudd heard the truth in what she was telling him and also sensed the sadness in her voice. "Ellen," he began, not sure exactly what it was he wanted to ask.

There was something in his voice she didn't want to hear right now. Whether it was sympathy or curiosity, she didn't want to deal with either one. "We'll talk about this later.

I'm going to go find your housekeeper while you spend some time with your daughter.''

Rudd stared at Ellen as she opened one of the doors off the hallway and closed it behind her. Ellen was going the wrong way. The door she had chosen would lead her to the back patio, and Mrs. Holloway was still in the kitchen preparing lunch. Ellen would have to open a few more doors before she would find the kitchen the way she was going.

He shook his head in bemused admiration. If anyone could find her way out of a maze, it would be Ellen.

A soft voice close beside him brought him back to his own maze. It was followed by a slight tugging on his hand. Glancing down, he saw Katie was looking up at him with a wide-eyed gaze, Annabel held tightly in the crook of her arm in an affectionate stranglehold.

''What it is, Katie?''

She bit her lip, then said something incomprehensible to him. Except for one word. The last one. *Señor.* He knew it meant mister, not Daddy. Bending his knees, he came down closer to her height. ''In English, Katie.''

Lowering her gaze, she spoke in a low voice. ''I need to use the bathroom.''

He straightened up, fighting a feeling of panic. He looked toward the door Ellen had used, hoping to see her open it and come racing to his rescue. It didn't happen. He was on his own. Irritated with himself for being such a coward, he glanced down at his daughter, who was looking at him with a quiet seriousness.

Extending his hand, he smiled down at her, hoping he was displaying more confidence than he was feeling. ''I'll take you.''

She timidly slipped her hand in his, and he realized it was the first time she'd touched him of her own accord.

Such a small gesture, but one that gave him immense pleasure.

Walking down the hall beside him, Katie surprised him by volunteering, "*Señora* told me not to speak my father's language. That I would get in trouble."

Out of the mouths of babes, he thought grimly. "*Señora* was wrong, Katie. You won't get into trouble. I would like you to speak English since I don't understand Spanish."

In her solemn accented English, she said, "I will try to remember, *señor.*"

Stopping at the small bathroom door under the stairs, he asked, "Here you go. Do you need any help?"

She gave him a very mature look. "No, *señor.* I'm a big girl."

He saw the way she clutched Ellen's doll in her arms, her actions disputing her words. Smiling down at her, he said, "I can see that. How about if I wait out here for you? Then we'll go to the dining room."

With her hand on the knob, she took a step, then hesitated. "Will *señora* be there?"

The decision was easy to make whether the *señora* liked it or not. "The *señora* will be having her lunch in her room. It will be just you, me, Ellen, and Annabel."

She nodded and pulled the door open.

Rudd leaned against the wall beside the door while he waited, a smile of satisfaction on his mouth. He'd just performed his first duty as a father, and all had gone fine. When he realized his automatic reaction was to tell Ellen about it, his smile widened. He wanted to share his minor victory with her. He wanted to share every part of his life with her. She might think their association was temporary, but she was wrong.

Without Ellen, he might not have learned Katie could speak English or made the progress he had in such a short time. It was as though she were the catalyst between two separate ingredients, making them join together in a unit they might not have without her. It was how she affected him, making him whole and complete. This weekend was a revelation in more ways than one.

The sound of the latch brought his attention back to the bathroom door, which was opening slowly. Katie's head peeked around the frame of the door, a worried frown tightening her mouth. When she spotted him, a look of relief crossed her face, making him wonder if she thought he might have left. Then she solemnly left the bathroom and walked over to him, clutching Annabel tightly in one arm. She stopped about a foot away and looked up at him with her usual too-adult expression.

Maybe he was rushing things, but there was something he needed to know. "Katie, do you know who I am?"

She nodded her head slowly.

"Who am I?"

"My Daddy."

The softly spoken word made the muscles in his chest tighten almost painfully. He never thought one word could sound so wonderful. Hoping he sounded calmer than he felt, he asked, "Did the *señora* tell you who I was?"

Katie's dark hair shifted on her shoulders when she shook her head. "Mommy put a picture of you by my bed. She said you were my Daddy and that I should include you in my prayers."

It wasn't easy, but somehow he managed to keep the shock from showing on his face. He had taken it for granted Katie hadn't been aware of his existence any more than he'd been aware of hers until after Cynthia's death. His ex-wife's generosity was hard to understand, but at the moment all he could do was be grateful. In spite of the nanny's attitude toward him, Katie didn't appear to be afraid of him, and he supposed he had Cynthia to thank for that. Gratitude was the last thing he ever thought he would feel toward his ex-wife, but for the sake of their child, he would try to forget the animosity that had been between them for so long.

He reached for Katie's free hand and placed it on his open palm. It was such a small hand, so delicate. His fingers slowly closed over hers as he said, "You have no reason to believe me, Katie, when I tell you that I would never do anything to hurt you. If there is something you want or something you don't understand or something I do that you don't like, I want you to tell me. I promise I'll listen. Can you do that?"

He remained perfectly still as she studied him thoroughly, her dark eyes meeting his unflinchingly. After what seemed like hours, she finally nodded her head.

Smiling faintly, he added, "And if you do something I don't like or say something I don't understand, I'm going to tell you. Do you think that's fair?"

Again she nodded. "Can I tell you something now?"

He wasn't sure he was ready, but he gave her a smile. "Sure."

"The *señora* made me sit on a hard chair when I was bad. I don't like that much. Will you make me sit in a chair when I'm bad?"

Ellen was right, he thought grimly. The nanny had to go. Thinking of Ellen, he wondered how she would answer his daughter's question. Surprising himself, he came up with his own. "If you do something you aren't supposed to be doing, it doesn't mean you are bad, Katie. If you do something I might not think is right, we'll sit down and talk about it. There will be no more sitting on hard chairs as punishment, I'll promise you that. But we are going to have to talk about some basic rules, the things you can do and can't do.''

"Like I have to keep my toys picked up and brush my teeth before I go to bed? Mommy told me those.''

He hadn't the faintest idea. He supposed he would learn as he went along. "Something like that, I guess.'' Straightening up, he still held on to her hand, extremely pleased when her little fingers clasped his. "Let's go find Ellen and have some lunch.''

It was easy to find Ellen. All he had to do was follow the sound of laughter. Entering the kitchen, Rudd stared at his usually dour housekeeper, who was sitting at the table with her shoes off and her feet propped up on one of the chairs. She was wiping tears of laughter from her eyes as she pleaded with Ellen, "Tell me you didn't really do all that.''

Ellen was standing with her back to the door and her arms elbow-deep in a sinkful of frothy bubbles. "Well, I didn't do it by myself. Tiffany was the one who crawled up on the counter and got all the ingredients out of the cupboard. I was in charge of stirring. Tiffany's idea of the proper ingredients was to chose them according to color. No matter what she added, the glop kept coming out a disgusting gray color.''

Mrs. Holloway dabbed the tears from her eyes with a corner of her flower-sprigged apron. "Did you actually bake this concoction?''

"Of course. We used one of Tiffany's mother's fancy platters to put the finished product on, and frosted it with powdered sugar and water mixed so thoroughly it was like cement by the time it hardened. To give you an idea how great Tiffany's mother is, she valiantly cut off a piece and exclaimed how wonderful the cake was, even though it tasted like something left in an attic for about a year.''

That set the housekeeper off again. After the laughter slowed, Rudd spoke from the doorway. "Maybe you could whip up one of those cakes for the *señora*."

Some of the bubbles went flying when Ellen whirled around from the sink. Her gaze went to Rudd holding his daughter's hand, a pleased expression making her eyes dance.

"Hi, you two. I hope you don't mind, Rudd, but I took a tray up to Señora Santana's room. She won't be joining us for lunch."

"I had the same idea. You just beat me to it."

Centering her attention on Katie, Ellen asked, "I could use some help with these dishes, Katie. How about it? Would you like to wash dishes?"

The little girl's eyes widened, her dark eyes glittering with excitement. "I could do this?"

Extending her soapy hand out, Ellen nodded. "Sure. I'll show you. Rudd, pull a chair over to the sink while I roll up her sleeves."

Since he couldn't think of a single reason not to, he did as he was told.

A few minutes later, he watched as Katie happily splashed around in the bubbles, occasionally even actually washing a cup or a saucer which Ellen took from her and placed in the dish drainer next to the sink. Rudd somehow had ended up being responsible for Annabel and accepted the charge with as much gravity as possible.

Tucking the doll into the crook of his arm, Rudd positioned himself so he could see his daughter's face. She was smiling, a genuine, happy, life-is-good smile that warmed his heart. When Ellen handed her the spray nozzle and showed her how to work it, Katie giggled.

Rudd closed his eyes briefly as pleasure rocketed through him. Such a simple thing. A child's laughter. His child's laughter. It was the first time he'd heard her laugh. He opened his eyes. She was like a cardboard cutout suddenly coming to life in front of him. And he had Ellen to thank for the miraculous transformation.

Ellen ended up getting as much soapsuds and water on her as Katie did. The front of her sweater clung damply to the shape of her breasts, drawing Rudd's gaze away from his frolicking daughter. When his body reacted to the tantalizing sight, he had to put some distance between them to give himself time to gain control.

He sat down abruptly across from his housekeeper, who immediately popped up like a jumping jack. Lifting his hand, he gestured for her to sit back down. "Everything seems to be under control, Mrs. Holloway. Take advantage of having your kitchen taken over and relax."

"But, Mr. Lomax," she protested, clearly not comfortable to be sitting at the same table as her employer.

"Just enjoy the show," he drawled.

Ellen had something to say about Mrs. Holloway's protest, which he should have expected. She seemed to have something to say about everything. "Lunch is all ready. Mrs. Holloway and I set the table out in the solarium." Drying her hands on a towel, she lifted Katie's hands out of the water. "Let's get you dried off so we can eat. I don't know about you, but I'm starving. You're going to love the lunch, Katie. Mrs. Holloway and I put our heads together and came up with some food appropriate for a picnic in a jungle."

Oh Lord, Rudd groaned silently. Now she was rubbing the front of her sweater with the towel. To get his mind off the desire to yank the towel away from her and replace it with his hands, he asked, "Did you do the cooking?"

"Mrs. Holloway did the honors." She stopped brushing her sweater. "Wait a minute. Have I just been insulted? I can cook, you know."

"Not from what I heard a minute ago. Gray glop and cement frosting? Yum, yum."

Helping Katie down from the chair, she said, "Tiffany and I were only seven years old at the time. I've learned a few things since then."

"I'm counting on it."

Ellen made a scolding noise with her tongue. "Such a skeptic. You can either eat with us or you can toast a hot dog over a Bunsen burner like you do in the lab."

Pushing himself away from the table, he followed Ellen and Katie out of the kitchen. "I don't toast hot dogs over Bunsen burners at the lab. I usually don't eat lunch."

"Well, you're going to today. Mrs. Holloway went above and beyond the call of duty even though her bunions are killing her. The least we can do is eat her cooking."

Rudd had to walk a little faster down the hall in order to keep up with her. Katie, he noticed, was practically running. They were like two objects being tossed along by a tidal wave called Ellen Sheridan. "Is that why you were doing the dishes? So Mrs. Holloway could get off her feet?"

Ellen stopped at the leaded glass door leading into the solarium. "That and the fact I like doing dishes."

Piping up from between them, Katie said, "So do I. Could I do them again?"

Grinning, Ellen said, "Sure you can."

Rudd wondered if he should be warning Katie about the possibility of other new experiences she might have before the weekend was over. He could have used a warning or two himself.

"You did a terrific job, Katie," he said lightly as he reached across Ellen and opened the door. "Maybe we could ask Mrs. Holloway to put the dirty dishes in the bathtub. Then you can take a bath and wash dishes at the same time. That way you won't get your clothes wet."

Katie's head tipped back so she could see her father's face, her blue eyes bright with excitement. "Could I really?"

Chuckling, Ellen shepherded the little girl into the solarium. "I think your father was just kidding, honey."

The air in the solarium was considerably more humid and about ten degrees warmer than the rest of the house. Rudd had forgotten how many plants there were in the solarium. Or how big they'd grown. He'd arranged for a gardener to come once a week to tend to his mother's plant menagerie as she'd asked him to do, but other than that, he rarely came into this part of the house. Pushing aside several hanging fronds belonging to a large fern, he saw that the glass patio table had been cleared of some of the smaller plants and prepared with place settings for three people. There were several covered dishes situated around a delicate, pink violet that had been placed in a rustic basket in the center of the table.

There was a perfectly good dining room they could have used, but Ellen had chosen a room that resembled a jungle.

It seemed as though Ellen had thought of everything, including several phone books stacked on one of the wrought-iron chairs for Katie. It was something he wouldn't have even considered as necessary.

Ellen's choice of proper lunch fare, however, did manage to cause him to raise an eyebrow or two. He could honestly say it was the first time he'd ever eaten toasted cheese sandwiches that had been cut into a variety of animal shapes, evidently by an assortment of cookie cutters. Nor could he remember ever dining on green beans that had been mixed with some sort of creamy soup and sprinkled with crushed potato chips. The pièce de résistance was a silver platter piled high with homemade french fries.

He gingerly picked up a teddy bear-shaped cheese sandwich and placed it on his plate, ignoring Ellen's smile as she handed him the platter. Instead, he concentrated on Katie's obvious enjoyment as she calmly nibbled off the head of a duck. He'd always considered his memory as being better than average, but he certainly didn't recall ever having any animal-shaped cookies baked by Mrs. Holloway.

Of course, there was also the off chance that Ellen had brought cookie cutters with her. Any woman who saved a doll from her childhood would no doubt have a supply of cookie cutters around someplace just for such an occasion as this.

The few times he'd dined with his daughter in the past, Katie had just picked at her food while the *señora* supervised the adult-style meal that she'd evidently chosen to be served. He hadn't paid much attention to what he'd eaten, but the menu had been plain and drab compared to today's unusual spread. So had the conversation, which had been almost nonexistent.

That wasn't the case today. With Annabel propped up on Katie's lap, his daughter munched away happily, even pretending to feed a french fry to the doll once in a while. Ellen kept the conversational ball rolling, somehow encouraging Katie to join in, although he couldn't pin down exactly how she was doing it. She didn't ask questions or prod or pry, just chatted away about an assortment of things that managed to interest Katie. Whether it was the jungle atmosphere or Ellen's fertile imagination, Rudd found himself as spellbound as his daughter when Ellen spun a web of tales. Eventually, Ellen narrowed her subject matter to one geographical area. She covered the Boston Tea Party, the famous Old North Church, and tantalized Katie with descriptions of all sorts of other fantastic sights in Boston that the little girl really must see some time.

Rudd knew what she was doing. Ellen hadn't pulled any punches when she gave him her opinion about taking his daughter back to Boston to live with him.

It wasn't all that long ago that he was patting himself on the back for coming up with a clever solution to his problems with Katie by bringing Ellen to Nantucket. An hour after Ellen had arrived at his summer house, she'd discovered Katie could speak English, told him to fire the nanny and demanded he take his daughter back to Boston. He no longer thought of comparing Ellen to a hurricane or a tidal wave. Steamroller was more like it.

"Don't you agree, Rudd?"

He blinked and met Ellen's amused gaze. "About what?"

"About Katie needing new clothes."

Rudd glanced at Katie's white shirt, remembering the long, dark green skirt and black socks. "That's up to her. Would you like some different clothes, Katie?"

The little girl's slender shoulders rose and fell. Undaunted by Katie's lack of enthusiasm, Ellen asked, "Do you have a favorite color, Katie?"

Nodding, Katie answered, *"Rojo."*

"Perfect," agreed Ellen.

Rudd wasn't so sure. "Is that some new shade I'm not familiar with?"

It took Ellen a few seconds to figure out that he hadn't understood Katie's answer. "Her favorite color is red."

"What about pink?" he asked Katie, liking the idea. Seeing Katie's nose crinkle up in disapproval, he added, "You don't like pink?"

"I don't like that funny sticky hair."

Ellen burst out laughing. "Not punk, Katie. Pink." Ellen pointed at the delicate, pink violet in the basket on the table. "Pink."

Katie studied the blossoms with her serious gaze. Then she shook her head. *"Rojo."*

"Okay," Ellen said with a grin, pleased that Katie was asserting herself. "Red it is." Placing her napkin on the table, she pushed her chair back. "As soon as Katie and I help Mrs. Holloway with the dishes, maybe we can go see what Nantucket has to offer in the way of little girl's clothes."

Katie only heard the part about washing dishes. With Annabel tucked under her arm, Katie slid off the chair and skipped out of the solarium.

Even though Rudd couldn't remember eating anything, he pushed his plate away. "What's this about shopping?"

Ellen began to gather their dishes. "She needs jeans, T-shirts, some pretty underclothes and different shoes. She's four years old, not a dowdy eighty-year-old. If we can't find what we need here on the island, there are some great children's stores in Boston. Lord, I sound like Tiffany."

"Ellen," he cautioned. "Slow down. I'm still trying to get used to the fact Katie speaks English."

She didn't want to slow down. She wanted Rudd to whisk his daughter away to Boston and be a father to his child and live happily ever after. It seemed so simple, so basic. She continued clearing the table. It gave her hands something to do to prevent her from shaking some sense into Rudd. Holding the dishes, she paused and stared into space, debating her next move.

Rudd saw the faraway look in Ellen's green eyes and instinctively wanted to make it go away. When lightning is spotted in the sky, it makes sense to get out of its path when there is a danger of it striking.

"Ellen?"

She didn't even blink, much less look his way. She was obviously deep in thought, and he knew that could only mean trouble.

Rudd's chair scraped against the red tile floor as he pushed it back and stood up. He took the stack of plates from her and put them down on the table. "Lord, I can't believe this. You've got me doing things I would never have thought I'd ever do." He had her attention now. She was looking at him as though he had lost his mind. She might be right. In a calmer voice, he said, "Ellen, I brought you here to act as interpreter, not to rearrange my life."

Her green eyes were shadowed by confusion. "I'm not trying to rearrange your life."

"What else would you call it? Don't get me wrong. I appreciate what you've done, but you're pressing too hard, too fast, too soon for too much. One minute you're telling me to take Katie back to Boston, then discussing shopping expeditions in front of her so I don't have any choice but to go along with you unless I want to end up looking like a giant Scrooge. I don't like being manipulated, Ellen. I like to do things in my own time at my own pace. I even occasionally like to decide how I run my life all on my own. Aside from a disastrous marriage, I haven't done too badly."

Ellen bit her lip for a moment. "I'm sorry," she said quietly. "I was only trying to help."

Good Lord, he thought. He felt like he'd just whipped a defenseless puppy. "I know you mean well, and I'm sounding ungrateful. Oh, hell," he said disgustedly. "This is coming out all wrong."

Ellen held up her hand in a placating gesture. "I understand. I've been told often enough that I rush into things headfirst without looking where I'm going. It looks like I'm doing it again. I thought I'd learned not to butt in where I'm not wanted." She covered up the hurt his words had caused by giving him a mocking smile. "I'm not totally stupid. I see what I'm doing now."

Rudd hated knowing he had been the one responsible for putting that shadow of pain in her eyes, even though its origin came from her relationship with her father. "Ellen, I didn't say you were—"

"Yes, you did, but it doesn't matter." She reached over and lifted the plates off the table. "I'd better get these back to the kitchen so Katie can do her thing." She stopped. "Unless you don't want her to wash dishes."

"I don't care if she washes dishes. You're misunderstanding me."

Holding the stack in front of her like a shield, she added, "I won't say anything more to Katie about going shopping. You're right. I was out of line. It's your decision. I won't interfere again."

She started to walk away from him, but he reached out and grabbed her arm to stop her. She had to scramble quickly to retain a hold on the plates so she wouldn't drop them.

"Leave the damn plates alone," he demanded as he took them from her again and returned them to the table. "Dammit, Ellen. You're twisting what I'm saying all out of proportion. Without your intervention, I would never have known Katie understands English. You've worked miracles in a short period of time."

"And you're grateful," she said softly. "I heard you. I don't want your gratitude. What I want is for you to be a real father to your daughter."

In case she tried to take off again, he moved his hand to her shoulder to keep her in front of him. It seemed like forever since he'd touched her, and he was stunned by how delicate her bones felt underneath his fingers. "Why is it so important to you for me to try out for Father of the Year?"

"Why is it so hard for you to be a father?" she retaliated with more heat than she'd intended. "Do you have any idea of how much your daughter needs you?" She didn't give him a chance to answer. "But it's easier to concentrate on your work, isn't it? To put your child on hold until you can fit her in. Time goes by awfully fast, Rudd. Before you know it, she'll be all grown up and you will not have had one damn thing to do with that process. She'll have nothing but neglect to look back on when she thinks about her father. It might be enough for you, but it won't be enough for Katie."

He could feel her tension under his hand and heard it in her voice. "Are you talking about Katie now, or yourself?"

Instead of denying it, she lifted her chin and faced him defiantly. "Maybe a little of both. Having been raised by a cold, unfeeling parent, I feel I can speak with some authority on the subject."

"The circumstances are different, Ellen. Your father chose to be a father in name only. I want to be Katie's father, but I don't know how."

"Well, you certainly aren't going to learn anything this way. You've ignored her for four years, so why rush into anything now, right? See Katie a couple of hours once a week. Forget about her the rest of the time. Don't go to her school programs or her graduation from high school or college. Don't pay her tuition to college. Tell her it will mean more to her if she works for it herself. Don't ever hug her or kiss her or listen to her problems. When she eventually leaves home, see her once a year on your birthday when she brings you a card because she doesn't know you well enough to know what you would like for a gift. If that's the type of relationship you want with Katie, then you're going about it the right way."

"That's not what I want," he argued, stepping aside to put distance between them and clenching the back of the chair. "You don't know me well enough to know what I want, Ellen."

Ellen ignored the hurt his words caused. "I know what you don't want. You don't want me or your daughter or anyone else to get close to you. Well, you just keep pushing people away, Rudd. It won't bother me. I'm used to it. I've been pushed away by the master. Keep your daughter in a safe, little compartment in your life and take her out when you feel it's convenient. Just don't be surprised if your daughter isn't satisfied with being a part-time member of your family when she gets a little older."

"Don't compare my daughter's life to yours. Or me to your father. There are no similarities at all."

"Aren't there? Do you really want to wait twenty years and find out that it's too late to do anything about it? My father couldn't care less, but you might. Think about it. And while you're at it, think about whether or not your feelings for your ex-wife carry over to your daughter. And to me."

She didn't wait around for his response. She grabbed the plates and brushed past him and left the solarium.

Chapter Thirteen

Rudd didn't follow her this time. He spent the first few minutes simply staring at the door Ellen had closed all too quietly behind her. Then he began to pace back and forth on the tiled floor, not an easy thing to do with so many plants in the way. Ellen's accusations were ringing in his ears like a discordant echo. It took a couple more minutes of relentless pacing to get over wanting to shake Ellen until her teeth rattled.

Once he was past that, he thought about everything she had said. Not only had she revealed a great deal about her own life, but she had exposed a little too much about his.

He stopped pacing to stand in front of the double glass doors that opened out onto the terrace behind the house. Usually he enjoyed the scenery around Serenity Lodge, but now he didn't even see it. All he could see were Ellen's blazing eyes. For someone who declared she couldn't get angry at anyone, Ellen thrust a pretty mean spear when she aimed it, he mused. In the process, she had pointed out things about himself he wasn't too pleased to find were there.

He hadn't looked at bringing Katie to Nantucket as putting her in a temporary slot in his life. It had seemed like the perfect solution, a way of letting his daughter gradually get used to him.

Now his motives sounded less noble. He had to consider whether what Ellen had said was partly true, that he had brought Katie to Nantucket for his sake, not for the child's. Ellen made it sound like he was the one who needed the distance.

And that part of his motivation was not wanting to face a reminder of his ex-wife on a daily basis.

He turned around abruptly and stared at the door Ellen had used a few minutes ago. She was making him open doors inside himself, and he didn't like what he was finding on the other side.

It was a full thirty minutes later when he finally left the solarium. As he was passing the door leading into the kitchen, he could hear sounds of activity, but he didn't go in. He had a few things to discuss privately with Señora Santana before he joined the other ladies in the kitchen.

Ten minutes later, he came back down the stairs. How blind he'd been. Bringing the Spanish woman to Nantucket had been a big mistake. Instead of providing Katie with someone familiar who could help her make the transition to her new life, he'd brought a bitter woman along who resented him. In the nanny's mind, he had two strikes against him. He'd married her precious Cynthia and taken Katie to America. The truth had come out in a raging tirade when he'd given her notice. Señora Santana had hoped he would be dissatisfied with a child he couldn't communicate with and send her back to Spain with the *se-ñora,* who considered Katie more her child than Rudd's.

Why hadn't he seen what the woman was doing? Maybe it was because he'd been overwhelmed with parenthood suddenly thrust on him. Being responsible for a small child still scared the hell out of him. But he was more frightened of losing this chance for a family.

Entering the kitchen, he found Katie standing on a chair pulled in front of the kitchen counter, a dish towel wrapped around her small waist. Mrs. Holloway was showing the little girl how to put spoonfuls of chocolate chip dough onto a cookie sheet. There was a dab of flour on Katie's cheek and a small smear of chocolate near her mouth, proof that not all the chips had made it into the batter.

Two of the players were accounted for, but one was missing. Ellen was nowhere to be seen. Six months ago, he'd run away from her because he'd instinctively felt she would disrupt his carefully planned life. Now, he didn't want it any other way.

"Don't tell me. Let me guess," he stated as he stuck a finger into the bowl of dough. "Ellen had another wonderful idea, and it had to do with baking cookies."

Mrs. Holloway answered, even though he hadn't actually asked a question. "Miss Sheridan did suggest Miss Katie might like to try her hand at baking some cookies."

"It sounds like her." Brushing a little of the flour off Katie's cheek, he asked, "Are you having fun?"

She nodded her head vigorously. "*Si.* I mean yes."

He glanced down at the spoonfuls of dough on the cookie sheet on the counter. Baking cookies wasn't something he knew all that much about, but even to his inexperienced eye, some of the dollops of dough looked a wee bit on the large size.

"Why isn't Ellen here supervising?"

Bending over the oven to slide one of the filled sheets inside, the housekeeper's reply was too muffled for Rudd to hear.

When she straightened up, Rudd stated, "I didn't hear what you said, Mrs. Holloway. Where did you say Ellen was?"

"She left."

Rudd stiffened. "What do you mean, she left?"

The housekeeper frowned. "I don't know how else to say it, Mr. Lomax. When Miss Sheridan returned to the kitchen after lunch, she helped Miss Katie with the dishes, then thanked me for the lovely lunch, hugged Miss Katie, said she was glad she'd had a chance to meet her, then she left the house."

He quickly went through a mental list of Ellen's options. "Do you know if Ellen phoned for a taxi?"

"I don't believe so. She didn't ask for the number of the taxi service or for the phone book to find one."

Since he had the keys to his car in his pocket, that meant Ellen was on foot. Unless she was adept at hot-wiring a car. At this point, her possessing that particular dubious talent wouldn't have surprised him. Just in case, he left the kitchen for a few minutes to check to see if his car was where he had left it. When he saw that it was still parked in front, he returned to the kitchen.

He could have asked Mrs. Holloway to watch Katie while he went after Ellen, but he didn't. What he did do, however, was ask his housekeeper to do a few things for him up in Katie's room. Then to her amazement and a little of his own, he rolled up his shirtsleeves and assisted his daughter with her cookie baking.

When the final cookie was out of the oven, he helped Katie wash her hands and face, untied her apron, fastened the coat Mrs. Holloway had fetched for her, then drew Katie along with him out of the house, taking the small case he'd asked Mrs. Holloway to pack with some clothes for Katie.

As he closed the front door behind them, Katie asked, "Where are we going?"

Taking her hand, he said with a smile, "We're going after a hurricane."

She struggled with the unfamiliar word. "What's a hurlicane?"

He opened the car door and helped her onto the seat. Fastening her seat belt, he explained, "A *hurricane* is a powerful force that creates a lot of trouble in its path."

"If it's so much trouble, why do you want one?"

"In this case, the hurricane has blond hair and green eyes."

"Oh," Katie said, nodding her head slowly. "Ellen."

Rudd grinned at his daughter, pleased with her perception. "That's right, Katie. We're going after Hurricane Ellen."

There was only one logical place Ellen could have gone, and that was the windmill. Even though logic and Ellen didn't necessarily go together, he drove directly there, keeping a lookout for the figure of a woman walking alongside the road just in case she hadn't reached her destination yet. What bothered him more than the thought of her walking the mile to Willa's place was the possibility that she might not remember the route they'd taken and was wandering around lost. The windmill was a place to start looking for her, so he would start there.

The small windows were dark as he pulled up in front of the windmill. After he helped Katie out of the car, he felt her fingers clinging to his hand. Looking down, he saw her staring up at the large blades with wide, startled eyes.

"Don't be frightened, Katie. This is a windmill."

"A windmill?" she asked, not only having difficulty pronouncing the word, but obviously not understanding what it meant.

In the time it took to reach the front door, he'd explained what the building had once been used for and why it was called a windmill. He kept the explanation brief, not because he was afraid of boring her, but because his mind was more on the woman he hoped was inside.

Since the door was unlocked, Rudd assumed Ellen had found the key where he'd left it above the door. That meant she was there. Relief washed over him.

When he opened the door, he saw the unlit lantern on the table. There was enough light coming from the windows to enable him to see the room clearly enough to discover that Ellen wasn't there. When his shin knocked into a solid object near the door, he looked down and saw that Ellen's case was on the floor instead of in the bedroom where he'd taken it earlier. It looked as if he'd arrived none too soon. Although, where she thought she would be going was a mystery.

The fire in the wood stove had burned down to ashes, but the room was still reasonably comfortable. Katie released his hand and walked over to the grinding stone. He left her there while he stepped around the barrier to the sleeping area to see if Ellen was there. She wasn't.

He came back and stood looking around the room as he debated where Ellen could be. She'd obviously come back and packed her case. His lips tightened into a straight, tense line. So where the hell was she now?

He struck a match and put it to the wick of the lantern. Then he got the fire in the stove going again. If he was alone, he might not have bothered, but he had someone else to consider now. He was so preoccupied with worrying about Ellen, he didn't realize how naturally he was assuming the role of a father.

He helped Katie take off her coat, shifting Annabel from one arm to the other in the process. Then he took off his own and flopped it over the back of the couch. As his gaze roamed around the room, he noticed the wooden supply cabinet where Willa kept her art supplies. One of the cupboard doors was slightly ajar. It might have been that way for weeks, but he didn't think so. Going down on one knee, he opened the door and looked inside. There was a stack of sketch pads still in their plastic wrap covers, another pile of pads that had been used, some charcoal sticks, and a supply of pencils. Since he'd never looked inside the cupboard before, he had no idea if anything was missing or even moved.

A voice beside him asked, "What's in there?"

"Drawing materials."

"*¿Qué?*"

Turning his head, he looked at her. "What?"

"Yes."

Feeling as though he'd just stepped into an Abbott and Costello routine, he said, "Speak English, honey. I don't know what you want."

"What are drawing materials?"

"Oh, I see. *Qué* means what." Answering her question, he said, "These are drawing *materials.*" He took out one of the unused sketch pads and a set of colored pencils. "You can draw pictures on the pages, then color them. You can use these pencils to draw on the paper, if you want."

With a little frown, she looked down at the things he held in his hand. "Draw?"

It took a few minutes to get Katie settled at the worn desk and to get the wrapping off the pad of paper. His

ability to draw measured on the scale with his talents for
singing, gourmet cooking and golf. Next to nil. Fortu-
nately, Katie's enthusiasm for this new activity made up for
his pitiful attempt to draw a cat, and he was chagrined to
see that her rendering came out much better than his.

Leaving Katie happily scribbling away, he walked to the
window that looked out behind the windmill. The branches
of the trees were bending and whipping around by the
force of the wind. It wasn't the sort of weather suitable for
taking out a small child, or for an adult woman to be taking a stroll in. He couldn't explain why he knew Ellen was
near. It was just a feeling he had, which was odd for a man
who was more comfortable with facts, figures, and for-
mulas than intuition.

But he couldn't deny the feeling, even if he didn't understand it. Ellen was here. He didn't like the idea of her
wandering around the property in this weather, but there
wasn't much he could do about it at the moment. As badly
as he wanted to find her, he couldn't leave his daughter
alone, nor could he drag the little girl outside into the cold
weather to search the property. He was going to have to
wait for Ellen to come back to the windmill. He seemed to
be spending a great deal of his time waiting for Ellen in one
form or the other.

As he stared out the window, his attention was caught
by a brief glimpse of something red through the shrubs and
trees. A few minutes later, he saw it again and recognized
it as Ellen's jacket. Then Ellen stepped out of the dense
woods, and he could see her clearly. The knot of tension
eased in his stomach when he saw that she was all right. He
could make out the flat object she held clutched to her
chest with one arm and recognized it as one of the sketch
pads from the cupboard. It didn't seem like a very good

day for her to go sketching in the woods, but apparently that's what she'd been doing.

He saw her suddenly stop walking and stand still as she looked in the direction of the windmill. He doubted if she would be able to see him at the window, but she would see the light and realize he was there. What he didn't know was whether that would make a difference about her returning to the windmill. Even from this distance, he could see how stiffly she was holding herself, and he didn't think her rigid stance was due entirely to the cold weather.

She couldn't stay out there all day. A muscle in his jaw clenched. The hell she couldn't. If there was a woman more stubborn than Ellen Sheridan on the island, he couldn't imagine who it would be.

Glancing at his daughter, he saw she was engrossed in the colored pencils and paper. "Katie, I'm going outside for a minute."

She jerked her head around to look at him. "Can I go, too?"

"It's too cold, Katie," he explained patiently as he opened the door. "I'm just going to step out to bring Ellen inside. While I'm gone, don't go near the fire."

Katie shook her head emphatically and scrambled down from the chair. "No! I don't want you to go."

Startled, Rudd stood stiffly in the doorway and looked down at the little girl clinging to his leg. There were no tears, but she looked up at him with wide, frightened eyes.

He felt oddly humble. Even though he didn't feel he'd done anything to deserve her devotion, he was overwhelmed by the emotion she was creating deep within him. What Ellen had said earlier in the solarium came back to him. Katie hadn't understood why he kept leaving her at the end of every weekend any more than Ellen did, and Katie expected him to leave her again.

Gently prying her arms from around his leg, he knelt down on one knee and clasped her shoulders. "I'm not leaving you for long, Katie. I was just going outside to bring Ellen in."

"You are coming back?"

He couldn't stand the appeal in her eyes. "Get your coat, Katie. You and I'll go get Ellen together, okay?"

Before he'd even finished, she'd torn away from him and run over to her coat. It took a second or two for her to untangle one of the sleeves before she could finally put it on. The zipper took even longer, but Rudd waited, debating whether or not to assist her or if it was better to let her do this sort of thing for herself. One of the lessons he was learning in this new position as a parent was that when he thought he'd solved one problem, two more popped up.

The feeling of inadequacy had crept back just when he thought he was handling things pretty well, but he shoved it aside when he saw that Katie had managed to get the coat fastened all by herself. He extended his hand out to her.

Ellen hadn't moved. She was still standing near the woods. Holding Katie's hand, Rudd walked slowly toward her, not only because of Katie's shorter legs, but because Ellen looked tense enough to dart back into the woods at the slightest provocation.

When they stopped a few feet away from her, Ellen smiled faintly at Katie, then raised her gaze to meet Rudd's. Her shoulders lifted in a self-deprecating gesture. "This is the story of my life. I try to make a grand exit and discover I have no place to go."

"For someone who said she can't blow off steam, you did all right in the solarium."

There was a strange catch in her voice. "I was inspired."

"You didn't have to leave, Ellen."

"I thought I did. Coming back here seemed appropriate somehow. I seem to be tilting at windmills like Don Quixote, with as much success."

"I thought that way not too long ago, but a certain woman set me straight about a few things."

Ellen glanced away, then brought her gaze back to his. Lifting her chin, she said, "I wouldn't put too much stock in what that woman told you. She doesn't always know what she's talking about."

"In this case, I think she was right on the money. She's wiser than she thinks she is."

When he saw her shiver, he wasn't altogether sure it was caused by the weather. He reached out to take her arm, his intention to bring her back to the windmill, but she took a step backward. Puzzled by her reaction, he dropped his hand. "Come back to the windmill with us. It's too cold out here for you and for Katie."

He knew if he had put his request any other way, Ellen might not have agreed to return with him. For Katie's sake, she would do a great deal more than she would do for herself.

Ellen nodded her assent. She certainly hadn't accomplished anything out here. Ever since she'd left Serenity Lodge, she'd felt perverse, restless, and frustrated as hell. And scared. This was the first time she'd let her temper explode, and she'd directed it toward the one man she cared about. All her self-doubts had come rushing back in a torrent, and she'd been caught in the backlash. The walk in the woods hadn't eased any of her tension as she'd hoped it would. Going back to the windmill wouldn't change anything, either, except she would be warmer. She was also going to have to deal with Rudd, but that couldn't be helped.

Katie apparently took Ellen's agreement for granted as she offered her free hand to Ellen. As they walked back toward the windmill, Katie swung the adults' arms back and forth, obviously content and happy. Ellen envied the child's ability to adjust so easily to the changes in her life.

Once inside, Ellen set the sketchbook down before removing Katie's coat, then her own. Katie showed Ellen the drawings she'd made and after they were properly admired, the little girl asked Ellen to draw with her. Before Ellen could agree, Rudd asked Katie to draw on her own for a little while. He wanted to talk to Ellen.

"I'd rather draw with Katie," argued Ellen. "I think I've said enough for one day."

He took her arm and drew her away from the table. "Then listen for a change."

She didn't like the sound of that. Resigned to having to listen to recriminations, she sat down on the couch, folding her legs under her and turning slightly sideways to face Rudd as he sat down beside her. Close beside her. She would have moved away from him if she could, except she was already pressed up against the arm of the couch.

His gaze flicked to her suitcase still sitting by the front door. "You said you would stay for the weekend."

"As you can see, I'm still here."

"Only because you haven't found a way off the island."

"There is that," she admitted.

"Do you usually go around dropping bombs, then run away before they go off?"

"It looks that way," she said vaguely, wondering where this was heading.

Rudd felt his body tighten when he saw her teeth clamp down on her bottom lip. It was a sign of her nervousness and wasn't done to arouse him, but that's what it did.

Lifting his hand, he slid his forefinger across her lip to force her to release it. She raised her gaze to meet his, a puzzled frown forming when he continued to stroke her bottom lip.

She brought her hand up to move his finger away, but all he did was turn his hand over and close his fingers around her hand. Bringing their clasped hands down to his thigh, he said, "You'll just have to wait until tomorrow to leave the island. But you won't be bored. We have a lot to do until then."

Ellen had always prided herself in having the ability to catch on rather quickly to new situations, but for some reason her brain had taken a vacation without giving any advance notice. "We do? Like what?"

"It wasn't that long ago I heard you mention that Katie needed new clothes. I know a great deal about a number of things, but shopping for a little girl's clothes isn't one of them. While we're at it, I'd like you to pick out some nightclothes for her. She's spending the night here with us."

Ellen had heard the word *thunderstruck* before but had never known exactly how it felt until now. "And Señora Santana?"

He smiled faintly. "Never satisfied, are you? Señora Santana is going to be taking a return trip to Spain in the next couple of days. She wasn't happy about it even when I softened her termination with enough severance pay to tide her over comfortably until she finds another position."

"You're really going to have Katie stay here overnight?"

"Yes, Ellen," he said patiently. "I'm really going to keep Katie here with us. Why are you frowning? I thought that would make you happy. Isn't that what you wanted?"

She bit her lip again but stopped abruptly when she saw his gaze go to her mouth. "It doesn't matter what I want. You have to want it. You're the one who will be taking care of her." Now it was her turn to respond to his expression. "Why are you shaking your head?"

"*We* are going to be taking care of her."

"We?" she asked hesitantly, not sure she wanted to hear the answer. "What do you mean *we?*"

He gestured with his free hand, pointing at her, then himself. "I'm going to need all the help I can get to assimilate Katie into my life. Katie and I will both benefit from a woman's touch. Your touch."

She tried to pull her hand away from his grip, but that action only resulted in his fingers tightening around hers. "I've interfered enough. You were right when you pointed out that what you do with your daughter is none of my business."

"I don't recall saying that, but if I did, I was wrong. I've been wrong a lot lately, but that's going to change. There are going to be some major adjustments for both Katie and me to make. Your instincts have proven much better than mine. This was your idea, so you're responsible for seeing it through."

"Exactly what does that mean?" she asked cautiously. "You don't need my help with Katie any longer. She speaks English, remember? My short-term job as interpreter lasted about five minutes."

"Your job description has changed."

Feeling as though she'd somehow skipped a couple of pages in an important part of a story, she asked, "I have a job description?"

"If you need one. Whatever it takes."

She wished he wouldn't rub his thumb over the back of her hand in that slow, tantalizing motion that was affecting the way her lungs dealt with her breathing. At the moment, they had shut down temporarily. She started to bite her lip in consternation, then remembered what he'd done the last time she did that. A shiver of awareness skidded along her spine as she relived the memory of how he'd stroked her mouth.

It was necessary to clear her throat before she asked, "Why don't you just tell me what this is all about in twenty-five words or less?"

"When we leave Nantucket tomorrow, my daughter will be going with us."

She let his words filter through her sluggish brain a couple of times just to make sure she'd heard him correctly. "Oh, Rudd," she said softly. "That's wonderful. You won't regret it."

He smiled. "I'll remember you said that after we get through the first week."

There was that *we* again. "You and Katie will be fine."

"I wish I had your confidence. You'll have to keep reminding me of that when we get back to Boston." He stood up abruptly, bringing her with him. "We'd better get going before the stores close."

Since shopping had been her idea, she couldn't think of a single thing to say to talk him out of it, but she really wanted to know what he meant about what was going to happen when they returned to Boston. She was beginning to get the impression that the *we* he kept talking about included her. But that was crazy. He meant himself and Katie.

At least for the rest of the day, she was definitely part of the *we*. Tiffany would have been proud of her. With absolutely no help from Rudd except the use of his charge cards, she outfitted Katie with an assortment of clothing from the inside out. Aside from an occasional raised eyebrow, Rudd paid for the purchases without comment. His reward was seeing the excitement in his daughter's eyes as she tried on one brightly colored outfit after the other. He marveled at the enthusiasm both Ellen and Katie maintained through the whole shopping expedition. It was as though each item gave them a shot of adrenaline, an added incentive to move on to the next.

The new clothing certainly made a difference in Katie's appearance. It hadn't taken Ellen long to replace Katie's original, dull clothing. Rudd's daughter marched out of the first store wearing a red denim skirt, white cotton sweater, and red denim jacket with an assortment of colorful patches all over it. It was as though Katie had stepped from old-world Spain to downtown Beverly Hills. Ellen had also managed to arrange Katie's hair into some kind of ponytail effect at one side of her head.

By the end of an exhausting couple of hours, Rudd was relieved to hear Ellen ask Katie if she was hungry. The little girl nodded her head eagerly, which was all Rudd needed to steer them toward a restaurant.

For Katie, dining in the restaurant was a new experience. For Rudd, it was a chance to sit down. For Ellen, it was an adventure in subtle torture when Rudd slid onto the padded seat of the booth next to her, leaving her very little space to breath. Which wasn't all that necessary anyway, since she was having a difficult time accomplishing that simple little task when she could feel his strong thigh pressed against hers.

She must have eaten something, although later she wouldn't have been able to say what it was. Her mind was on other things. Like wondering why Rudd continually found occasions to touch her. Maybe other women would accept his actions as normal, but she was aware of every incident. He'd taken an astonishingly long time to fasten her seat belt when it had only taken him a few seconds to secure Katie's. He'd let his hand trail down her spine after helping her on with her coat. When he wasn't touching her, he was watching her with a soft smile shaping his mouth.

The more distance she tried to put between them, physically and emotionally, the more he seemed to want to be closer. It had been a mistake to come to Nantucket. She should have listened to her first instincts instead of letting sympathy for Rudd's little girl overcome her good sense. She'd accomplished what she had hoped to do and that was to help Rudd communicate with his daughter. Now that wasn't a problem. What *was* a problem was getting through one more night. And a boat ride across the Sound.

She just wished he would stop touching her, reminding her of what might have been and would never be.

By the time they returned to the windmill, Katie was practically asleep on her feet. It took a little searching through the various packages for Ellen to find one of Katie's newly purchased nightgowns and a few minutes more to get the little girl into it. When Rudd tucked his daughter in bed, he learned one more little fact about her he hadn't known before. She needed a night-light on in order to sleep.

Coming around the grinding stone area, Rudd immediately searched for Ellen. He was past fighting the automatic need to look for her whenever he entered a room. He'd finally accepted she was necessary to his peace of mind. It might have taken him a while to figure things out, but now he had and he was anxious to put his plans in action.

Since the room was fairly small, it was easy enough to see that Ellen wasn't there. Clamping his hands on his hips, he muttered a satisfying but ineffectual curse under his breath. Why in hell couldn't the woman stay where she was supposed to be? he asked the room silently. A glance at the low table showed him the sketchbook was where she'd left it, which meant she hadn't gone off drawing again. Considering it was almost nine o'clock in the evening and dark outside, it wouldn't be the best time for sketching, not that that would stop her, he thought ruefully.

He couldn't very well go out looking for her and leave Katie alone in the windmill. But he walked to the back door and yanked it open. Stepping outside, he strained his eyes to look out at the bluff where she'd been walking earlier. The full moon gave the land an eerie glow, shedding enough light for him to discover that Ellen was nowhere to be seen.

A scraping sound drew his attention to his left, and he jerked his head to look in that direction. Ellen was leaning against the side of the windmill, her arms crossed in front of her.

"What in hell are you doing out here?"

"Looking at the moon."

As much as he was enjoying the sight of the moonlight glimmering in her eyes, he was freezing. "Couldn't you do that from one of the windows inside?"

"It's not the same."

Moon watching hadn't been high on his list of priorities. Especially when it was like stepping into a refrigerator. His lightweight shirt was poor protection against the cold night air. She at least had the sense to put on her jacket, which was more than he could say for himself.

"You're going to have to control this preoccupation you seem to have with washing cars and staring at the moon in cold weather." A dark cloud was sliding across the moon, partially obliterating the bright circle. "Dammit, Ellen. Come inside."

He had expected her to argue, not to brush past him and hurry back inside. By the time he had opened the door to follow her, Ellen was sitting on the couch with a sketch pad propped up on her raised knees. She still had her jacket on and was engrossed in sketching. He watched her for a few minutes. At one point, she tucked a strand of hair behind one ear and ran the tip of her pink tongue over her bottom lip as she concentrated on what she was doing.

The sight of her moist tongue stroking her mouth affected him on a deep, masculine level. It was unfortunate he couldn't do a damn thing about it with his daughter in the next room. He could wait. He'd waited his whole life to find the other half of himself. A little longer wouldn't make any difference.

Watching her was no great hardship, so he simply stood and waited for her to finish whatever it was that had caught her attention. After a few minutes, she sighed contentedly and flipped over the cover of the sketch pad.

"Are you finished?"

She jumped. His mouth twisted into an ironic smile as she looked up at him with wide, startled eyes. She'd forgotten he was there. He would have felt insulted if he didn't have the same reaction when he was interrupted while involved in his own work.

As he walked toward her, he said, "I take it inspiration has struck a mighty blow."

She removed her jacket. "I'm working on a series called Nightglow. Our inspired art director has decided we should do a line of linens in dark greens, navy, and black." Changing the subject, she asked, "Is Katie asleep?"

"She fell asleep almost as soon as her head hit the pillow."

"She's had a busy day."

When he sat down close beside her, she sprang up off the couch as though she'd been shot out of a cannon. "I think Katie has the right idea. I think I'll turn in, too."

He reached out and clamped his hand over her wrist as she took a step past him. "Not yet. We have a few things to straighten out first."

His tone was as uncompromising as his hold on her wrist. Instead of going through an undignified tug-of-war with him, she gave in to the unrelenting grip of his fingers and sat back down. She could have wished for a little more room between Rudd and the plump arm of the couch, but she wasn't going to have her wish granted. His hip was pressed against hers, his hand sliding down from her wrist to thread his fingers through hers, resting their clasped hands on his hard thigh as he had before. With her free hand, she tightened her hold on the sketchbook on her lap so she wouldn't do anything incredibly stupid—like flinging herself into his arms.

Satisfied that she was going to stay put at least for a while, he leaned back. There was a thread of mocking humor woven through his voice when he said, "Of all the times during the last six months when I thought about what I would do if I was ever alone with you, I never once considered having a small chaperon in the next room."

She was stunned by his casual statement. Lord knows, she'd thought enough about him during the last six months. It was astonishing to hear he'd conjured her up in his mind, as well.

Rudd propped his feet up on the low table in front of him and let his body relax into the lumpy cushions of the couch. "I don't understand why women find shopping so exciting. It's exhausting. A game of racketball is a cakewalk compared to following you two around a mall."

"Tiffany considers shopping an art form," she murmured absently. When she noticed his expression had changed from amusement to a frown, she asked, "What's that look for?"

"What look?"

"You get that same expression every time I mention Tiffany."

"What expression?"

"It's sort of like the look Mr. Phillips had on his face when we refused to dissect frogs in biology class. A resigned tolerance for the feebleminded kind of look."

"Who's Mr. Phillips?"

"Our high school principal. Don't change the subject."

He reached over and took the sketchbook from her. As he leafed through some of the pages she'd filled, he said, "I don't understand women like your friend, Tiffany. I like this sketch of Katie. You caught the expression in her eyes perfectly."

"Don't try changing the subject." Ellen reached over and took the sketch pad away from him. "What type of woman do you think Tiffany is?"

Making a gruff sound of impatience, he said, "I really don't want to get into this tonight, Ellen. There are a lot more important things to discuss right now."

She lifted her chin and glared at him. "You started this. You just said you didn't like my best friend. I want to know why."

He knew that look. A mule could take lessons on being stubborn from this woman. "I didn't say I didn't like her. All I said was I don't understand women *like* her."

Tossing the sketchbook on the low table in front of the couch, Ellen crossed her arms over her chest. "Women like Tiffany are warm, generous, loyal, and caring. There's a lot more to Tiffany than shopping."

Disarming her in the only way he could think of at the moment, he took her hands in his and unfolded her arms from the shield she'd put up against him. Keeping her hands between his, he said, "Tiffany and women like her are fancy, decorative desserts. They are pretty to look at and sample, but not something you would want to have as a steady diet. Your friend lives to shop. You said so yourself. There are more important things in life than material possessions. Women who consider spending money their life's work and don't think they need to do a thing to earn it other than be beautiful aren't worth discussing."

"Or marrying?" she asked quietly.

He gave her a blank look, then slowly smiled. "Touché." Releasing one of her hands, he slipped his arm around her and brought her slender body firmly against his side. He felt her resistance. "Relax. I want you closer so we can talk quietly. I don't want to wake Katie."

Ellen tried to relax, but it wasn't possible. If she was any closer to him, she'd be sitting on his lap.

Sighing heavily, he said, "This is as good a time as any to get my ex-wife out of the way, I suppose, although it isn't what I wanted to talk about tonight."

The heat emanating from his hard, solid body almost made her forget what they *were* discussing. She let her gaze lower to where he was holding her hand in his, his thumb slowly stroking across her palm. "Rudd, if you don't want to tell me about your ex-wife, you don't need to. You have a right to your opinion about Tiffany, even though I don't agree with it."

"Don't backslide now. One of the things to remember when you're having a fight is not to back down if you think you're right."

"I don't want to fight with you."

"I don't feel like fighting with you, either." He sighed heavily. "It's not something I enjoy talking about, but we might as well get it out of the way. I should have told you about my ex-wife before, when you attacked me for how I've been ignoring my daughter. It didn't occur to me until you left the solarium that you thought I'd been ignoring Katie since she was born, not just the last couple of months."

"What else would you call it?"

"I would call it not knowing I had a daughter until I heard from my ex-wife's lawyer after she died."

Ellen could only stare at him as she absorbed what he said. Shock was still in her eyes when she asked, "Your ex-wife didn't *tell* you about Katie?"

He shook his head, smiling faintly at the astonishment in Ellen's voice. "We got married for all the wrong reasons. Looking back now, I can see I was a selfish jerk for the two miserable years we were married. I wanted the conveniences of a wife who would have meals ready, be a willing bed partner, and raise my children, leaving me free to become the greatest scientist since Pasteur. Her reasons for marriage were a chance to stay in the States and a free bank account, which she could use to decorate the house and herself. Unfortunately, I was just getting started in my career and wasn't making all that much money, at least not enough for her standards—which were very high."

Ellen looked for bitterness or even pain, but apparently he didn't regret the divorce, only the reasons for the marriage.

"When Cynthia asked me for a divorce, she thought I would put up a fight about agreeing to end our marriage, which I guess is why she didn't tell me about the child. She got her divorce and settlement before she left for Spain. The first I knew about Katie was when the lawyer contacted me after Cynthia had been killed in the car accident.''

Indignation overcame the shock. "How could she keep your child from you all that time?"

As much as he appreciated the way Ellen was taking his side, he had to be honest with her. "To be fair, I wasn't the most congenial person to live with. She often accused me of putting my job before her, and to some extent, she was right. My work was my first priority, which didn't leave much time for her. I don't know why she felt she had to keep my own child's existence from me, though. I don't know if she thought I wouldn't care about having a daughter or if she was simply punishing me for neglecting her."

Ellen had tightened her fingers around his without even realizing she was doing it. "Maybe a little of both."

"Maybe. I'll never know if Cynthia ever planned on telling me about Katie. I learned earlier from Katie that Cynthia told *her* about *me*. Katie said that her mother had put a picture of me next to her bed so she knew who I was."

"So that's why Katie wasn't afraid of you in spite of the way Señora Santana tried to undermine you."

"I'd like to think it's my charming personality," he said with dry humor. "But I think I have my ex-wife to thank for Katie's acceptance of me more than anything I've done since I've known her."

"You're not being fair to yourself, Rudd. You're very good with her, whether you realize it or not. You treat her as though she's a person, not an inanimate object. You don't talk down to her or ignore her."

He brought their clasped hands up to his mouth and touched the back of hers with his lips. "I wouldn't have been able to get as far as I have with her if you hadn't discovered she speaks English."

Her heart thudded, then started to rock uncomfortably in her chest. The very air seemed to change and electrify around them like a sudden summer storm. She was aware that he wasn't holding her hand so tightly that she couldn't draw it away. It was the last thing she would want to do.

Turning her head slowly, she met his gaze. "What are you doing?"

"Not as much as I would like to do," he said softly. He gathered her into his arms, easily lifting her across his thighs. "I'll settle for this for now."

Chapter Fourteen

Logic, caution, and common sense were words with little meaning when Ellen lifted her face to meet Rudd's descending mouth. For once, she didn't try to protect herself from future pain but gave in to the need for a moment's pleasure.

He took her mouth with undisguised hunger. There was no tentative exploration or teasing gesture. His lips demanded a response she willingly gave. She was vaguely aware of his hands sliding down to her hips and shifting her so she was lying across his thighs. The impact of her soft breasts against his hard body had her moaning softly in the back of her throat.

"Rudd," she said achingly.

"I know," he murmured against her lips as though she'd asked a question.

Slanting his mouth over hers, he deepened the assault, and Ellen willingly slipped into the next stage of sensuality. She thought she knew what desire was, but this was like nothing she'd ever experienced before. She no longer wanted to hold herself back from him. This might be all she would have, and she wanted to grab ecstasy with both hands and hold on to it as long as she could. Need clashed with passion as she slid her hands over his shoulders and around his neck to hold on to the man who was as caught up in the magic as she was.

The oil in the lantern was running low, the light dimming slowly to create an intimate glow to the room. The wind blew against the outside of the windmill, rattling the glass in the windows, but it was snug and warm inside.

Rudd knew he should stop. He was only torturing them both, but it felt so good. *She* felt so good. He'd managed to hold on to the reins of resistance up until now, but he felt them slipping through his fingers.

The ache to have more of her was both pleasure and pain. He'd wanted women before, but never craved the taste, the feel, the essence of a woman until Ellen.

He stroked the straight line of her spine under her shirt, his fingers smoothing over her silky skin. He felt her shudder under his hand, her reaction to his caresses tightening the primitive call inside him. He kissed her more deeply, his head spinning when she opened herself to him in silent invitation. The satisfaction of knowing he'd brought her to this point sent an exultation through him.

She was as caught up in the sweet agony of desire as he was.

Holding her securely against him, he shifted and fell back onto the cushions, bringing her with him. He made a raw sound of pleasure when he felt her weight along his hard body. His mouth became as impatient as his hands, searching and arousing, inciting and seducing.

He threaded his fingers through her hair to keep her mouth locked to his until she was as breathless and as mindless with passion as he was. Her legs were entwined with his, her hips rocking and arching sensuously against his hard body. Hunger became a writhing need, twisting through him. The heat radiating from her made him feel as though he was burning up, and he wanted more of her fire.

Opening her shirt, then his own, he groaned roughly when her bare breasts were crushed against his chest. Her head fell back when he took her full breasts in his hands, her eyes closed as a shudder ran through her. Raising her upper body slightly, the action brought her lower body more firmly into his, searing him with desire.

When he breathed her name, her hair slid over her shoulders as she brought her head forward slowly and opened her eyes. Her shirt fell off one bare shoulder as she looked down at him. He could see the heated arousal in the depths of her green eyes and knew it mirrored his own.

His control was as fragile as this new turn their relationship had taken. He brought his hands down to hold her hips still, pressing her down against his hard loins.

"Ellen," he groaned.

"I'm here," she breathed.

He closed his eyes when she stroked her hands over his bare chest before following the path she made with light touches of her moist lips. Each time she moved to find another taste, another texture of his skin, her hips ground into him.

With a hoarse sound of enchantment, he cupped the back of her neck and brought her mouth to his again. He slipped his other hand between them, laying his palm over her stomach, then sliding it down to the juncture of her thighs. He nearly exploded when she arched into his hand.

Almost mindless with the taste and the feel of her, he tore his mouth away from her and buried his face against the subtle curve of her neck.

"Oh, Ellen," he murmured with naked longing. "This is killing me."

Shifting onto his side, he held her tightly pinned between the back of the couch and his long frame as he fought to gain command of his raging senses.

For a long time, he simply held her to him, waiting for his blood to cool, pulling badly needed air into his lungs. One of her arms lay over his waist, her hand still and warm on his back. Her breathing was as ragged as his.

When he thought he could look at her without losing his hard-won control, he eased away from her enough to enable him to see her face. He almost lost the frail hold on his body when she slowly raised her head and met his gaze. Bewildered and aroused, she looked at him.

"Do you understand why I stopped? It's not because I don't want you. I think I've made it clear enough that I do. It's not the right time."

Her body was still throbbing with need, making it difficult for her to think sensibly about anything except wanting him. Sighing heavily, she murmured, "Katie."

He ran his hand in a soothing gesture over her side, stopping when the feel of her was having the opposite effect on both of them. Unable to stop touching her completely, he left his hand on the sweet curve of her hip.

"I'm going to have to ask you to be patient, Ellen." A ghost of a laugh escaped his throat. "Something I'm having a little trouble dealing with myself right now. I'm only just beginning to understand all the changes Katie will bring into my life."

She smiled faintly as she traced the firm line of his jaw with her fingertip. "And this is one of them."

"This is definitely one of them," he said resignedly. "I haven't a clue how I'm going to work this out, but somehow there will be time and privacy for us."

She wanted to believe him, but he could be speaking in the heat of the moment and not really mean it later. She trusted him with his daughter, but she still couldn't trust him with her heart. She started to move so that she could sit up, but there wasn't enough room to accomplish that since Rudd wasn't taking the hint to give her more space.

"I'm barely hanging on as it is, Ellen. You rubbing against me isn't helping much."

"Lying here together isn't helping, either. It would be better if I sit up and you stay at one end of the couch and me at the other."

The only concession he made was to roll onto his back so she wasn't pressed intimately against him, compromising by keeping her locked to his side. He pressed her head onto his shoulder. "I would do just about anything for you but that. Stay here with me. I want to hold you through the night."

It's where she wanted to be, but she still had to ask, "And tomorrow?"

He took a deep, shuddering breath and closed his eyes. "We'll take care of tomorrow when it comes."

She bit her lip, then murmured, "We're going back to Boston tomorrow."

He opened his eyes and turned his head toward her. "You're worried about the boat trip."

That's not all she was worried about, but she let him think it was. "I don't think worried quite covers it."

"When are you going to tell me why you have such a fear of boats?" He could feel the tension stiffening her body. "If you feel you can't make the trip again, we'll book a flight at the airport so you don't have to worry about it, but I wish you trusted me enough to tell me what happened. How many other people know?''

She trusted very few people in her life. Smiling faintly, she held up one finger from Rudd's chest.

''Tiffany?'' he asked softly.

''Hmm. I've known Tiffany most of my life. She's always been there when I needed someone.''

Rudd's hand joined hers, and he raised another of her fingers to join the other one, indicating he wanted her to add him.

''I don't have the same track record with you. Technically, we've known each other six months, but sometimes I feel like I've known you all my life.'' His voice was low and serious. ''Let me in, Ellen.''

The lantern chose that moment to flicker out, leaving the room in near-darkness. Only a vague light came through the small windows from the waning moon.

The intimacy of the darkness made it easier for Ellen to confide in Rudd. ''When I was six, I was taken aboard a boat after three men kidnapped me.''

His arm tightened around her as though she were being threatened again. ''Go on,'' he said huskily.

''That's about it. They didn't hurt me other than tie my hands and put tape over my mouth when they took me from the house. After a long car ride, one of them flung me over his shoulder as though I were a duffel bag and carried me down a dock. I remember seeing the wide boards and the backs of his canvas shoes. It's odd what you remember.''

''Or what you'd like to forget. And I'm asking you to remember it all over again. Just this once, honey. Tell me what happened.''

''They took the boat out onto the water, then anchored it. I was kept in a small cabin, tied up except for once a day when they fed me peanut butter and jelly sandwiches and let me go to the bathroom. To this day, I can't face peanut butter and jelly. After five days, they pulled up the anchor, brought the boat back near the dock, threw me overboard, and left me in the water."

The dispassionate way she related the story told Rudd more than the actual words. He fought down the rage at the nameless men who had done this to her. "Then what happened?"

"A fisherman saw the men throw me overboard and fished me out of the water. When he saw that I wasn't hurt, just cold and scared, he took me to a restaurant close by where they had a phone. Luckily, Mercedes had taught me my address and phone number, and she came with the gardener to pick me up in Cape Cod after the owner of the restaurant called her."

He hated the thought of her being so young and alone and defenseless for five days. If anyone had done that to his daughter, he would have wanted to kill them. "Why did it take so long for your father to pay the ransom?"

"He didn't."

Rudd shifted her so that she was propped up on his chest and he could see her face. His voice registered his shock. "Your father didn't pay the ransom? Why not?"

"During the drive back when Mercedes thought I was asleep, I heard her and the gardener cursing out my father for refusing to pay the money the kidnappers demanded. It took a little while longer for me to learn what the word ransom meant. And what not paying the ransom could have meant."

He was just learning about it, and it turned his stomach to think of what could have happened to the small child. Needing to feel her safe and secure in his arms, he pressed her head down to his shoulder and held her against him.

"How long did it take you to realize that your father put money ahead of his own daughter?"

"I was a fast learner," she said drowsily.

"What kind of man is he? To treat his own child like that is barbaric."

"I have the dubious honor of resembling my mother, who had the nerve to run off with my father's law partner. Pride means a great deal to Paul Sheridan. Too many people knew of my existence and praised him for raising a child all on his own. He couldn't send me away to get rid of me for fear the newspapers would hear about it."

He ran his fingers through the soft hair at the nape of her neck, gently stroking the tension he could feel under his hand. "You haven't been very fortunate with your set of parents. No wonder you had a problem with my treatment of Katie when you thought I could go four years without seeing her."

"I told you I was a fast learner," she mumbled sleepily, nuzzling her face into his shoulder. "Even when I thought you had neglected her for four years, I knew you care for her now."

His hand cupped the back of her neck. He could tell by her breathing that she was falling asleep. Staring up at the ceiling, he hoped she could still adjust to accepting things quickly. He'd wasted six months. He wasn't wasting a minute longer than he had to, if he could possibly help it.

He tightened his arms around her, hating the barrier of clothing between them. He wanted to feel her skin heat under his fingers, learn her soft textures and intimate curves, and claim every tantalizing inch of her.

He was hard and aching—and helpless to do anything about it. But soon, he promised himself. Somehow he would take her and make her his.

* * *

When Ellen awoke the next morning, she had the couch
all to herself. It took a few minutes for her to remember
where she was. And why. She flicked back the blanket that
was over her. She didn't remember being covered by a
blanket, but then she didn't recall Rudd leaving her, either. As she sat on the edge of the couch, she looked
around. The person she was looking for wasn't anywhere
in the room.

Her foot caught on the fringe of the blanket as she stood
up and took a step. Once she was untangled, she walked
around the grinding stone and found the bed empty, too.
Katie was no longer asleep, and the bed was made up as
tidy as it'd been when they'd arrived yesterday.

Ellen slowly returned to the couch and folded the blanket before sitting back down. She rested her elbow on her
knee and leaned her chin on the palm of her hand. There
was little food in the windmill, and Rudd had probably
taken Katie back to his house for breakfast. It made perfect sense. Rudd was just being considerate and letting her
sleep while he took care of his daughter—which was the
way it should be. It was really childish to be feeling left out
and forgotten, even if that was a perfect description of how
she felt.

She looked down at the sketchbook lying on the table
where she'd thrown it the night before. Before she'd slept
in Rudd's arms. Maybe for the last time. Feeling sorry for
herself was something she wouldn't allow. She grabbed the
sketchbook with one hand and her jacket with the other.
Sitting around sulking wasn't accomplishing anything. She
might as well work, since there wasn't a car handy to wash.

She had one arm in a sleeve when the door opened, and
Rudd stood in the doorway looking remarkably wide

awake and cheerful when she was feeling more in the mood to kick something.

"Good, you're awake." He walked over to her and assisted her with her jacket. "I've got our cases in the car. If we hustle, we'll just make it."

She balked when he took her arm and drew her with him toward the door. "Wait a minute. Make what? Where are we going?"

"To the airport. The flight leaves in about thirty minutes."

She stuck her hand out to grab the door he'd left open. Holding onto it, she said, "But I haven't had a chance to say goodbye to Katie."

Prying her hand away from the door, he slipped his fingers through hers and tugged her out the door. "You don't have to say goodbye to her."

Ellen stared at him. She couldn't believe he could be so cavalier about her attachment to his daughter. "I guess I don't," she muttered under her breath.

Stopping, he leaned over and kissed her lightly. "Poor baby. You aren't awake yet. Mrs. Holloway packed some breakfast rolls and a thermos of coffee for you. You can have some on the way to the airport."

Her free hand went to her mouth, which was still tingling from the brief contact with his, as she stumbled along beside him. Maybe she was still asleep and having some sort of weird dream.

Maybe this wasn't really the man she loved, just a dream about someone who looked a lot like him.

She stopped walking. Where did that come from? She jerked her head around and looked at Rudd as though she'd never seen him before. He had stopped along with her and was staring at her with a perplexed expression on his face.

"Ellen? Are you all right?"

She shook her head, but it didn't help clear up a single thing. Good Lord, she thought as she closed her eyes and raised her free hand to her forehead. Of all the stupid idiotic things she'd ever done in her life, this one had to take the top prize. She was in love with a man who couldn't wait to get rid of her.

Rudd reached out and trailed the back of his fingers over her jaw. "You aren't afraid of flying, too, are you?"

Numbly, she shook her head. "I'm not afraid of planes, just boats."

That was all he needed to hear. It would have been inconvenient if he had to come up with an alternate means of getting off the island, but they were leaving today if he had to rent a hot air balloon.

He opened the door of the passenger side, and Ellen started to step around him to get in, but he held his arm out to stop her. Leaning down, he spoke into the car. "Scoot over, honey."

Ellen took a step backward. She was in love with a crazy person who was talking to cars.

Rudd stepped out of her way. Sliding onto the seat, Ellen was stunned when she saw Katie sitting in the middle of the seat. No wonder Rudd had said she didn't have to say goodbye to Katie. The little girl was going with them.

Katie was holding Annabel on her lap. "We're going for a plane ride, Ellen."

Ellen answered weakly, "So I hear."

"I'm going to Boston to live with my Daddy."

Ellen watched Rudd walk around the front of the car. "It looks that way."

When Rudd slipped behind the wheel, he smiled at Katie, then glanced past her to Ellen. "You're looking a little pale, Ellen." He indicated a canvas bag on the floor at her feet. "You'd better have some of that coffee. It'll make you feel better."

He was expecting a lot from a cup of coffee, she thought as she took the thermos out of the bag and shakily poured herself a cup of the steaming liquid. Grasping the cup with both hands, she took a scalding sip and waited for the caffeine to kick in.

She'd managed another cup by the time they reached the small airport. Rudd shepherded Ellen and his daughter onto a chartered plane, talked a few minutes with the pilot, then sat down across from Ellen and Katie.

"There are some books and a couple of games in case Katie gets restless. She probably won't need them, though. We'll be landing almost as soon as we get in the air."

"Coffee and breakfast rolls for me. Books and games for Katie. A chartered flight to Boston. You've thought of everything."

His gaze narrowed. Somehow her statement didn't sound like a compliment. "Probably not, but between the two of us, we'll manage."

She should be pleased he was thinking of Katie and himself as a team already. It was more than she'd hoped would happen this weekend. Rudd was taking his new position as a father seriously. It was what she had wanted all along. Sometimes it wasn't all that satisfying to have one's wishes come true as it was supposed to be.

She would be less than human if she didn't feel let down because she was no longer needed by either Rudd or his daughter.

She was so preoccupied with her thoughts, she didn't realize the plane had left the runway and Rudd was speaking to her. Blinking, she said, "What?"

"I said I've made arrangements for my car to be at the airport instead of parked at the marina where I'd left it."

"That's nice," she said vaguely.

He'd seen her more animated than this when she was asleep. Unfortunately, with Katie sitting beside her, this wasn't the time to ask her what she was so preoccupied with.

He didn't mind that she was grouchy in the morning. He could think of several creative ways to change her distracted expression to the smoky look she got in her eyes when she was aroused.

Forcing his mind on more mundane matters, he said, "I thought having my own car at the airport would be easier and more comfortable than taking one of those hair-raising taxi rides from Logan Airport to my place."

"That's very considerate of you."

Her polite tone was beginning to irritate the hell out of him. "I'll remember you said that when we go directly to my place. You're spending the night."

That woke her up. "Where'd that come from? We agreed on this weekend. That was all."

"We have a new agreement."

"Since when?"

"Since last night," he said pointedly, his gaze sliding down to her mouth.

His attention was caught by a movement from his daughter. He noticed Katie's head was switching back and forth from him to Ellen as though she were watching a tennis match, her puzzled expression making it clear she didn't understand the rules of this game the adults were playing.

Making an effort to calm down his temper, he said soothingly, "This was your idea, Ellen. It's only fair that you help get Katie settled in. For one thing, my place is going to need some drastic changes. Think about it, but you don't have long to mull it over." He glanced at his watch. "We'll be landing in a short time. It isn't a very long flight."

Ellen didn't know whether to stare, shout, or shake her head.

Rudd turned his attention to Katie. "Are you and Annabel enjoying the plane ride?"

"*Si*. I mean yes. Is that man you were talking to the one driving the plane?"

"He's the pilot. You want to go see how he flies the plane?"

"Can I?"

"May I," he automatically corrected. He leaned forward and unfastened her seat belt. "For you, kiddo, the sky's the limit."

Smiling, he looked at Ellen, expecting her to respond to his clever turn of phrase. She was staring out the small window next to her seat.

A little later, when the pilot informed Rudd that they would be landing soon, Rudd escorted Katie back to her seat. Ellen was still staring out the window. After he got Katie settled again, he reached across Ellen and fastened her belt for her. When she didn't turn to look at him, he let his hand linger on her thigh. He felt the muscles tense under his hand and moved his fingers in a caressing motion meant to soothe, the material of her slacks sliding slowly under his fingers. The effect on him was anything but soothing.

She slowly turned her head to look at him. Her lips parted slightly, tempting him with the memory of how her mouth had tasted under his last night. He heard her sharp intake of air when his hand glided farther up her thigh. He stopped only when she placed her hand over his.

"Isn't this better?" he murmured.

Swallowing with difficulty, she asked in a voice soft as velvet and hot as whiskey, "Better than what?"

"Better than the boat."

"Yes." She curled her fingers around his. "But I would have survived."

"I'm not sure I would have," he murmured truthfully.

"Thank you, Rudd," she said seriously. "I wasn't looking forward to taking the boat back to Cape Cod."

He tightened his grip. "Thank you," he returned.

Her gaze went to his mouth, then raised to meet his eyes, her own registering her confusion. "For what?"

"For finally trusting me enough to tell me why you don't like boats."

Memories of the previous night brought a faint flush to her cheeks and were reflected in her eyes for him to see. "You're welcome."

The drone of the engine and the close proximity of his daughter reminded him this wasn't the time or the place for what he wanted to do. That would wait for long hours in the dark and even longer in the daylight.

His mouth twisted into a mockery of a smile. Tightening his hold on her hand briefly, he consoled himself with a promise. "I'll accept a proper thank-you later."

Returning reluctantly to his seat, he fastened his own seat belt.

Closing his eyes, he leaned his head back. The only thing he could do was wait for the plane to land so he could put the rest of his plans in action. And it couldn't be too soon for him. If he hadn't been so stupid about wasting six months, she'd be in his bed now. It wasn't going to be much longer.

Chapter Fifteen

When the plane landed, Ellen and Katie were whisked efficiently from the plane to the car. Rudd kept a running commentary with Katie on all the things she was seeing as they drove along. Ellen became as interested as Katie when she saw they were in a part of Boston she'd never been in before. It appeared to be an older part of town with little shops, the occasional warehouse, and rows and rows of small houses built around the turn of the century.

Rudd slowed down as they passed a corner grocery store with a sign in Japanese below large lettering that spelled out Yamamoto Groceries. A few minutes later, Rudd pulled into a paved parking area next to a long, dark green building. Reaching above the visor, he depressed a button on a remote control device and the garage door in front of the car began to rise slowly. Once it stopped, Rudd put the car in gear and drove into the building.

After Rudd parked the car, he got out and came around to open the passenger door for Ellen. She made no move to get out. Her attention was on the view she had through the windshield. At first, she stared at the reflection of herself, the car, and the lush foliage of the plants lined up along the other side of the car. The wall opposite was covered by a mirror from floor to ceiling as far as she could see.

When she didn't make any move to leave the car, Rudd reached across her and unfastened her seat belt. "You can get out now, Ellen. We're here."

She jerked her head around. "Rudd, you drove into the building."

"It looks that way, doesn't it."

"There are mirrors all along one wall."

"I noticed," he said with amusement.

She tore her gaze from the mirrors and met his. "Why?"

"This place was once a dance studio." He took her arm and helped her out of the car. "Now it's where I live."

"Why do you live in a converted dance studio?"

Smiling, he repeated her own words to her. "It's home."

Was it any wonder she would love a man like this, she mused as she smiled back at him. "Well, I like it."

"I'm glad, because I wasn't looking forward to finding anywhere else that would hold everything we need."

He didn't have a thing to worry about. This place was a child's dream. "How long have you lived here?"

"I understood you living in your apartment for twelve years more than I let on. I've lived here since I was at MIT. The grocery store on the corner and this building used to belong to the Yamamoto family, and they let me rent it from them. Their son was my best friend. Still is, for that matter."

The rest of his explanation had to wait until he helped Katie out of the car. "I stayed on here when Tommy went out to California to another school and bought the building from the Yamamotos when they were having problems paying their taxes. I wanted you to see it in case you didn't think this place would be appropriate for Katie."

"Are you kidding?" she answered, as she gazed around the spacious building. "This is a wonderful place for a child. Especially if she wants to become a ballerina."

He grinned down at his daughter. "You heard the boss, Katie. It passed inspection. Let's go pick out your room."

The little girl took his hand, her eyes wide and spellbound.

Ellen slowly followed them as she took in her surroundings. The mirror gave her two views of the area that was obviously where Rudd spent a great deal of his time when he was home. On the wall opposite the mirrors was a large entertainment center with every electronic device designed for viewing and listening pleasure. Nestled around a large, oriental carpet was a six-foot-long sofa covered in dark blue fabric. When she came closer, she could see narrow peach stripes running diagonally throughout the material. An easy chair faced the entertainment center, its seat cushion showing it had endured considerable use. Next to the chair was a table with several books stacked on it, bookmarks marking the places Rudd had temporarily stopped reading. A long, goosenecked floor lamp extended up and to one side of the chair. There were two other upholstered chairs and more tables, one low and wide situated in front of the sofa.

Dividing the living area from whatever was on the other side was an extended folded screen consisting of four panels. On the other side of the screen was a room that was Rudd's office. There was a large desk with a computer on one end, a well-worn leather chair, and bookcases stuffed with imposing volumes of leather-bound books. The rooms had solid walls. The door of the first one she approached was open, enabling her to take a glimpse inside. The most prominent item of furniture in the sectioned-off area was a king-size bed covered in a lush, dark green satin duvet. The headboard was made of dark wood and was ornately carved in an oriental theme of storks, Mount Fuji, and trees. On top of a low dresser with a mirror above the cherry wood surface was a Lladró figurine depicting a small child holding a bouquet of flowers. The stance of the child reminded her of her own painting, the one Rudd had stared at for so long that night in her apartment. Now she knew why it had caught his eye. The figurine told her this was Rudd's bedroom.

The sound of small leather soles on the wood floor drew her attention away from Rudd's bedroom and the thoughts that had come unbidden of Rudd's tall frame sprawled out on the wide expanse of satin...and of her lying beside him.

Turning, she smiled at Katie as the little girl came skipping toward her. Ellen was amazed at the change in the child in such a short time. The miracle was love, and Katie was blossoming under its effects. Katie smiled almost all the time, giggled, and had the confidence to know she could be petulant and pouty on occasion, and still be loved even when she was being disciplined.

"Ellen, come see my room," she ordered as she tugged at Ellen's hand.

As she responded to Katie pulling her along, Ellen saw Rudd standing near one of the doorways waiting for them to join him. He had his hands shoved into the back pockets of his jeans, his eyes shining with his amusement at Katie's excited reaction to her new living quarters.

Standing beside him, Ellen watched Katie skip over to a brass bed that was almost as high as she was. Annabel was lying on the multicolored quilt covering the bed. A white dresser was the only other piece of furniture.

Ellen tore her gaze from Katie. "She's obviously made her decision."

"It looks that way. There were two other rooms for her to pick from, but she wanted this one. One of the first things we need to get is a set of steps so she can get into the bed by herself. I suggested we get a different bed, but she wants this one. I don't imagine my mother will object too strongly that her granddaughter has taken over the room she uses when she comes for a visit."

"I don't see a kitchen."

"This way." He took her hand in his usual possessive way and drew her along with him to another screen extending across the end of the building.

Stepping behind Rudd and around the screen, Ellen saw a modern kitchen built into the wall. Instead of a regular dinette table and chairs, there was a plank table big enough to seat ten people, with benches on either side, situated several feet from the counter. A sink was built into the counter. The prerequisite stove and refrigerator were in place, as well as a rack of copper pots and pans hanging from a wrought-iron rack that had been built over the stove. The cupboards above and below the counter were made of teakwood and gleamed in the reflected light from the fluorescent lighting built into the ceiling.

Before she could ask her next question, Rudd turned her around and guided her toward the mirrored wall. Smiling down at her, he said, "I should have shown you this room first."

When she was several feet from the wall, Ellen saw a latch attached to the mirrors just before Rudd reached around her and took hold of it. He opened the mirror-covered door to reveal a spacious bathroom. Ellen stared. It was as big as her bedroom. The shower alone took up as much space as her bed would.

Giving Rudd an arch look over her shoulder, she murmured, "More mirrors."

"Hmm. It presents interesting possibilities, doesn't it? I never really thought much about them until now." His hold tightened as he brought her closer with the pressure of his hands. "There is one thing that needs to be changed about this place as soon as possible."

"What's that?" she asked breathlessly, her gaze going to his mouth as he spoke.

"Privacy. Katie's room is at a considerable distance from my bedroom, but I have a sudden urge for sound-proof walls and a door that can be locked."

Mesmerized by his low, husky voice and the feel of his warm hands, Ellen raised her gaze to meet his. How could blue eyes blaze with such heat? she wondered abstractedly. How could her heart beat so rapidly and still keep her alive?

She leaned into him, and he lowered his head. Only inches away, Rudd cursed under his breath. "I want you so badly I ache. I don't dare kiss you right now. If I do, I might not be able to stop."

She ached, too, but knew he was right. A deep, shuddering breath escaped her and she took a faltering step back. Though she wanted his mouth on hers, she understood his reasoning for not kissing her, and she fell in love with him all over again because of his thoughtfulness. He was a sensitive, caring man who didn't want to expose his daughter to things she wouldn't understand. The little girl had enough adjustments to make without having a third person interfering in the time she had to become acquainted with her father.

For that reason, she said, "I'm not staying here tonight, Rudd."

"I know." He rested his forehead against her briefly, then looked down at hers. "I shouldn't have suggested it under the circumstances. But I'm calling a locksmith first thing in the morning."

Desire was like molten glass running through her veins. Knowing she was in love with him only added to the hunger tightening her body.

She was unaware of the naked longing in her eyes, but Rudd saw it. Unable to resist the compelling warmth in her eyes, Rudd let his hands flow up her rib cage, sliding them under her breasts, his thumbs stroking the tips into hard buds. Hearing her shuddering breath, he moved his hands higher, taking the fullness of her breasts in his hands. His fiery gaze locked with hers, and he felt as though he were burning up from the inside out, and all he was doing was touching her. When they finally did come together, he knew they were going to go up in flames. And he could hardly wait.

His own breathing halted when Ellen raised her arms and wound them around his neck, bringing her pliant body into his. She buried her face into his neck and made a low, whimpering sound that vibrated through him like a tuning fork.

Desire gripped him with talons of fire, scorching his control and searing his blood. He was hard and throbbing, his body responding to the primitive need to claim the woman he held in his arms.

In the small recesses of his brain that were still able to think coherently, he was aware of Katie's happy chatter as she played with Annabel in her new room. As much as he loved his daughter, he would have liked her to be anywhere but where she was at this exact moment.

His hands were unsteady when he clasped her wrists and brought her arms down. He threaded his fingers through hers, unable to let her go completely.

His voice held the torment his body was experiencing when he said the name of his desire. "Ellen?"

She trembled as she drew back. She closed her eyes for a moment while she tried to steady her breathing and her racing heartbeat. When she opened them again, she said shakily, "It's a good thing I'm not staying here tonight."

His eyes darkened as he looked down at her, his needs fighting with his common sense. He started to draw her back into his arms, but she resisted.

"We're supposed to be the adults. We can't be thinking of ourselves right now."

His mind told him she was right. His body was screaming for satisfaction. "We can't go on much longer like this either, Ellen."

"But not at Katie's expense," she insisted. "She has to come first."

He buried his face in her neck to absorb her scent and the softness of her skin. It was going to have to last him through the long, lonely night. When he finally raised his head, he touched the side of her face, running the back of one finger over her cheek. "I'll let you go tonight, but I want you to come back tomorrow night."

She would have agreed to just about anything, as long as he wasn't going to insist she stay tonight. Now that she knew she was in love with him, her resistance was next to nothing.

The simple task of taking Ellen to her apartment took considerably longer than it would have if she hadn't reminded Rudd he needed to get a few grocery items, such as milk, for his daughter. They spent an hour in the Yamamoto store where Rudd put everything in the cart that Katie pointed to, while Ellen took it all back out again. Ellen marveled how a child unfamiliar with American products could unerringly chose only items with enough sugar in them to keep a dentist in business for a year. Ellen picked out healthier foods, making a point of filling the basket with things Rudd wouldn't have any difficulty in preparing.

She'd been introduced to Mrs. Yamamoto, a tiny gray-haired woman with dark, twinkling eyes and a warm smile. It was love at first sight when Mrs. Yamamoto met Katie. In an excited rush of Japanese and English, the little woman made Rudd promise to bring Katie to meet the rest of the family as soon as possible.

To Ellen's surprise, she'd been included in the invitation.

When Rudd finally stopped in front of her apartment building, Ellen said her goodbyes in the car rather than wait for Rudd and Katie to walk her to her door. She knew Rudd didn't like her suggestion, but she hurried into the building before he could argue about it.

Two hours later, after accomplishing absolutely nothing except staring at the painting of the child in a meadow, Ellen was resorting to a long soak in her bathtub when the phone rang. When it kept ringing, she realized she'd forgotten to turn her answering machine back on after listening to the messages when she arrived home. By the time she climbed out of a slippery tub, wrapped a towel around her wet, bubble-coated body, and made it to the phone in her bedroom, the phone stopped ringing as she reached for the receiver.

She slumped down on the bed and stared at the phone, willing it to ring again. It could be any number of people calling, but she had a feeling it had been Rudd.

She debated calling him just to make sure everything was all right. What if Katie was sick? she thought helplessly. What if Rudd was ill? Even though it was irrational thinking, considering they were both perfectly healthy when she'd seen them two hours ago, she still conjured up demons.

She should have stayed with them. No, she insisted silently. She'd done the right thing. She needed to start pulling away from Rudd before she became so hopelessly involved, it would kill her when he felt he could do without her.

Her damp skin was beginning to feel uncomfortably cool as she waited in case he phoned again, and she was beginning to feel equally foolish for sitting by the phone like some lovesick teenager.

Standing by her bed, she loosened the towel and began to dry off more thoroughly, nearly jumping out of her skin when the phone beside her bed jangled loudly. The towel dropped out of her hand as she reached for the phone.

"Hello?"

A cross voice barked, "Where the hell were you?"

"Hello, Rudd. And how are you?"

"You know how I am. Frustrated as hell. Answer my question. Where were you? I was about ready to bundle my sleeping child in a blanket and go over there."

"Well, as you can tell, I'm here, and I'm fine. Did Katie give you any trouble about going to sleep?"

The edge wasn't in his voice quite as much when he answered, "Either she's worn out from the trip on the plane and all the excitement or my rendition of Dr. Seuss's *The Cat in the Hat* was so boring it put her to sleep."

Ellen was feeling a definite draft without the towel, although the sound of his voice was warming her blood. Even though Rudd couldn't see her, she felt absurdly exposed talking to him when she was stark naked. She bent down to retrieve the towel and tried to wrap it around her, which was difficult to accomplish with one hand. The receiver slipped out of her hand, and she caught it just before it hit the floor. When she brought the phone back up to her ear, she could hear Rudd practically yelling her name.

"For Pete's sake, Rudd. Your shouting is going to wake Katie. I just dropped the phone when I was picking up my towel, that's all."

"That's all," he said in a choked voice. "As in, that's all you're wearing?"

She sank down on the edge of the bed, her knees suddenly incredibly weak. The shivers skidding over her skin were caused by his voice and not the coolness of the room. "I was in the bathtub when you called the first time."

"Why isn't that making me feel better? Have some mercy, Ellen. I've already had one cold shower, and it didn't work. Knowing you are naked and damp and scented from your bath isn't helping at all."

Ellen bit her lip, then forged ahead with what she had to say. "Rudd, I've been thinking."

His groan came clearly over the line. "Ellen, that doesn't make me feel any better, either, especially if you've been thinking about us as graphically as I have."

Using the philosophy that medicine goes down better if it's gulped rather than sipped, she said, "I think we should stop seeing each other."

There was no response for almost a whole minute. She couldn't even hear him breathing. Then he murmured, "If that's what you call thinking, you're in worse shape than

I am. Listen carefully. I'm not going to stop seeing you, and you aren't going to stop seeing me. In fact, we're going to be seeing a great deal of each other without our clothes on just as soon as I figure out how to manage it."

"But, Rudd..."

"Get dressed," he snapped. "I'm going to get Katie and come over there."

"No! You can't drag that child out in the middle of the night."

"And you can't make a statement like that and expect me to accept it."

So much for taking a stand. He'd just knocked her feet out from under her. "I have reasons for thinking that not seeing each other is the best thing to do, Rudd."

"I'm sure you do, and they're probably as crazy as you thinking I'm not going to fight you on this."

"Rudd, I—"

Ellen was left holding the receiver with no one on the other end. Rudd had hung up.

Replacing the receiver, she flung her arms over her head as she fell back on the bed and closed her eyes. She'd tried to give him an out, but he didn't take it. Or was she only trying to protect herself? Whatever the reason, she knew she was right to stop things from going any further between them.

Opening her eyes, she stared at the ceiling fan hanging over her bed. At the moment the blades were stationary, but they required only a switch to begin twirling around and around in an endless circle. Like her thoughts. When she was with Rudd, her doubts were relatively stationary, but when she was alone, they began to whirl around in her mind, confusing her.

She'd told Rudd that children didn't come with guarantees. Neither did love. It could be given and shared and even one-sided, but love couldn't be forced down someone's throat like bitter medicine. She had learned at a very young age that caring for someone didn't mean her feelings would always be returned.

Suddenly, she sat up. That's why she was so frightened. She was afraid her love for Rudd wouldn't be returned. Loving Rudd had brought her alive, and she didn't ever want to go back to simply existing. Falling in love with Rudd had completed her in a way nothing else ever had. She didn't want to lose it any more than she wanted to stop breathing.

Her father had killed any ounce of feeling she might ever have had for him early in her childhood. For a long time, she'd felt it had been her fault that he hadn't cared about her. It had taken years to develop a sense of self-worth, but there were still remnants of self-doubt lingering deep inside her, making her feel insecure about her relationship with Rudd.

But just because her father hadn't found her worth loving didn't mean she was unlovable. Rudd wanted her. It was a start.

Jerking the towel around her, she knotted it above her left breast and walked over to stand in front of the mirror attached to her dresser. She gazed at her reflection intently. Everything she had or was she'd accomplished alone. Her education, her friends, her career, her self-esteem. Whatever she'd wanted, she'd worked for, fought for if necessary.

Could she do any less for love?

She gave herself a mock salute before dropping her towel and slipping between the sheets of her bed. Some of her best planning had been done while she was lying in bed late at night.

Except all she could think about now was how it would feel if Rudd was beside her, holding her. Inside her.

That last thought had her moving restlessly in the bed, unable to find a position where she would be comfortable. The smooth fabric of the sheets seemed rough to her sensitized skin. Her legs became entangled in the sheets as she rolled over, switched to her back, then shifted again and again.

When her doorbell rang, she suddenly froze. It couldn't be her doorbell at this time of night. Not even Tiffany would come calling this late. It was probably someone who had the wrong apartment. She flopped over onto her stomach and covered her head with her pillow. She was going to ignore it.

Whoever it was didn't go away. The doorbell rang again several times, then went on in a long, solid tone. She had two choices, ignore it or answer it. Ignoring it was becoming increasingly impossible when the noise began to jangle along her nerve endings like jagged slivers of ice.

Ellen yanked the pillow away and struggled with the tangled sheets to free her legs. When she was finally able to stand, she grabbed her black satin robe and shoved her arms in it on her way toward the front door.

By the time she reached the door, the doorbell had been abandoned and a fist had taken its place.

Ellen yelled through the door, "Stop hammering on the door and go away. I don't want whatever you're selling."

"Open the door, Ellen. Now."

She made a startled sound. "Rudd?"

"Yes. Open the damn door."

Her fingers were unsteady as she fumbled with the dead bolt lock. Finally, she managed to unlock it and turned the knob. It was torn away from her grasp when Rudd planted the palm of his hand on the flat surface and gave it a shove.

As she stood in the doorway, she was about to ask him what in the world he was doing, pounding on her door in the middle of the night, when he put his hands on her waist and lifted her out of the way. Kicking the door shut with his foot, he hoisted her up into his arms and stalked down the hallway to her bedroom.

The room spun around her as he stepped sideways through the doorway and dropped her onto the bed. Following her down, he pinned her hands to the bed, his weight holding her in place.

"Rudd, have you lost your mind?"

"Yes," he muttered grimly. "And it's all your fault. You're driving me crazy."

"Me? What have I done?"

"At my place, you kissed me with all the passion any man could ever hope for, then tonight you tell me you don't think we should see each other." Shifting onto his side, he released one of her hands and brought his hand down to the opening of her robe. "Well, I'm going to see every delicious inch of you tonight, sweetheart. And you're going to see all of me."

Ellen felt cool air on her bare skin when he flipped the front of her robe away. She gasped when she felt his hand on her stomach. His fingers left a searing trail as he moved his hand over her in a slow, possessive motion. She shivered as his touch incited her blood to riot, hot and fiery, in her bloodstream.

"Rudd," she groaned as her legs moved restlessly under his.

His mouth came down to cover hers, eliminating any objection she could make. His tongue surged into her warmth with undisguised desire and need. His hunger for her was being fed by the fear of losing her, and he needed to claim her in the most elemental way possible. He branded her with his taste and his touch, fanning the smoldering flames that had always existed between them.

His fingers tightened around the hand he was holding over her head when he felt her legs part for him and her hips arch into his hard body. Her mind might not want him, but her body did. It was something, not all he was going to have from her, but it was a start.

Breaking away from her mouth, he buried his face in her neck as he tried to rein in his raging hunger.

Raising his head, he looked down at her. "Touch me, Ellen." He released her hand and opened the front of his shirt, his gaze never leaving her face.

She brought one hand to his chest, her fingers sliding over his heated skin and the hard muscles underneath. Her other hand came up to stroke and caress his taut stomach, his hard nipples, then up to his shoulder and into his hair. Clenching her fingers, she pressed him toward her, her moist lips parting in unspoken invitation.

His hand shaped her thigh, her hip, and finally cupped her breast. Breaking his mouth from hers, he left a scalding, moist trail over her skin until he found her breast and the hardened nub at the tip. He heard her cry out softly, his own response a moan of aching pleasure as he took her in his mouth.

Lingering over her burgeoning softness, he sucked in his breath raggedly when he felt her hand slide across his stomach and fumble with the opening of his jeans. The knowledge that she was responding to needs of her own was more intoxicating than the finest whiskey, and he wanted to drink his fill of her.

Unwilling to move away from her even briefly, he slid his arms under her to keep her clamped to his chest, making a sound deep in his throat when her breasts pressed into his solid body. His fingers tore at the opening of his jeans. He shoved the barrier of denim and cotton down his legs and kicked them off the end of the bed.

She arched her back when he slid his hand lower and pressed against the center of her femininity, and she cried out his name. The sound shattered his control.

He covered her, his mind nearly exploding when he felt her legs part, her hips tilting in an invitation as old as time. He looked down at her, searching her eyes even though he wasn't sure what he was looking for.

Until he saw it. She raised her long lashes slowly and met his gaze with a heated arousal in the depths of her green eyes. He wasn't alone in the maddening spiral of need. As long as he had Ellen, he would never be lonely again.

"Hold me," he murmured hoarsely. "Don't ever let me go."

His body began to merge with hers, and Ellen closed her eyes until Rudd said huskily, "No. Don't shut me out. Look at me."

He was held spellbound by the way her eyes glazed with pleasure when he entered her fully. He held his body still to allow her time to adjust to him, even though it required an extreme effort not to give in to the raging need driving him.

Holding his gaze, Ellen smoothed her hands over his back to his hips, her fingers insistent and strong as she pressed him into her throbbing heat. He shuddered against her, then fell into oblivion.

Chapter Sixteen

Rudd kept Ellen locked in his arms as he waited to get his breath back and for the world to right itself again. If things were different, he could think of nothing more wonderful than remaining right where he was for the rest of his life. But once his heart rate became relatively normal, his mind also began clicking back into place. He had responsibilities waiting for him somewhere else.

The reluctant way he moved to his side made it obvious it wasn't what he really wanted, his expression one of regret as he watched Ellen slowly open her eyes.

His voice was raspy with emotion and awakened need. "Are you all right?"

Giving him a faint smile, she said softly, "I'm not sure. I haven't made it all the way back to earth yet."

Not bothering to hide the regret he was feeling about leaving her, he said, "I can't stay."

"I know. We... This shouldn't have happened."

"Honey, this was inevitable." Leaning on his elbow, he kissed her softly. "Don't regret it."

She was offended that he could think she would be sorry she'd made love with him. And that's what it had been for her. *Love.*

"How could I regret something so..." She couldn't think of a word to describe what they'd shared.

"So..." he prompted.

"Ask me later when I can think straight."

He brushed a strand of damp hair away from her face, his touch gentle, his smile tender. "Well, when you do fully recover, we're going to have a nice, long talk. Maybe not so nice if you keep giving me that garbage about not wanting to see me again."

"I didn't say I didn't want to see you again. I said I thought we shouldn't see each other for a while. You need time to spend with—" Her eyes suddenly widened and she struggled to sit up. "Oh, my God! Where's Katie?"

He brought her back down and settled her on his chest. "Take it easy. I went next door and dragged Mrs. Yamamoto away from her television set and plunked her in front of mine. I told her there was a major emergency. I had to take care of someone who'd lost her mind."

Feeling guilty for creating so many problems for Rudd, Ellen pushed against his chest until he released her. She pulled the sheet up to cover her breasts and leaned back against the headboard. "I thought I was doing the right thing."

"You thought wrong." Rudd levered himself up so he was sitting beside her, the sheet falling to just below his waist. "The right thing is for us to be together."

It was difficult to remember all her arguments for her decision when she could feel the warmth of his body so close to hers. She was still vibrating from the pleasure she'd experienced in Rudd's arms. It wasn't going to be easy to make him understand.

"Rudd, you need time to adjust to this major change in your life. I would only complicate things. You need to concentrate on your daughter."

In one swift motion, he reached for her, lifting her over him so that she was facing him, her legs straddling his thighs. Cupping her face in his warm hands, he held her only inches away. "Call me greedy, but I want both you and my daughter. Nothing you've said or done has made me think I can't have both."

"You have to be fair to your daughter, Rudd. She deserves all of your attention right now."

"I realize there are going to be problems, but we can work them out. I'm not letting you out of my life, Ellen." He trailed his fingers down her neck, her breasts, her hips. Then lower. His smile was softly sensual when he saw her eyes glaze over as he slipped his hand between her thighs.

"Do you still want me to leave you alone?"

She gasped when she felt him stroke her sensitive flesh. "You don't fight fair."

With his hands on her hips, he positioned her and slowly lowered her on him. "Do I feel as though I want to fight with you?"

Her fingers gripped his shoulders as he filled her.

Every cliché about Mondays seemed to apply from the minute Ellen's alarm jarred her awake the next morning. It was raining outside and, at work, the art director was distributing his own brand of thunder and lightning inside. The deadlines he'd set earlier were changed to yesterday and projects originally approved were considered garbage. Ellen wanted to suggest she and the other artists would stand a better chance of getting the designs completed if he would limit his three-hour-long chewing-out sessions to ten minutes.

The only thing she could honestly say she'd accomplished was that she got through the day without thinking of Rudd every minute. Every *other* minute, maybe, but there were a few seconds when his face didn't appear or she didn't relive being in his arms the previous night.

When she woke up, he'd been gone. The sheet and blanket had been straightened and spread over her, but his side of the bed was cool to the touch. She understood why he'd had to leave, but she still wished she could have awakened in his arms.

Since she didn't get much done during the day, she decided to take work home with her. She filled her art portfolio with an ambitious assortment of drawings. If she worked all night every night for the next week, she wouldn't be able to finish every sketch she'd included, but that didn't stop her from adding a few more design ideas. Work would give her something to do to fill the long, lonely hours of the night.

When the phone on her desk rang, she jumped and three drawings slid out of her hand. Grabbing it, she said crossly, "What?"

Chuckling, Rudd said, "You're in a good mood."

Her mood suddenly got better. She sank down in her chair. "It's been one of those days."

"I want to take you away from all that. Come to my place instead of going home. You can relax while I fix dinner. And don't start in about how we shouldn't see each other again or I'll bring Katie, Annabel, and Mrs. Yamamoto's nephew, who is training to be a sumo wrestler, to back me up to show you the error of your ways."

She found herself smiling even though he wouldn't be able to see her amusement. "You do know how to turn a girl's head. What's on the menu?"

He chuckled again. "For a woman of your discriminating tastes, I've gone all out. We're having hot dogs and beans out of a can. It was Katie's idea after she saw an advertisement on TV this morning."

"Perhaps it would be a good idea to start governing what she watches on television. I was going to say I would bring dessert, but I can't think of a single thing that would go with that."

"What does your Palmer's Etiquette say to do?"

"I don't think bringing a bottle of wine would be appropriate."

"Just bring yourself." He sighed deeply. "Believe me, you're all I want."

It was a good thing she was sitting down. The husky tone of his voice caused an intense feminine response from her. Her sigh was ragged. "I'm as crazy as you are."

"Does that mean you're coming?"

"That means I'm leaving right now."

She could almost see him smiling when she heard him say, "Drive carefully."

She might have been imagining it, but she sensed a certain smugness in his tone. And why not, she considered. Everything was going his way. Why wouldn't he feel smug?

"Rudd, there's something we need to talk about. Tonight is as good a time as any."

He made a disgruntled sound. "I thought we'd settled everything last night."

Leave it to a man to consider that once they'd made love, everything was going their way. "We haven't settled anything. We will tonight."

"I can hardly wait," he groused. "Honk the horn when you get here, and I'll open the garage door for you."

Ellen hung up the phone and set her portfolio down beside her desk. She wasn't going to be doing any artwork tonight. She was going to take the biggest chance she'd ever taken.

Rudd was waiting near the garage after he opened the door in response to her blaring horn. When she approached him, he snaked his arm around her and brought her close to his body. His kiss was intimate and welcoming, making her feel that she'd finally come home.

But this wasn't her home.

When Katie came running up to her, she hugged the little girl, marveling again at the changes in Rudd's daughter in such a short time. Katie's smile came naturally, her dark eyes glowing and happy. Her ponytail was a little off-center, but Rudd had at least tried and would get better with practice.

The first part of the evening was spent eating the meal Rudd had prepared with Katie's assistance as she stirred the beans and franks. Afterward, Ellen helped Rudd and Katie set up a miniature railroad Rudd had purchased that day. Ellen ignored the fact that crawling around on her knees didn't do her rayon trouser suit much good. She didn't care.

Several times, she sat back and watched Rudd with his daughter. He was so patient with her, yet maintained a gentle discipline. He was gradually giving the child necessary boundaries interspersed with affection.

After seeing them together, Ellen knew she had made the right decision.

Once Katie was asleep, Rudd led Ellen over to the couch and pulled her down beside him. He propped his feet up on the low table in front of the couch and took her hand.

Placing their clasped hands on his thigh, which she was discovering was something he was fond of doing, he smiled at her. "Hi."

"Hi."

"I'm learning that my days are going to be chopped up into segments. This segment is ours."

Even though his eyes were warm with pleasure, she could see how tired he was. That was understandable, considering he couldn't have gotten much sleep last night. He was being pulled in a number of different directions all at once, and that had to stop.

She shifted her position so she was facing him, her fingers tightening around his. "Rudd, we need to talk."

He sighed heavily, a puzzled look entering his eyes. "This sounds serious."

"It is."

"Is this about last night?"

"Not in the way you mean. I don't regret last night. I only regret that it's another complication in your life. *I'm* another complication, which is the last thing you need right now."

"I thought I made it clear last night what I needed."

Memories of the night they'd spent together interfered with the point she was trying so hard to make. Tugging her hand away from his firm grip, she stood up and took several steps away from him.

Turning around, she said, "I think it would be best if I left you alone with Katie for a while. At least a week, maybe longer." She expected him to protest. When he didn't, but just continued to look at her with his dark, fathomless eyes, she went on, "You and your daughter are only now getting acquainted, and there are a lot of adjustments for both of you to make. All of your attention should be on her, not shared with me. There is also a great deal you need to accomplish before you go back to work next Monday. You need to find someone to take care of her during the day, and work out some sort of routine you can live with. I'll just be in the way of all that.''

She had blurted out her arguments all in one breath and had to stop to pull badly needed air into her lungs. Rudd continued to watch her, but he made no comment. Her nerves were in tatters as it was. His lack of response wasn't making her feel any better.

''Dammit, Rudd! Say something.''

The word he chose was straight out of a barnyard.

Ellen blinked, shock draining the color from her face.

''Don't use Katie as an excuse, Ellen. Bringing her here was your idea and now you want to back out of your responsibilities to both of us because you're running scared.''

''I'm not. I'm thinking about you and Katie. It has nothing to do with last night.''

''I think it does. What was last night to you, Ellen? A one-night stand? Just good sex, but not good enough to want the complication of a child to go along with being involved with the father?''

The unexpected attack had her taking a step back. ''That's not fair.''

''Probably not,'' he admitted. ''But I'm not feeling particularly fair right now. I don't know of any man who likes being kissed off after he's made love to a woman.''

Her pain-filled eyes brought him off the couch. Her expression was similar to the way she'd looked when her father had dismissed her at the restaurant. Even her fingers were clenched into fists like before.

Fight, dammit, he thought fiercely. *Fight for what we can have.*

He stopped in front of her and lifted a hand toward her, needing a physical connection with her. ''Don't,'' he pleaded when she flinched away from him before he could touch her. "Don't pull away from me."

Her voice was frigid with control. "I think I should go."

"Not yet. Not this way." *Not ever if he could help it.*

Ellen was barely holding on. "This was a mistake. I need to go."

Rudd shook his head, suddenly aware of what she really needed. *Love.* He'd never known anyone who needed to love and be loved more.

"Ellen, look at me."

He sucked in his breath when she raised her eyes and he saw the haunted sadness in their depths.

His hands came up to cup her face. "Ellen, I love you. I want you as part of my life."

Her mouth dropped open, and all she could do was stare at him. Then tears filled her eyes, and he became a blurred image. He loved her?

The next thing she knew, he was lifting her off her feet and into his arms. She sobbed into his shoulder as he carried her into his bedroom and gently put her down on the wide bed. He left her briefly to shut the door quietly. A few seconds later, she was nestled against his warm body, held securely by his arms around her.

When her tears had dwindled to an occasional sniffle, he brushed them away from her cheeks. "I won't go a week without you, sweetheart. Not even one day. It's just not possible."

Wiping her eyes with the heel of her hand, she asked, "But Katie needs you."

"She needs both of us. I understand why you are thinking of her before yourself, but you have to understand that I have enough love to go around to include both you and Katie. I'm not your father, Ellen. I don't plan on putting either of you in separate rooms to visit occasionally. Katie might as well get accustomed to having you with us, because that's the way it's going to be from now on."

Ellen was still trying to absorb that he'd said he loved her. "You can't."

Because he knew her, he knew exactly what it was she thought he couldn't do. "I can and I do love you."

"You're just grateful for my help with Katie."

Even though he knew the reasons for her insecurity, it didn't stop him from hating the fact that she still didn't trust him enough with her heart. Since she didn't believe him when he told her, he would show her how much he loved her.

He rolled over and covered her, arching his hips into her. "Does this feel like gratitude?"

It was just as well she couldn't come up with an answer, because he didn't give her a chance to give it to him. He kissed her, taking her mouth with tender passion.

She clung to him, desperate to believe he could love her. She gloried in the sweep of his hands, the solid feel of his hard body pressing her into the mattress.

Like a beggar at his door, she was willing to take whatever he was willing to give her.

Last night their coming together had been like a fiery explosion. Tonight was like an erupting volcano: hot, molten, a slow slide down into a valley of sweet satisfaction.

Holding her shoes in her hand, Ellen pushed open the door of Katie's bedroom. The carousel night-light on the dresser glowed dimly, giving enough light for Ellen to see the small form on the bed. Katie had kicked her covers off, and Ellen stepped inside the room so she could pull the quilt back over the sprawled figure. She smiled when she saw Annabel tucked into Katie's arm.

Ellen left Katie's room and walked quietly down the hall to where her car was parked behind Rudd's. The weak dawn light coming through the windows near the ceiling was enough for her to see her way without bumping into any plants or furniture.

She was trying to figure out how she could open the large door without waking Rudd when she caught a movement out of the corner of her vision. Startled, she jerked her head to face whatever it was. Her reflection shimmered back at her. She saw a woman dressed in rumpled clothing, hair mussed and untidy, with her shoes clasped in her hand.

Her image mocked her. She was exactly what she saw, a woman sneaking out of a man's house rather than face him.

Chapter Seventeen

Rudd yanked his jeans up from where they'd landed on the floor. He was going to do it this time. He was going to put his hands around Ellen's soft, delicate neck and throttle her.

The next time he got her in his bed, he was going to handcuff her to the damn headboard. He didn't like waking up and finding her gone.

Barefooted, he left his bedroom and headed toward the kitchen. Coffee, lots of it, and then he was going to Carstairs Designs and drag her out of there so he could have a nice, long chat with her about the error of her ways.

At first, he thought the idea of coffee was why he was actually smelling the rich scent in the air. Then he heard his daughter giggling.

Rounding the screen sectioning off the kitchen area, he stopped and stared.

Katie was carefully setting a knife next to a plate on the table, her small tongue sticking out between her lips as she concentrated on the task. Ellen was standing at the counter with her back to him.

She hadn't left after all.

He was so surprised at seeing her, he couldn't move. Until she raised her forearm to swipe at her eyes. She was crying!

His anger forgotten, he went to her and turned her around, his arms wrapping around her. "Shh. It's all right. Don't cry."

She made a strangled sound and pushed against his chest. "I'm not crying."

He looked down at the tears rolling down her cheeks. Brushing one away with his thumb, he asked, "Then what is this? Some new type of makeup?"

Sliding out of his arms, she reached over to the counter. She held up an onion. "I was slicing onions for an omelet."

He leaned against the counter. "Well, don't do that again." He smiled faintly when she raised a brow at his grumpy demand. "So sue me. I don't like to see you crying."

"What you need is a cup of coffee," she said as she poured steaming coffee into a mug and handed it to him.

He met her gaze and held it with his. "When I awoke alone, I thought you'd left."

A remnant of the anger he'd felt then remained in his voice. He deserved honesty and she gave it. "I almost did."

"It's a good thing you didn't. While I was putting on my pants, I'd come up with several interesting things to do to you when I came after you."

Her eyes widened at the implied threat, but her reaction was the opposite of fear. She smiled. "I'm almost sorry I didn't leave. Now I'll never know what interesting things you'd planned to do to me."

He cupped the back of her neck. Leaning forward, he kissed her. Not the way he would have liked, but his daughter was only a few feet away and it was too soon to give her lessons in sex education.

Ellen was as aware of Katie's presence as Rudd was. She also noticed the question in his eyes he didn't ask. She'd admitted she'd almost left that morning while he was asleep. He had no way of knowing she'd decided to stop running away from the possibility of being hurt again by him.

It had occurred to her that she had worked for everything worthwhile she had in her life. Why would her relationship with Rudd be any different? She wanted to be in his life and was willing to accept whatever capacity that might be. In a very short time, they had gone from acquaintances to lovers. With time, who knows what could happen? Time and fate could also bring their relationship to an end, but she would grab whatever happiness she could in the meantime.

Rudd stroked his thumb over the side of her jaw, placing his finger under her chin in a silent command to look at him. Before he could ask why she'd stayed, Katie was tugging at his shirtsleeve.

"Daddy, come see what I did."

His shocked gaze met Ellen's for a second, then he looked down at his daughter. She had called him Daddy!

His hand trembled slightly when he smoothed his hand over her silky hair. "What is it you wanted to show me?"

Ellen swallowed with difficulty as she watched Katie lead her father over to the table. In the brief glance they'd shared, she'd seen the emotion in his eyes. He'd made her a part of his elation, and she knew it was something she would never forget.

Shortly after eating the breakfast she'd prepared, Ellen left to go back to her apartment for a quick shower and to change before going to work.

For the next three days, she juggled work and evenings spent with Rudd and Katie. She didn't spend the night again, refusing when Rudd asked her to stay. She'd meant what she'd said to him Monday night. He had a lot of adjustments to make, and Katie had to come first. She also didn't think it was a good idea to expose Katie to the fact that Ellen was sleeping with Rudd. Katie might be only four years old, but they were adults and had to set an example for the child.

Rudd hadn't liked it each night when she'd gathered her things to leave his place. By Thursday night, he was downright cranky about it. They'd had dinner with the Yamamotos, spending a hilarious time sitting on the floor around a low table eating an astonishing assortment of oriental dishes. Ellen couldn't begin to remember everyone's names or even to count how many members there were in the large family. Katie had been given a beautiful kimono of her own, which she wore during dinner and wanted to keep on when it was time for her to go to bed.

When Rudd went with Ellen to her car after Katie was asleep, he said crossly, "I don't like the idea of you driving home at this hour alone. Stay. I'll sleep on the damn couch, and you can have my bed since you're worried about what Katie will think in the morning."

"We've been over this, Rudd. It would be too confusing for Katie."

He sighed as he held her close in his arms. "All right, but can I hate this?"

Her sigh was an echo of his. "I'm not real wild about it myself."

"I can't even kiss you the way I want to or I won't be able to stop." He framed her face with his hands and looked intently down into her eyes. "Things are going to be different when we get married."

"Married?" she asked with a gulp. "You and me?"

He ran the back of his fingers over her cheek. "Isn't that what two people do when they love each other?"

"I haven't thought that far ahead."

"Apparently." He was also aware that she hadn't said she loved him, either. He placed his fingers under her chin so she had to look at him. "You're going to have to think about it now."

"It's too soon," she argued inadequately.

"It's not soon enough if we could get married tomorrow. Dammit, Ellen. I want you with me."

She slumped against the door of her car. "I didn't expect this."

"What did you expect?" Sexual frustration and a gut-wrenching fear that he was losing her made his voice rougher than he intended. "Are we supposed to keep drifting along with you returning to your apartment every night when you should be in my bed with me? You might be satisfied with this arrangement, but I'm not. This isn't natural. We should be together in every way."

His mention of marriage had stunned her completely. "I need time to think."

Anger and fear made him stubborn. "Why?"

Defensive, she said, "It's a big decision to make."

"I don't know why. Either you love me or you don't. Either you want to live with me or you don't. What's so hard about that?"

His relentless attack accomplished what nothing else would have. She told him the unvarnished truth. "I'm afraid of disappointing you."

He stared at her, his expression utterly baffled. "What?"

Damn him. He wasn't going to be satisfied until she'd ripped out her insides and handed them to him. Well, if that was what he wanted, then that's what he damned well was going to get. Then she would leave and try to put herself back together again.

Anger glittered in her eyes as she took several paces away, then whirled around to face him. "Rudd, you were raised in a close family. I could hear the love in your voice when you told me about your mother and your father when they made you go to that science camp. There was affection in every word when you mentioned Willa Chase. You've been surrounded by love and you know what the feeling is like. I grew up in a house where the only person who was remotely fond of me was the housekeeper. I would be cheating you and Katie by accepting love from you when I don't even know what the emotion is myself."

He shook his head in bemusement. How could an intelligent, talented, sensitive woman like her be so incredibly blind?

He held out his hand. "Come here."

She looked down at his hand as though it held a live snake. "No."

"Then I'll come to you."

And he did. Instead of taking her hand, he wrapped his arms around her and held her tightly. "Ellen, I've never met anyone more capable of love than you. It's remarkable, considering the bastard of a father you ended up with, but you have more love within you than anyone else I know. I saw the people at your birthday party who like you and care about you. I met your friend, Tiffany, who threatened me if I hurt you because she loves you. You kept a doll you've had since childhood because you love her.''

He held her away from him so he could see her face. "You wouldn't have made love with me unless you loved me. You wouldn't have stayed Monday night unless you knew it would have hurt me if you'd left. You wouldn't have hounded me into bringing my daughter back to Boston unless you cared about her. Don't say you don't know what love is. You give love with every breath you take. Let me give you mine."

Her hand shook when she brought it from around his neck to place it along his face, enjoying the feel of his rougher skin. "I never want to hurt you or make your life more difficult."

"The only way you could hurt me is by staying out of my life." His thumbs caressed her firm jawline. "I've been alone for a long time, Ellen. I didn't realize how lonely I'd been until I had dinner with you that night six months ago. You filled an empty space deep inside me I didn't even know was there."

She laid her head on his shoulder as his arms came around her. His words echoed how she'd felt most of her life. It was beginning to sink in that she would never be alone again.

For a few minutes, they simply stood in each other's arms, peace and contentment overriding the passion laying just under the surface.

"Rudd?"

"Hmm?"

"You haven't asked me."

"Haven't asked you about what?"

"You said things were going to be different when we got married, but you never *asked* me to marry you."

Tightening his hold on her, he looked down into her eyes. "Ellen Sheridan, you are going to drive me crazy the rest of my life but I don't want it any other way. I love you. Will you love me and live with me and marry me?"

Her eyes glowed with joy and love. "Yes."

"Which?"

She frowned. "Which what?"

"Which question did you answer? I asked you three different questions."

Her eyes glittered with amusement. "Yes, I love you. Yes, I'll live with you, and yes, I'll marry you."

Lowering his head, he spoke against her mouth. "It's about damn time."

He sealed the promises she'd made by kissing her deeply and for a very long time. By the time he raised his head, his breathing was as ragged as hers.

"You're not going home tonight."

She smiled softly and tightened her arms around his neck. "I *am* home."

Rudd grinned down at her as he slipped his hand under her knees and lifted her up into his arms to carry her into his bedroom. Their bedroom.

* * * * *

It's Opening Night in October—
and you're invited!
Take a look at romance with a
brand-new twist, as the stars
of tomorrow make their
debut today!
It's LOVE:
an age-old story—
now, with
*WORLD PREMIERE
APPEARANCES* by:

Patricia Thayer—Silhouette Romance #895
JUST MAGGIE—Meet the Texas rancher who wins this pretty
teacher's heart…and lose your own heart, too!

Anne Marie Winston—Silhouette Desire #742
BEST KEPT SECRETS—Join old lovers reunited and see what
secret wonders have been hiding…beneath the flames!

Sierra Rydell—Silhouette Special Edition #772
ON MIDDLE GROUND—Drift toward Twilight, Alaska, with this
widowed mother and collide—heart first—into body heat
enough to melt the frozen tundra!

Kate Carlton—Silhouette Intimate Moments #454
KIDNAPPED!—Dare to look on as a timid wallflower blossoms and falls in fearless love—with her gruff, mysterious
kidnapper!

**Don't miss the classics of tomorrow—
premiering today—only from**

PREM

™

In the spirit of Christmas, Silhouette invites
you to share the joy of the holiday season.

Experience the beauty of Yuletide romance with Silhouette
Christmas Stories 1992—a collection of heartwarming stories by
favorite Silhouette authors.

**JONI'S MAGIC by Mary Lynn Baxter
HEARTS OF HOPE by Sondra Stanford
THE NIGHT SANTA CLAUS RETURNED by Marie Ferrarella
BASKET OF LOVE by Jeanne Stephens**

This Christmas you can also receive a FREE keepsake Christmas
ornament. Look for details in all November and December
Silhouette books.

Also available this year are three popular early editions of
Silhouette Christmas Stories—1986, 1987 and 1988. Look for these
and you'll be well on your way to a complete collection of the
best in holiday romance.

Share in the celebration—with Silhouette's
Christmas gift of love.

SX92

THE DONOVAN LEGACY
from Nora Roberts

Meet the Donovans—Morgana, Sebastian and Anastasia. Each one is unique. Each one is . . . special.

In September you will be *Captivated* by Morgana Donovan. In Special Edition #768, horror-film writer Nash Kirkland doesn't know what to do when he meets an actual witch!

Be *Entranced* in October by Sebastian Donovan in Special Edition #774. Private investigator Mary Ellen Sutherland doesn't believe in psychic phenomena. But she discovers Sebastian has strange powers . . . over her.

In November's Special Edition #780, you'll be *Charmed* by Anastasia Donovan, along with Boone Sawyer and his little girl. Anastasia was a healer, but for her it was Boone's touch that cast a spell.

Enjoy the magic of Nora Roberts. Don't miss *Captivated*, *Entranced* or *Charmed*. Only from Silhouette Special Edition. . . .

Take 4 bestselling love stories FREE

Plus get a FREE surprise gift!

Special Limited-time Offer

Mail to Silhouette Reader Service™

In the U.S.	In Canada
3010 Walden Avenue	P.O. Box 609
P.O. Box 1867	Fort Erie, Ontario
Buffalo, N.Y. 14269-1867	L2A 5X3

YES! Please send me 4 free Silhouette Special Edition® novels and my free surprise gift. Then send me 6 brand-new novels every month, which I will receive months before they appear in bookstores. Bill me at the low price of $2.96* each—a savings of 43¢ apiece off the cover prices. There are no shipping, handling or other hidden costs. I understand that accepting the books and gift places me under no obligation ever to buy any books. I can always return a shipment and cancel at any time. Even if I never buy another book from Silhouette, the 4 free books and the surprise gift are mine to keep forever.

*Offer slightly different in Canada—$2.96 per book plus 69¢ per shipment for delivery. Canadian residents add applicable federal and provincial sales tax. Sales tax applicable in N.Y.

235 BPA ADMC   335 BPA ADMQ

Name _____ (PLEASE PRINT)

Address _____ Apt. No. _____

City _____ State/Prov. _____ Zip/Postal Code. _____

This offer is limited to one order per household and not valid to present Silhouette Special Edition® subscribers. Terms and prices are subject to change.

SPED-92   © 1990 Harlequin Enterprises Limited

TAKE A WALK ON THE DARK SIDE OF LOVE

October is the shivery season, when chill winds blow and shadows walk the night. Come along with us into a haunting world where love and danger go hand in hand, where passions will thrill you and dangers will chill you. Come with us to

In this newest short story collection from Silhouette Books, three of your favorite authors tell tales just perfect for a spooky autumn night. Let Anne Stuart introduce you to "The Monster in the Closet," Helen R. Myers bewitch you with "Seawitch," and Heather Graham Pozzessere entice you with "Wilde Imaginings."

Silhouette Shadows™
Haunting a store near you this October.

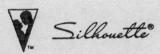

VOWS
A series celebrating marriage
by Sherryl Woods

To Love, Honor and Cherish—these were the words that three generations of Halloran men promised their women they'd live by. But these vows made in love are each challenged by the tests of time....

In October—Jason Halloran meets his match in *Love* #769;

In November—Kevin Halloran rediscovers love—with his wife—in *Honor* #775;

In December—Brandon Halloran rekindles an old flame in *Cherish* #781.

These three stirring tales are coming down the aisle toward you—only from Silhouette Special Edition!

SESW-1

Dear Reader,

Welcome to Silhouette **Special Edition** . . . welcome to romance. Each month, Silhouette **Special Edition** publishes six novels with you in mind—stories of love and life, tales that you can identify with—romance with that little "something special" added in.

This month is packed full of goodies in celebration of Halloween! Don't miss the continuation of Nora Roberts's magical new series, THE DONOVAN LEGACY. This month we're proud to present *Entranced*—Sebastian Donovan's story. And in November, don't miss the third of this enchanting series—*Charmed*.

October also launches a new series from Sherryl Woods—VOWS. These warm, tender tales will light up the autumn and winter nights with love. Don't miss *Love*—Jason Halloran's story in October, *Honor*—Kevin Halloran's story in November or *Cherish*—Brandon Halloran's story in December.

We're also pleased to introduce new author Sierra Rydell. Her first Silhouette **Special Edition** will be published this month as a PREMIERE title. It's called *On Middle Ground* and is set in Alaska—the author's home state. This month, watch for the debut of a new writer in each of Silhouette Books's four lines: Silhouette **Special Edition**, Silhouette Romance, Silhouette Desire and Silhouette Intimate Moments. Each book will have the special PREMIERE banner on it.

Rounding out this exciting month are books from other favorite writers: Andrea Edwards and Maggi Charles. And meet Patt Bucheister—her first **Special Edition**, *Tilt at Windmills,* debuts this month! Her work has been much celebrated, and we're delighted she's joined us with this wonderful book.

I hope you enjoy this book and all of the stories to come.

Sincerely,

Tara Gavin
Senior Editor
Silhouette Books

"Our previous meeting reads like a poorly written script for a soap opera,"

Ellen said to Rudd. "Two people met, had dinner and a few laughs, a good-night peck on the cheek and a tidy exit. Then the curtain went down. The end."

"We must have had two different sets of scripts. I don't recall kissing you on the cheek. I remember how soft you felt, how you moved against me, how you nearly made me go up in flames. If I hadn't stopped, we would have finished the kiss in your bedroom and not come out for days."

She couldn't look away from the heated awareness in his dark eyes. Her chest began to hurt; and she realized she'd been holding her breath. Her pride forced her to pull air into her lungs and answer, "I'll stick with *my* script."